# Books by John Triptych

Wrath of the Old Gods series (in chronological order)
The Glooming
Pagan Apocalypse
Canticum Tenebris
The Fomorians
A World Darkly
Eye of Balor
Mortuorum Luctum

Expatriate Underworld series
The Opener
The Loader

Dying World series
Lands of Dust
City of Delusions
The Maker of Entropy

The Amoralist series
A Man of Leisure
Savage Wanderings

# Lands of Dust

## The Dying World Book 1

John Triptych

Copyright© 2016 by John Triptych
All rights reserved.

J Triptych Publishing

This is a work of fiction. All names, characters, places, and events either are the product of the author's imagination or are used fictitiously. Any resemblance to actual persons, living or dead, events, and/or locales is entirely coincidental.

Cover by Deranged Doctor Design (http://www.derangeddoctordesign.com/)
Interior formatting by Polgarus Studios

*For Jim Henson and E Gary Gygax..*

## Author's note:

Dear reader, I would like to thank you for purchasing this book. As a self-published author, I incur all the costs of producing this novel so your feedback means a lot to me. If you wouldn't mind, could you please take a few minutes and post a review of this online and let others know what you think of it?

As I'm sure you're aware, the more reviews I get, the better my future sales would be and therefore my financial incentive to produce more books for your enjoyment increases. I am very happy to read any comments and questions and I am willing to respond to you personally as quickly as I can. My email is jtriptych@gmail.com if you wish to contact me directly. Again, thank you and I hope you enjoy reading this book as much as I enjoyed writing it!

Please join my exclusive mailing list! You will get the latest news on my upcoming works and special discounts. Subscription is FREE and you get lots of FREE books! Just type this link to your browser: http://eepurl.com/bK-xGn

*Night-walkers, Magians, priests of Bacchos and priestesses of the wine-vat, mystery-mongers practised among men.*
- Heraclitus

*All other things have a portion of everything, but Mind is infinite and self-ruled, and is mixed with nothing but is all alone by itself.*
- Anaxagoras

*Nothing is more active than thought, for it travels over the universe, and nothing is stronger than necessity, for all must submit to it.*
-Thales

## Chapter 1

Across the night lands, two cloaked figures ran desperately beneath the moonlit sky. Solid dunes of fine dust were all around them, and the reflected luminescence made it look like they were in an ocean of brightly colored ash, with undulating sand drifts resembling static, unmoving waves that crested and dipped across the landscape. The taller one had set a relentless pace across the firm, sandy ground. The shorter of the two was trying hard to keep up, but kept stumbling forward, barely keeping his balance and slowing their progress. The taller one grabbed the other by his elbow and pulled him in an effort to go faster. After what seemed like an eternity, the little one began to tire and had to be dragged forward, his exhaustion finally getting the better of him.

The taller man stopped as he scanned the nearby terrain. He was sure the enemy was close and they would soon be caught. They had been running for five days now, resting while the sun was up and moving during the night. Now their food and water were all gone. The leather map he had in the fur pouch he was carrying had showed him this was the way, but there was nothing but sand all around them- they were utterly lost. He bent down and stared at the small figure kneeling by him. "We must strive on if we are to get to safety. We cannot tarry long here. You must get up."

With short, labored breaths, the smaller figure looked up at him and the hood of the little cloak fell back, revealing a young boy with short, golden blond hair and pale skin. "I… I cannot go on, Aertos. I am t-too tired."

The taller man threw off the hood of his own cloak, revealing a bald, smooth head. His nose was sharp and he was beardless, as most men were these days. It seemed that those who could still grow hair on their chins had largely died out many generations ago. "If you cannot run, then you will die. Is that what you want?"

But the boy was too exhausted. His body was spent after fleeing the moment the sun had set. The child let out a soft moan as he fell on his hands and knees. He just wanted to rest, to close his eyes, and sleep on the cold, dusty ground. If he could just have a brief moment to recover, then he could run again. Right now, his feet and legs were hurting, his lungs ached with a burning pain as he still hadn't gotten his breath back. He needed a drink of water, but he knew they no longer had any.

Just as Aertos tried picking the boy up with both hands, he saw them. Two cloaked figures crested a dune at the edge of the horizon, headed their way. He could see they were armed, one carried a longbow, its white-boned construction was highly visible in the moonlit night. It meant that their pursuers had been tracking them all this time. With a hiss of desperation, Aertos grabbed the child and placed him over his shoulders. Then he turned once more and ran.

The chase continued as Aertos sprinted up and down the dunes. The boy hung desperately over his shoulders. Since Aertos was the one doing all the running, their pace quickened considerably. He had known they would be pursued the moment they made the escape from the citadel. The boy was held in such high value to them, they would be willing to kill any traitor who would dare steal him. If Aertos was to be caught, then they would surely flay him alive for his treason. He dared not think any further about the consequences. Aertos had already made a vow to himself that they would never take him alive. His goal now was to get the boy to safety, his own life no longer mattered.

Glancing briefly behind him, Aertos let out a short sigh of despair. His pursuers had slowly closed the gap. The two men were now only a hundred yards away and getting closer. He needed to do something or they would catch him within the hour. His lungs were now searing in pain and his arms felt leaden from lugging the boy. The only thing fueling Aertos's relentless pace now was his own desperation. If the two men got to within thirty yards, they might decide to use their weapons, but that would mean they would have to pause as the taller of the two would have to ready the bow.

Aertos made another glance behind him as he crested another low lying dune. He could clearly see his two pursuers now. Urien was the shorter one, and Estragon had the bone bow. They had known each other ever since all three had been assigned to the citadel. So it was his own friends who had been tasked to pursue and kill him. How ironic it all was. Aertos kept on running as he spotted a low lying wadi up ahead, the small, dried riverbed looked largely untouched by men for the past several hundred cycles. An idea came into his mind, it would be a desperate gamble, but it was his one chance to shake them off, albeit temporarily. Gathering his thoughts, Aertos used his remaining reserves of energy to run directly towards the edge of the wadi.

Just as he got to the lip of the trench, Aertos immediately used his mindforce to push his body forward, his sudden jump powered him over the twenty foot gap and across to the other side. He ran for another twenty yards, then turned and waited while catching his breath. Just as the two men pursuing him used their own mindforce to propel themselves above the edges of the wadi, Aertos held out his hand and used his remaining Vis to mentally throw up a column of loose sand at their faces, temporarily blinding them. The two men were immediately inundated by a barrage of dust as they momentarily lost their concentration. Urien cursed aloud as he fell sideways, but managed to hold onto the top edge of the sand wall, while the much bigger Estragon completely lost his footing and fell head first into the sandy gorge, his longbow still in his hands.

Aertos turned around and started running once more. Up ahead, he could no longer see the horizon. Everything in front of him seemed opaque, not even the light from the moon above could illuminate the inky, swirling blackness in front of him. Not seeing any other choice, he dashed forward anyway. Whatever lay ahead out there had to be better than the things they would do to him if he was brought back to the citadel.

His pacing soon began to slacken as the hard sand on his feet began to loosen up. Every time he put his foot forward, his boots would get sucked in and needed a lot of extra effort to pull them back out. During his cycles as an apprentice, Aertos was taught by his teachers that the wastes had many variations of sand; some were hard as packed stone, while the loose patches were to be avoided. He had heard tales of men being sucked underneath the pools of moving dust that acted like water, their cries of terror forever silenced as they drowned not in any liquid, but were swallowed up by grains of fine particles. It was a kind of death that instilled fear among his peers.

Aertos grimaced as he kept on going, the pain in his aching legs was pure agony. The only thing that kept him moving was his sheer force of will and the hope that the flatlands ahead of him would be packed more tightly. The boy whimpered slightly as Aertos continued to carry him, but his gait was awkward due to the extra weight on his right shoulder. Just as he pulled his left foot out from the loose floor, his fatigue and unbalanced stance made him slip, and both fell forward onto the soft ground.

The boy rolled forward onto the fine dirt but he quickly got up. Aertos pulled himself up while both his hands dug into the loose earth until he was on all fours. As he glanced over his shoulder, Aertos noticed Urien and Estragon had gotten out of the wadi and were now trudging their way slowly towards him. It was apparent that his pursuers were as exhausted as he was since they didn't use their Vis for another jump. The boy noticed the two men and took off running on the harder packed soil. With a hiss of desperation, Aertos changed direction as he started following the lad.

By the time he had gotten to the area with the compact sand, the boy was about ten yards ahead of him. Aertos could see a vast wall of dust in front of them, rising hundreds of feet high. The boy stopped and just stared at the monstrous waves of ash swirling in the air. So that was why the horizon suddenly became opaque, there was a large storm just ahead of them. The boy turned, giving him a look of despair as he just stood there while the wind began to pick up around them. If they kept moving, then they would surely be lost within the raging tempest ahead.

Just as Aertos pulled himself up onto the hard packed earth, a bone arrow embedded itself on the back of his lower leg. He screamed and fell forward onto the ground. As he glanced behind him, he saw that Estragon had his bow out and was notching another arrow with it. He cursed at himself for not being more alert.

"Aertos!" the boy cried as he ran back and started pulling him up. Urien drew his dagger as he slowly got closer, only the loose soil was keeping him from getting there quickly. Estragon aimed with the bow and fired off another arrow, but Aertos held out his hand and used his mindforce to deflect the projectile off into the night.

Grabbing the boy by his collar, Aertos drew him close to whisper in the child's ear. "You must go. I will hold them off as long as I can. Lose them in the storm!"

The boy started to cry as the salt tears ran down his dusty cheeks. "No, no. I will not leave you."

Aertos grimaced. He could no longer control his right leg as the sharp pain was replaced with an agony of burning fire. Estragon must have had the tips of the bone arrow poisoned. It meant he was dead either way. "Do not argue with me, boy. Run. Run now! Quickly!"

The boy kept trying to pull him up until Aertos finally pushed the child away. There was a pained expression on the boy's face- a sad mixture of grief and desperation, but the child finally understood as he got up and started running towards the incoming storm. Aertos turned around, just as he noticed Urien had gotten close and was about to stab him with a dagger.

Aertos managed to grasp Urien's wrists as both men struggled on the ground. Urien was on top of him as he used his mindforce to press the dagger down towards the other man's throat. Aertos used his own Vis to hold back the weapon, but the poison in his wounded leg had already begun to dull his concentration. A few yards behind them, Estragon couldn't use his bow for fearing that he might hit his own ally, so he placed the weapon onto the ground while holding his hands in front of him, and he started to use his thoughts to unpack the dirt around Aertos.

With his other leg still functioning properly, Aertos bent his good knee and used it to kick Urien's left torso. The other man grunted in pain as he fell sideways, but he was able to hold onto his dagger. Estragon concentrated as he tried to push Aertos into the loose sand, but his victim was able to roll away at the last minute, just as a hole opened up from where he had been lying in. Aertos kept rolling until he had some distance in between and then tried to stand up. Urien managed to get up to one knee and he threw the dagger, using his mindforce to propel the bronze blade with enough power to connect with his target before the other man could counter it.

Aertos sensed the blade whistling through the air, heading towards him. He put his hand up to try and deflect it using his mindforce, but his numbed senses were too late to react. The dagger plunged into his throat, tearing into his windpipe and cutting the main arteries before embedding itself into his neck bone. Aertos let out a gurgle as he fell backwards into the sandy ground, blood spurting from his opened throat. As the darkness began to envelop him, a final bright tinge of hope settled into his fading thoughts. He hoped the boy would be safe. Then he died.

Urien stood upright and made his way to the dead man. Estragon was now at the edge of the hard soil as he pulled himself up. Urien bent down and retrieved his dagger from Aertos's corpse while looking around. He noticed that the boy was about fifty yards ahead of them. "Estragon," he said. "Get the boy."

Estragon grunted as he ran ahead of his partner. He was one of the tallest Magi in the citadel compared to the others. His forehead was balding, but the sides above his ears still had long black hair that drooped down his shoulders. Estragon had thought about using his bone bow, but their orders were to bring the boy back alive so he couldn't risk a shot. As he began to close the distance to the child, the wind suddenly picked up in intensity, and he was soon enveloped in a column of sand. Estragon screamed and he was quickly half-blinded, he could barely notice the outline of the boy ahead. He tried to move further, but he could no longer see anything in front of him.

Just as Urien was about to follow his partner into the dark horizon up ahead, he saw Estragon make his way back towards him. The other man was alone. "Where is the boy?"

Estragon grimaced as he used his arm to wipe the dirt from his eyes. "The child kept going, he ran into the storm!"

Urien cursed. "We were tasked to bring the boy back, we cannot return without him!"

"But it is impossible! I had to retreat, I cannot see anything out there."

Visibility had suddenly gone away. Both men were quickly engulfed in an ash filled darkness as the moonlight above them disappeared. They tried to push forward, but the air currents became so strong, they were suddenly unable to see one another. Urien tried to use his mindforce to clear a small space of air in front of his face, but he was too exhausted and the winds too powerful.

Estragon stood beside him as he cupped his hand over his mouth in order to be heard. "We need to find shelter, quickly!"

Urien shook his head violently. "We have to find that boy!"

While the two of them kept arguing, something large stirred underneath them. It had been hibernating deep beneath the loose sand, but the sandstorm had awakened it. When it extended its sensory tendrils along the waves of loosening dust, it immediately sensed prey, its long sleep having given it an appetite. Now it was time to feed.

Urien sensed it first. For a brief moment, he thought the shifting sands below his feet were merely being stirred up by the howling zephyrs of air. All of a sudden, the entire ground around the both of them started moving as they both fell onto their backs. As he tried to get up, Urien saw something huge come out from under the sand, it was large enough to grab onto Estragon and pull him back down into the ground. Urien could hear his partner's hapless screaming even with the intense sandstorm raging around him. He turned and tried to run, but he was soon knee deep in loose ground. Urien cried out in desperation as he tried to grab hold of anything that could pull him back out into the harder packed sand. He used his hands to try to feel his way forward until he touched something long and ropey. Urien immediately grabbed onto it with both hands, thinking it was some sort of line with which to pull himself to safety. Just as he managed to pull his body forward, the rope he was grasping suddenly had a life of its own as it coiled around his arms. Instead of getting himself on harder ground, he was suddenly being dragged deeper into the loose terrain.

Urien had suddenly remembered the teachings of the late, lamented Grand Magus Ontoro with regards to surviving in the desert. The long dead Magus had given a lecture to his class about the more dangerous creatures living out in the wastes. One particular animal hunted at night and used tentacle-like appendages to find its prey in the sand. This creature was quite huge, and the largest specimens known had eaten men whole. *It was best to avoid creatures such as those*, the Grand Magus had said. *The only way to defend against it was to run.*

Realizing his fate, Urien managed to let out one bloodcurdling scream before he was swallowed up by the shifting sands.

# Chapter 2

It was close to high noon when Nyx finally sensed the sand dargon's presence. She had just recently celebrated her sixteenth cycle, and her mindsense had been growing steadily by the day. Elder Zedne had been right, the moment her loincloth had tasted its first blooding, her powers of prescience increased in both scope and intensity. At first, her newly acquired senses had been a terrifying experience, an endless stream of conversations among voices that manifested inside her mind. For the next few weeks, she lay in her hut, clutching her head and screaming, begging for the sounds to stop. Elder Zedne and her brother spent those painful days by her side, gently coaxing her to develop the thought blocks to ensure her mind would not be overwhelmed by the sheer barrage of stimulation and emotions all around her. Even then, Nyx had heard stories of Strigas going mad and unleashing their powers amongst their own family, in a crazed fury that ultimately ended in death. In her case, it was only through the timely intervention of the protector that she was finally able to silence the incessant voices and waves of feelings that nearly consumed her. From that day forward, Nyx idolized the one woman who ventured into her mind and told her that everything would be alright.

Nyx stood up on the crest of the dune as she wrapped her leather cloak tightly around her thin body. She could sense the dargon sleeping beneath the sea of dust, not far from her observation point. Now that they had found their prey, the hunt would begin. Nyx reached for the mirrored crystal in her pouch and took it out. She held it to the general direction of her older brother, who had been sitting near the edge of another knoll several hundred yards away. By tilting the crystal at an angle, she used the sun's reflection as a shiny beacon to attract him. Within a few minutes, her brother had noticed and began to use his own crystal to alert the next man in the relay, until the alert made its way to the base camp.

The hunting party had been deployed in a V-shaped formation, with Nyx at the extreme edge of the left wing, while the village protector, who was also a Striga, at the opposite end from her. The bottom of the V was their base camp, where they would retire for the night after spending all day at the hunt. If either of them had detected the hidden sand dargon, they would pass on the message using their mirrored glass along the line until everyone was alerted, then the entire group would converge on her position. Nyx grinned with satisfaction. This was only the second hunt that she was a part of, but already she would have the honor of being the one who found the beast they had been hunting for these past few days. It was the first time she had used her powers to find prey by using her mental feelers to probe the ground around her, and she was extremely proud of herself. Not bad for an orphan girl who grew up amongst the elders of the tribe.

Her brother Jinn was the first to arrive as he ran up the dune to where she had been sitting. He had been the closest relay to her, so it was only natural he reached her before the others did. Like his sister, Jinn had bronzed skin and black, curly hair, a natural adaptation to the people of the wastes. Jinn carried a slightly curved bone spear with a flint head attached to its point. He sat down beside her, cradling his weapon. "Well done, Sister! Are you sure it is the beast we're looking for this time?"

She gave him a playful slap in the arm. "Yes, it is. It is a sand dargon alright. Our protector taught me how to sense it."

Jinn pulled out a waterskin from beneath his leather cloak and took a sip. "I hope you're right this time. Two days ago, your Vis told you it was the sand dargon, but what jumped out behind the dunes instead was a dust beetle."

Nyx slapped her brother in the arm a second time. "Silence! This time it is the real thing, I promise. If it is not, then may Duun take my life and spill my essence to the wastes."

Jinn shook his head while stowing the waterskin beneath his cloak. "Do not mock the gods, sister."

"I am not making fun of the gods, I am confident that it is truly the beast that we have been hunting for all this time. We shall feast back in the village within two days," she said assuredly.

Jinn got up to one knee as he noticed Krag, the group's lead hunter making his way towards them. "I hope you are right, sister. This is my sixth hunt and the last two did not turn out so well."

Nyx looked at her older brother. "Oh? But I thought the last hunt was a success, the party brought back two octapedes, each one was over two feet long. That was a great feast we had."

"We had to range far and wide- and for almost a whole moon- just to get those two and we were lucky," Jinn said softly. "The larger octapede was a mother to its last youngling. I have this terrible feeling that our patron god Duun no longer favors us and there are no more beasts left to hunt."

"Silence, Jinn," Nyx said. "Do not say such bad things."

Krag had moved up to their position. His brown, leathery skin had been toughened after spending so much time in the wastes, and he consumed the smallest amount of water as compared to the others. While Nyx idolized the tribal protector, Jinn idolized Krag, for he was widely considered to be their best hunter.

The slight breeze whipped at Krag's shoulder length, thick black hair as he looked around. He surveyed what looked like a patch of loose sand towards the trough of a far dune. "Yes, that looks like the nesting place of a sand dargon, alright. You have done well, Nyx," he said.

Nyx grinned. "Thank you, chief hunter. This is a great honor for me."

Krag placed a hand above his eyes to shield them from the glare. "Seems like a big one too. I do not think we have hunted one this large for the last ten cycles. A major find indeed, you have the luck of the gods, girl."

Jinn squinted his own eyes as he imitated Krag. "How can you tell the size of the beast, chief hunter?"

Krag pointed at the edges of the patch. "When a dust beast burrows beneath the ground, you just have to notice how large the field is. A good rule of thumb is to divide the length of the outward edges of the loose sand by a third. Since I believe the size of that patch is between seventy-five to eighty feet, then the beast is probably a twenty-five or twenty-six footer in length."

Nyx was shocked. "A twenty-five footer? By the gods, I don't ever remember anyone in the village hunting a beast so large ever before."

"I remember hunting a very powerful dust beast long before you were born," Krag said. "Elder Pir was still young enough to hunt back then. It must have been close to thirty cycles ago. We stalked and killed the largest dargon ever known to the tribe. The beast was close to fifty feet long, and we lost two hunters that day." He looked at Jinn. "I was around your age, boy. Just barely eighteen cycles and it was only my second hunt."

Jinn grinned. "That must have been fun."

Krag nodded. "It was, but it was also hard, dangerous work. A sand dargon is not to be trifled with. It is not an octapede, or even a poisoned norpion. Dargons hunt those other beasts and consume them, just like we would eat our algae soup. You both must stay well away from the sand nest. Leave the killing to my hunters and the protector."

Jinn stood up. Even at his full upright position, he was still two shades shorter than the chief hunter. "But Krag, this is already my sixth hunt. Let me be part of your hunting group. Please."

Krag smiled and shook his head. "Too dangerous, Jinn. For a sand dargon this size, I will not allow anyone who has less than twelve hunts beneath their loincloth to be part of it. This beast is very dangerous, and I fear that some of us might not even return to the camp by tonight. Perhaps when you have more experience, yes?"

Jinn sighed. "But you yourself said a dargon this size comes but once in thirty cycles! We may not ever have this chance of finding such a magnificent beast ever again. Please let me become part of your group, I promise to obey every command and be careful. I beg of you."

Krag looked away as a half dozen more hunters began to converge on them. The young man was right. For a beast this size, they needed at least twelve hunters to make sure that it would not get loose when they confronted it. All he had left on his team were six experienced men. Jinn was still considered to be an apprentice, but there was no one else. With Jinn and the protector by his side, there would be nine of them.

While Krag stared at the other hunters readying their weapons, he started pointing towards the crest of the dune. "Donblis, Voot, and Geb, I want you three near the crest of that knoll. Hyr, Burd, and Nothgem, down over at the base of the loose patch, across from Nyx's direction. Go!" he said to them before looking into Jinn's eyes. "Very well, you will be part of this hunt. Stay here until we are all in position. Once the protector arrives, you will accompany her and stay close to her at all times. You must obey any command that I, or any hunter tells you. Is that clear?"

Jinn was now grinning from ear to ear. Finally! He would be part of this great hunt. "Thank you, chief hunter! I am most honored."

The six other men were already moving to take their positions as Krag hefted his bone spear and drew it from its fur scabbard. Like Jinn's, the shaft of his weapon was made from a curved rib bone of a long dead beast, a creature that died out thousands of cycles ago. Unlike Jinn's weapon however, his spearhead was made of steel- it was Krag's most prized possession and he took great care of it in between hunts. "Alright," he said. "You two stay here for now. Nyx, once the protector arrives, follow her instructions to the letter. Remember what I told you, Jinn."

Jinn nodded as the chief hunter left and began to make his way towards his team. The young man gripped his spear tightly while he knelt back down. He was already nervous and giddy with excitement. "May Duun guide my spear," he whispered.

Nyx giggled. "You better not mess this up, Jinn. Krag is a kind master, but he is fair and will not hesitate to criticize and punish when it comes to those that do not do well."

"Silence," Jinn said. He knew he was inexperienced, but if he followed their lead, then everything would go smoothly. "You heard what he said. All I have to do is to stay by the protector and all will be well."

Nyx patted him on the back. "I am sure this rite of passage will be easier for you than what I went through. Nothing could be worse."

Jinn turned and looked back at his younger sister. "Was the pain truly unbearable for you when the Vis manifested itself? You were in our hut for weeks, just staying in bed. I could see that you were in complete agony. The one time I tried to feed you, your bulging eyes stared back at me like you were in some great widdendream."

"It wasn't so much the pain, but rather the talking voices inside my head," Nyx said wistfully. "It was as if the mouths of the entire tribe were all right by my ear and they were shouting and screaming in unison, and I could not silence them. Every word, every thought, every flash of anger, every singe of pain, every tear-I could feel them all at the same time. I could not rest, could not sleep. The cacophony of feelings, of cries, it all came screaming at me and I could not shut it off. Once, I had wondered what those in a fit of madness would be thinking about in their minds. When the Vis appeared, that was when I knew what lunacy actually meant, having experienced it firsthand."

Jinn clasped his younger sister by her elbow. "I am gladdened that you made it through. I have heard so many tales of young Strigas who ended up killing themselves, but not before they destroyed the minds of those around them. It takes a strong will to survive that and I'm very happy that you did."

Nyx smiled. "Oh, I had plenty of help. Elder Zedne was able to calm me enough so that I could sleep every once in awhile. But the one who got me through the most was our protector, she was actually able to venture into my mind and instruct me as to how to place the thought barriers that would block off any senses. Once the protective wards were in place, she spent many days in teaching me on how to project my mindsense."

Jinn was intrigued. "When you said the protector went into your mind, how did that work exactly?"

Nyx closed her eyes and remembered what had happened as if it was yesterday. "It was like a dream. I had imagined myself by the dunes at the outskirts of the village, but instead of vermillion colored sand, it was white powder. Then I heard footsteps behind me and there she was, our protector just seemed to walk up to me slowly and she had a smile on her face. She told me that everything would be okay and soon enough, all the other voices that were shouting all around me were suddenly silenced. A great sense of calm washed over me while I finally relaxed my exhausted senses. Then she sat down beside me, and began to teach me thought chants to say over and over within my mind. That was when I was finally able to banish the daemons plaguing me from the moment the Vis came about."

"So it was all like a dream, you could picture yourself as if it was a vision?"

"Yes," Nyx said. "It was all so vivid. You remember when the elders staged a play for the entire tribe? When they all wore masks and pretended to be someone else in some other land? It was very much like that play, only it was real. The land around me seemed true as I could touch and feel the sand. When the protector held my arms I could sense her warm, soothing touch."

Jinn looked off into the distance. "Our protector must be a very power Striga if she is able to create visions like that. I remember when Elder Zedne came to heal me when that kiir worm tore my leg open. As she stitched my wound with sinew string, I could sense her thoughts as she made me fight through the pain, but in the end, she just dulled the agony, she didn't stop it."

"Elder Zedne is quite old now," Nyx said. "She is well past seventy cycles, I believe. Her power has been waning for a long time already. Our protector is much younger than that, probably just half her age."

"Yes, but I have heard stories about our protector, that she can kill other men with a mere thought. Elder Zedne was never able to do that in her entire lifetime."

"I have heard of those stories too," Nyx said. "Though I am not sure if I can believe them. Perhaps they are just tales, made up by the elders in order not to sow discord whenever the protector demands that we behave."

"Well, I would never willingly go against her," Jinn said as he turned around to look around. The other hunters waited patiently near the edges of the loose sand patch. "We have been lingering for some time now, I wonder when she will come?"

The protector was sitting inside the small tent at the edge of the base camp. Among her people, she had the authority to maintain order and peace, and was therefore highly respected. She was hurriedly going through a leather sack, trying to find the one piece she needed before joining the hunters at the other edge of the perimeter. As her hand clasped around its sharp edges, she triumphantly retrieved the steel spearhead from the bag and placed the shaft of her black spear across her lap. Taking a fist-sized rock, she pounded at the pin that held the flint spear tip until it was loose enough for her to pull out. Using her fingers, she plucked the pin out and the flint tip slid off from the wooden shaft. Then she placed the metal spearhead onto the empty edge and locked it in place with the pin.

Miri silently cursed at herself for being so unprepared this day. By the time the sun had come up, she was exhausted and unable to concentrate on the little tasks that needed to be done, from making sure that everyone's weapons were prepared, to keeping an accurate count on their water supply. Strange visions had kept her awake all night, and she had neglected to change her spear tip until the signal came when Nyx had found the dargon at the far end of the hunting zone. She could now sense, using her Vis, that everyone was waiting for her to show up so she needed to move quickly. After placing a bone knife in a small scabbard that was strapped to her boot, Miri got up and hurried out of the tent, her spear in hand.

The wind had picked up and it ran through her long, reddish hair as she sprinted towards where the hunters were. Unlike most of the tribe, Miri's skin had a slightly paler, amber tinge and her fiery hair made her initially stand out as a stranger to their ways. But her powers as a Striga were formidable, and once she had mastered her Vis, she was soon elevated to protector of the entire village. Her exceptional power with the mindsense was only equaled by her formidable fighting abilities. No one dared to cross her when she placed the gauntlet down and imposed her authority.

By the time she had arrived to where the youths were stationed at, she could sense the impatience of the others around her. Nyx and Jinn were the youngest members of this expedition, and she was not setting a good example for them. The goddess Karma would be very displeased with her unpreparedness. Now that she was with them, she needed to muster all the Vis within herself, for this particular beast was the largest they had encountered, and therefore the most dangerous. The moment she stood by them on the top of the dune, Nyx and Jinn bowed their heads slightly to her as a sign of respect.

Krag started giving her some hand signals while crouching near the edge of the loose patch, and Miri understood the plan almost immediately. She had been to countless hunting parties, and the tactics to take down large prey was always the same. The other hunters would serve to keep the beast within their perimeter, while Miri would use her mindsense to tame the creature well enough for the killing blow.

Miri placed a reassuring hand on Nyx's slender shoulder. The protector stood almost a foot taller than her novice Striga, but she sensed that Nyx would grow to be a powerful Vis user, and would eventually replace her as protector someday. "Nyx, you know what to do. Wait until we are in position, then I shall give you the signal. Everything will be fine, just remember the mating thoughts," she said to the teenage girl before turning to face Jinn. "As for you my young hunter, I want you to stay behind me at all times. Keep your spear pointed at the beast and do not move forward without my specific orders. If the dargon lunges at you, move back slightly but do not advance. Remember that your flint point is sharp, but it is also fragile, if you take a bad angle against the dargon, it will snap your spear in two."

Both Nyx and Jinn nodded anxiously. Miri turned around and ran down towards the nearby patch of loose dirt, followed closely by Jinn. Krag had already placed the hunters into position and they could finally begin. All of them held their spears out while crouching down, so as not to be target the moment the beast came to the surface. Krag got on one knee as he stayed at Miri's right flank, ten yards away. The chief hunter would use his spear to pierce through the dargon's ribcage, just behind its first set of forelegs, for that was where its heart would be located.

Everyone held their breath as they waited for the monster to reveal itself. Miri's concentration had now achieved a Zen-like calmness as she extended her mindsense along the pool of sand in front of her. Her thoughts seemed to flow out of her body, like an invisible coil of energy, as her feelings soon traveled deep into the granular soil until it touched the sleeping dargon that hibernated underneath. *Yes,* she thought. *It is a huge beast indeed. I must be careful, and use my Vis to keep it docile the moment it awakens.* She turned and nodded to Nyx, standing thirty yards away on top of the dune.

It was now Nyx's turn. The young girl closed her eyes as she began to generate the mind of a female dargon in heat. Remembering the skills she was taught to by Miri, Nyx immediately placed thought barriers around the dargon brain patterns she was creating, lest it overwhelm her own human personality. There had been tales of renegade Strigas, horrible women who roamed the wastes after they had abandoned their humanity and became like the beasts of the dust, both in deed and in thought. Nyx valued her persona so she made sure the created thought essence of a female dargon remained firmly in the distant recesses of her mind, to be shattered into inaccessible shards of forgotten memory once the hunt was over.

Miri could see that Nyx was in her mind trance as the younger girl's eyes had turned completely white. Now it was time to project the mating sense into the sand. The timing would be tricky for the faked thoughts would draw the beast up to the surface and then she needed to alter the dargon's mental patterns into one of docility once that was done. Miri began to concentrate as her Vis traveled from her mind and bridged the air between Nyx and the sleeping dargon. Within seconds, she was able to harness Nyx's mating call, and increased its intensity before flinging the unseen ball of senses into the sand beneath her.

Within seconds, they all sensed the ground stirring beneath them. The hunters began to clutch their spears tightly while they began to tense up. The mating call projection was meant to be very powerful, it was designed to overwhelm the dargon's defensive instincts and drive it into a mating frenzy in order to force the beast up to the surface. The center of the loose sand pool began to shift as a cloud of dust flew up into the air, followed by a frenzied roar. The more experienced hunters covered their eyes so that they would not be blinded by the airborne dust. Jinn was caught totally unprepared, particles of dirt seeped into his eyes the moment the patch erupted. The youth grimaced as he used his arm to wipe away the irritating grains, while squinting his eyes so that he could see what had just come out. As he looked over the protector's shoulder to finally see the beast, he gasped.

The nearly thirty-foot long creature that emerged from the sand patch was the stuff of nightmares. Its snout was as large as one of their two man tents, and filled with sharp teeth that resembled chiseled black obsidian. The sand dargon's neck tendrils were located just behind its eyes, and their ropy, five foot long tentacles wriggled in the air, excitedly searching for an imaginary female with which to mate. The beast had six stubby legs that could be folded into its torso, in case it needed to slither in tight spaces underground. Legends abounded that these fearsome beasts could burrow through solid rock, and their god was a mighty wyrm whose overall length stretched across the wastelands and lived in a monstrous cave deep below the world above. The sand dargon's eyes were like small slits, some people wondered whether the creature could even see with them.

Nyx momentarily faltered on her concentration as she stood like a statue, utterly astounded by the sight of the gigantic creature in front of her. Her mindsense lost its cohesion, and the telepathic bridge that connected her Vis to that of the creature quickly cut off.

For a brief moment, the sand dragon partially regained its senses. It realized it had burrowed out into the surface during the heat of the day and there were other, dangerous animals around it. Krag cursed and barked out orders to the other hunters as he started moving sideways, hoping to get to the creature's right side before it got out of control. The dargon thrashed about, and it smashed its long, scaly tail against one of the hunters who had gotten too close to it. The man flew backwards for ten yards before landing in a heap along the base of a nearby dune, his ribcage shattered. The other hunters kept their distance, using their spears to keep the beast within the perimeter.

Miri held out her hand and gritted her teeth. She immediately recalibrated her mindsense, throwing mental blocks into the creature's mind, dulling its defensive instincts. The dargon slowed and stopped thrashing, while its tendrils extended past its neck in an effort to discern what was going on. Krag was now in position as he stood just a few yards away from the creature's right ribcage. The chief hunter ran forward and drove his spear into the area just behind the dargon's foreleg, but the beast was still wary, and it was able to twist itself to face the incoming threat at the last second. Krag's spear narrowly missed the monster's heart as it dug in between the scaly rib plates before embedding itself along its side. The dargon roared in pain as it kicked back with its foreleg, snapping Krag's spear shaft in two. The chief hunter rolled sideways, but the loose sand upended his footing and he fell onto the ground. The dargon sensed his helplessness as it turned and charged at him.

Jinn cried out in alarm as he ran past Miri and thrust his spear at the dargon's left middle leg. The youth did not angle his weapon properly, and the flint spearhead shattered while barely piercing the monster's scaly hide. The dargon reacted as it whipped its tail in Jinn's direction, but Miri was able to pull the youth back to where she was. Nevertheless, the tip of the monster's tail caught Jinn's knee and sent him sprawling sideways into the dirt. With the dargon's charge momentarily halted when it attacked the youth with its tail, Krag was able to get up and retreat, narrowly avoiding the beast's snapping fangs by a mere foot. One of the other hunters threw his spear at the creature and the weapon embedded itself into the dargon's thick back. The beast's scaly hide was so thick, it barely noticed the spear in its body.

Nyx grimaced as she concentrated with all her might, throwing waves of mating thoughts at the dargon. The monster suddenly became confused, as if its survival instincts could not decide as to whether to search for the female on the surface, or to attack those men that wounded it. Miri sensed the beast's disorientated thoughts as she projected her Vis past the dargon's set of instincts and overwhelmed it. The creature stopped as its sensory tendrils rose up in the air, initiating its courtship ritual for an imaginary female of its own kind.

With the creature now vulnerable, Miri knew it was now or never. She immediately dashed around until she faced the creature's right side. Concentrating just a few inches from where Krag's spear tip was embedded. Miri charged forward and used all her strength to thrust the weapon deep behind the dargon's foreleg. The metal spearhead and the flexible wooden shaft drove itself deep past the dargon's ribs, piercing its pulsating heart. The creature made a loud snort as it suddenly became lethargic, its lifeblood seeping away into other parts of its body.

Miri began to pull her spear out. Krag ran over to her and helped as they both took out the black shafted weapon from the creature's side. As the spearhead exited the wound, there was a slight sucking noise while the blood began to pour out of the stricken dargon's rib. Krag was able to retrieve the tip of his own weapon as the beast lay down onto the sand. Great gusts of air exited the monster's snout as its breathing slowed and eventually stopped. The remaining hunters let out a yell of victory as the dargon's sensory tendrils wriggled for a few seconds, then became limp.

Nyx ran down to where her brother was. Jinn was sitting on the sand, grimacing in pain as he clutched his knee. "Are you alright?" she asked.

"The pain is intense," Jinn said softly. "But it shall pass."

Krag and two other men ran over to where the fallen hunter lay to examine him. Miri could sense the dargon's fading thoughts as it slipped into unconsciousness and then death. She turned around and started walking to where Krag was. "How badly is Voot hurt?"

Krag and the other hunter helped up the injured Voot by dragging him by his cloak on the ground. "His ribs are broken, but he will live."

Miri nodded before looking over at Nyx and her brother. "This could have been an even greater calamity if it were not for the luck of the gods. What happened?"

Nyx looked down in shame. "I am sorry, protector. When the beast came out of the sand I-I suddenly lost my concentration."

"This beast was quite powerful," Miri said wistfully. "It was my fault. I should not have entrusted the mating thoughts to you alone, I should have helped before refocusing my Vis for the taming trance."

Jinn stood up and tested his right knee gingerly. It seemed more like a bad sprain than a torn ligament. He could walk, but he would be limping for a few days. "Thank the gods you were able to defeat that creature, Protector Miri. I thought I would be dead for sure."

Miri frowned. "You should not have run forward at it like that. You disobeyed me and you might have been killed."

"When I saw Krag on the ground, I thought the beast would have had him for sure," Jinn said. "I merely reacted with my instincts."

"Only animals react with their instincts. We humans have the power of thought. There is a reason why I told you to stay by my side at all times during the hunt. Like your sister, you lost your concentration. It was by the sheer luck of the gods that another catastrophe did not occur," Miri said.

Jinn said nothing as he bowed his head in shame. His lips trembled and he was about to shed tears, but Miri walked up to him and placed a reassuring hand on his shoulder.

Miri smiled at them. "Despite your failure to follow my lead, you nonetheless proved your courage and you might have even saved our chief hunter. That is to be commended," she said to him before looking at Nyx. "As for you, I sensed that you were able to redouble your efforts after the initial setback. In the end, you proved to be the catalyst that brought this monster down. For that, I am proud of you both."

Nyx and Jinn looked at each other and grinned. The hunt was a success.

# Chapter 3

While the wounded man was carried back to the camp, the other hunters went to work. They used flint knives and axes to skin the creature, its scaly hide would be used in the making of their thick leathery cloaks, cuirass armor, and lining for their tents. In addition to being a hunter, Burd was a master bone worker. He supervised the careful removal of the dargon's ribcage. The rib bones would be reshaped in the coming weeks, and used to make spear shafts as well as lining for the inner part of their war shields. The curviest bones would be used to make bows. The smaller, thinner cartilages would be reshaped into arrow shafts. Powdered bone meal would be used as both fertilizer for the fungi farms and as medicine for the tribal healer. The thick leg bones would be used to make the handles for their flint axes, while the dargon's teeth and claws would be made into daggers and spearheads.

Every hunter had a secondary skill. Krag was the tribe's best sinew maker and he masterfully sliced the dargon's tendons from the joints before placing them into a skin sack of fermented algae wine, where they would be infused with the special liquid to make them more malleable. After a few moons, the flexible sinews would be stretched taught to make many useful items. The final end products would be used as rope, bowstrings, and slings. The dargon's stomach and intestines would be sewn and dried to make waterskins and sacks. The creature's heart and liver was a delicacy, and it was quickly cut up into pieces and stored in leather bladders. The two dargon eyes were given to Nyx and Miri respectively, it was their prize for baiting and killing the great beast. The animal's tiny brain would be taken back to the healer for study.

The hunters tried to save as much of the dargon's blood as they could. The body was not cut open until all available blood had been carefully drained and poured into bladders. The lungs were carefully unraveled and allowed to dry out in the sun, this part of the animal would be used to make fine cloth. The belly was diligently sliced open and every bit of fat was squeezed into leather skins- all this would be rendered down into oil back in the settlement. The remaining flesh was cut up for transport back to the village. It had been at least three moons since there was a feast, so everyone was in a great mood. By the time the sun had begun to set, all that remained of the dargon's existence were some crimson patches in the dirt. A few desert beetles came out of hibernation to feast on the little bits that were left behind, but two of the more enterprising hunters scooped up the bugs and placed them into their sacks for later consumption.

By nightfall, everyone was back in the camp. Dried manure was laid out and used as fuel for the smoldering fires. There were plenty of songs being sung and the remaining ration of algae wine was used up. Everyone was set to make the return journey back to the tribe's village at the crack of dawn. Even though Voot was in terrible pain, he nonetheless joined in the singing and took his full share of the residual wine before falling asleep.

Krag sat cross-legged by one of the bigger fires while he chewed on a hunk of meat. He needed to ask the bone maker for a new spear shaft. Krag felt himself lucky to have survived without a scratch and even recovered his metal spearhead. If he had lost that most prized possession he would have been in a worse mood. As it stood, he considered the hunt to be a great success. The village now had enough food to last until the next cycle, at least.

Jinn limped over and sat down beside him. Krag sensed that the youth wanted to say something, but he didn't seem to have the courage to do so. Jinn made a sideways glance at him before staring back into the glowing embers of the bonfire in front of him. The smoke gave off a ripe, pungent smell.

Krag swallowed the remaining piece of meat and looked at the younger man. "What is it?"

"I just wanted to say how sorry I am for disobeying the protector," Jinn said softly. "She told me to stay by her side, but like a fool I ran forward. I was lucky to only sprain the muscles of my knee."

"And if you had not run off like a fool," Krag said. "I might not be around to chastise you. It was a heroic thing you did, but you must take care to always follow the lead of the ones who have experience in this."

Jinn nodded. "You are right, Krag. I cannot believe how stupid I was today."

Krag let out a big, throaty laugh as he got up, patted the youth on the shoulder and grabbed a half empty wineskin that was lying nearby. "You are learning, boy! The fact that you came here to talk to me about it is a portent of your maturation. I believe you will become a great hunter someday. You will get better as you partake in more hunts- though I fear we may have slain the last of these beasts. This could very well be the final great hunt of our tribe."

Jinn had a quizzical look on his face as the older man sat beside him and began to drink the remaining wine. "What do you mean, chief hunter?"

The wine was having its desired effect. Krag shrugged as he stared into the glowing fire. "Think about it. The last time we hunted and fought a beast this size was over thirty cycles ago. Now, most of our hunts produce only smaller animals. The last expedition we did a few moons ago yielded nothing more than a pair of dwarf-sized octapedes. It wasn't even enough meat to feed the entire tribe for one meal. In my younger days, the smallest of them were around six feet, there was even a time when we brought back a queen, that beast measured twelve feet long, and it was a monster! The hunts we have had in the last three cycles have dwindled down to almost nothing. There was a time that even the wastes were teeming with all manner of beasts. Now, there is nothing but dust …and more dust. I fear that in the next few cycles, we will find nothing at all."

Jinn let out a deep breath. "Then what do we do, Krag?"

"I do not know," Krag said softly. "It will be up to the elders of the tribe to decide. Our hunts have been ranging farther and farther from our settlement, and they barely bring back anything. We are spending too much precious resources to organize these expeditions. If I were an elder, I would vote to uproot the entire tribe and make the journey to a better land, one that is teeming with beasts we could hunt."

"Where would these lands be?"

Krag shook his head. "I do not know that either, boy. There was a time when a Magi patrol would visit us, at least once every cycle, to see whether there were any children that possessed the gift of Vis, so that any boy who had the potential would be taken away by them to be trained as a Magus at one of their citadels. That was over twenty cycles ago. Now, very few outsiders ever come by our settlement any more. Many times during my own youth, we would sometimes encounter hunters from other tribes in the wastes and there would be much feasting and trading. Soon enough, these friendly meets dwindled to nothing. Five cycles ago, one of our hunts chanced upon an old village by the Stone Mountains, near the upper edge of the Silt Sea. It had been abandoned for some time. Many of the houses had already been buried in dirt. We found no one and nothing of value, so we moved on."

Jinn leaned forward so he could hear more, the pain in his right knee momentarily forgotten. "What do you think happened to them? The tribe that inhabited that settlement?"

"I do not know the answer to that either, Jinn," Krag said. "I only fear that our way of life is finally at an end."

Jinn bit his lip. "You should not be feeling so melancholy, especially at a time like this, chief hunter! We found a great sand dargon, perhaps there may be more in this area!"

Krag smiled. "I admire youth such as yourself for the unbridled optimism your generation always has. Perhaps you are right and I am wrong. Perhaps this encounter with a huge dargon is a good sign." He titled his head upwards and squeezed the waterskin to swallow the remaining droplets of wine still in it. "I shall drink to that!"

Jinn grinned. At least he was able to bring a smile to his mentor's face. "I wanted to ask you, Krag- I am going to need a new spear. If I do not get one, I may not ever be allowed to go on another hunt again."

Krag laughed again. "Fear not, boy! We have enough dargon teeth to make you a fine bone spear. Only instead of a fragile flint tip, you shall have a very sharp, very hard spearhead this time. Elder Brar is a master teether, and he will be delighted he finally has some new dargon teeth with which to work with. He has never forgotten to remind me to always find him some petrified teeth, as he fears his skills in tooth working have diminished due to a lack of practice."

Jinn was still unsure. "What about the other hunters? Would they not be given priority over me when it comes to having the best weapons?"

Krag gave him a playful punch in the arm. "Leave it with me, Jinn. I will make sure that one of the tooth heads will be yours. But you must promise me that you shall take care of it. A sharpened dargon tooth is far better than a flint head, but you must be responsible for it at all times. Make sure that you clean the tooth after every use and keep it away from the algae. Any liquid, such as blood, needs to be removed once you are done using it. If you do not do these things, your tooth spear will become as brittle as the flint ones."

Jinn nodded enthusiastically. "You have my solemn word that I will care for my future weapon as if my life depended on it."

"Good," Krag said. "A hunter's weapon is his most prized possession. Take care of it and it will not let you down. Once the others in the village see it, they will have even greater respect for you. Especially that betrothed girl you have, she will sing your songs every night!"

Jinn blushed. Like all young men his age, he was already destined to marry one of the females in the tribe, as per the custom. It had been arranged while they were still small children, due to the fact that the tribe needed constant new blood to replace those that had died. His wedding day with Kere the freckled girl was to take place in the next moon. As a youth of the tribe, he had a sacred duty to plant his seed in her, so that his people would survive. His sister on the other hand, was destined never to raise a family. Ever since Nyx had manifested her Vis, she was automatically excluded from any marriage arrangements. It was the tribe's sacred law that any Striga must remain childless and unmarried for the rest of their lives.

"A new tooth spear would surely impress Kere and her parents," Jinn said. "But I know what will make her desire for me even more powerful is if I could somehow get my hands on a metal tipped spear, like what you and Miri have. There surely is nothing better than having a weapon like that."

Krag smiled as he shook his head. "If you want my metal spearhead, then you must prove yourself. It is only passed down from the chief hunter to his successor."

"I shall work hard and let it be my one goal in life then, to become a chief hunter," Jinn said. "Does that also mean the same for our protector? If Nyx proves herself, will she also inherit Miri's black spear?"

"That remains to be seen, for Miri did not inherit her weapon," Krag said.

Jinn's eyes opened wide. "Oh? How did she come to acquire such a powerful spear?"

"Before you were born, Miri was but a young girl around the age of your sister, younger I think," Krag said. "Like you and your sister, Miri was a child of the wastes, a foundling. Elder Zedne's older sister Elipe found Miri as a baby, somewhere near the edges of the Silt Sea, and raised the child as her own."

"So that is why Miri's skin is somewhat paler than anyone else in the tribe! She was born an outsider."

"Yes, but she grew up amongst us, and she has earned her right to be a full member of the tribe," Krag said. "She is no outsider."

Jinn bowed his head down. "Of course. I would not question her dedication for protecting us. I am sorry for interrupting you, Krag."

"Good, now as for the rest of the tale, Miri eventually manifested her Vis and was soon called a Striga, like Elder Zedne was at that time," Krag said. "One day, a group of marauders attacked our settlement. I was but a young man myself back then. These powerful men were renegade Magi, either runaways or exiles from their order, and they were equipped with potent weapons and armor made of metal. Many of the tribe died defending the weaker ones that day- my father, Elipe, and the tribe's protector. Just as the brigands were about to slaughter the remaining youths and the wounded men, Miri challenged the leader of the marauders to a duel. If she won, the rest of them would leave the village peacefully. The enemy leader was so amused at the audacity of a young girl making such a bold challenge, he accepted."

"I had heard the stories of this battle as a child, but not with such detail," Jinn said. "Please go on, chief hunter."

"It was the most incredible battle I had ever seen," Krag said. "My own skull was bashed in, and I took an arrow in the leg, so my memories are somewhat hazy, but it was the first and only time I had ever seen a Striga fight against a Magus. The enemy leader was flying through the air, trying to use his mindforce to throw up a cloud of sand and he even tried to pin Miri to the ground with his Vis. They did a lot more things, but I can hardly remember it all, it is just a blur of recollections now. But Miri held her own, as she used her powerful mindsense to trick and disrupt her opponent's concentration. In the end, I no longer remember how, she drove a bone dagger through the enemy leader's throat. The rest of the marauders left peacefully and we buried our dead. They have not returned since that time, and Miri was unanimously elected by the surviving elders as the new protector. She has been defending us all ever since."

"So she earned the right to the black spear then?"

"The metal spear that she carries with her was the enemy leader's own weapon," Krag said. "She took it from his dead hands. The black shaft of that weapon is made from quetzal wood that once grew in abundance long before either of us was born. Quetzal trees were resilient, and would grow to reach up into the sky. Their wood was both hard and flexible. But these things called trees are all gone now- chopped up for building materials that ultimately rotted away or for the fire pit. That black spear shaft is all that is left of their legacy."

Jinn remembered the teller's stories of beings called plants and trees. Entities that could grow into mighty stalks that covered a once green land. The teller had told him that all the trees were now dead, driven to extinction eons ago. The only life that grew on the ground these days and could be farmed were the algae and the fungi. The young hunter could only imagine what a world in the past would have looked like, surely he would have gone mad at the first sight of such a vision.

There were shouts coming from the other side of the camp. The voice that called out to them was from Ruuk, the skinner. "Krag, come here quickly! We found something!"

Both Krag and Jinn got up and made their way over to the others. Spread out over a leather and bone table was the large stomach sack of the dargon. The beast's abdomen was carried back to the camp intact, because the skinner needed to carefully cut and peel away the right parts in order to save the membrane and eventually dry it out for use as lining for their bladders. A dozen people were standing beside Ruuk as he had sliced open the top part of the stomach, revealing its grisly contents. When Jinn limped over and stood behind Ruuk's shoulder, he immediately let out a yelp as he saw what was still inside the dargon's stomach. Nyx was standing beside her brother and she pulled him away, lest he start to vomit.

Krag made his way over until he was beside Ruuk the skinner. As he stared down at what was on the leather table, he realized it was the lower part of a human leg. Even the leather boot around the foot was still intact. Dargons were known to kill and eat people, but no attacks had been recorded for many cycles. "Were they men?" Krag asked.

Ruuk nodded. He was thick and stocky, and his arms were like stumps. "I think they were at least two men. I found three sets of hands, and at least one head. Looking at that well-made boot, it could not be from a tribe in the wastes, the leatherwork and the stitching of the sinew is too fine- it must have been made with a metal needle."

Burd was the master bone worker and he carefully took out the remains of a human torso from the interior stomach membrane of the slain beast. He carefully peeled back the partially digested loincloth. "At least one of the men was a Magus," he said. The Magi were the male counterparts of the Strigas, they were masters of the mindforce.

Jinn, having recovered his wits, turned around and looked at the bloated, slimy remains. "How do you know it was a Magus?"

Burd tilted his head impatiently as he held up the salient parts. "Look, boy, the loins were emasculated. Only the Magi practice this form of ritual."

Krag frowned. "What were the Magi doing out here? Were they coming to see us?"

Ruuk shook his head. "It has been many cycles since any of us has even seen a real live Magus. They stopped their patrols a long time ago. If they came out here, then there must be a reason for it."

Krag glanced at the master skinner. "How long do you think these men have been in that beast's stomach?"

"A dargon this size has very slow digestion," Ruuk said. "Looking at the carcasses, the beast must have eaten these men at least two days ago, maybe more."

The effect of the wine was beginning to dissipate from Krag's head, only to be replaced by a pounding headache. He didn't like this at all. He was an ardent worshipper of Duun, the god of the wastes, and signs such as this meant that bad luck was on the horizon. First they encountered the biggest sand dargon anyone had seen in thirty cycles, and now this. Duun's way was that of tranquility, for the days to remain constant, never changing. Life was supposed to be stable, not full of surprises. When things got interesting, it signaled a time of great change. And when change came about, it usually meant turmoil. This was not good.

Miri stood at the edge of the camp when the shouts of alarm were raised. She used her mindsense to get a glimpse of what the others were thinking of. Within seconds she already knew what they were talking about before she even needed to walk over there. While the others were celebrating this extraordinary day, the chief hunter was in a troubled mood. Miri was as worried as Krag, but she needed to maintain a calm exterior, for that was the way of the protector. The last thing that was needed was to show a sense of panic or concern, for that would demoralize the others. Whatever the challenge that lay ahead, she was confident she would be able to deal with it.

Nyx ran over to her and they both were standing at the edge of a dried riverbed. The illumination of the fires behind them cast long shadows along the dusty ground. "Miri, the hunters would like a word with you to discuss what they had just found," Nyx said.

Miri nodded without turning her head while she continued to stare out into the wastes. "I know what had happened, the bodies of two Magi were found in the beast's stomach."

Nyx was shocked. "Huh? How did you ... oh, you used your Vis! But I thought it was taboo to do that?"

"Normally it would be," Miri said. "But when everyone is suddenly excited, stray thoughts can sometimes make its way over to you, much like a grub worm will come out of the sands the moment they sense food. When that happens, it is best to let the other's thoughts flow through you like a current of warm air."

Nyx nodded. "I guess I placed too many thought blocks in my mind to be as sensitive to stray cerebrations like that."

Miri turned and looked at her. "Keep your thought blocks in place for now. Your power is still growing as you gain more maturity. I will teach you to be able to allow some flow of thoughts soon. But first, you must know how to deal with them should the intrusions become too much for your own mind to handle."

"I understand, Miri," Nyx said. "If I may ask, why did you not join the feasting earlier? Is something the matter?"

Miri looked back out into the distance. "I was late arriving for the hunt today. It seems that my mind has been preoccupied by something. I could not sleep the night before because some strange visions kept appearing in my thoughts, and no amount of my disciplines could seem to abate it. I was actually going to ask you about it whether you sensed it too."

"Oh? That is strange since I have not felt anything," Nyx said. "What kind of visions?"

Miri closed her eyes. "Visions of a storm. Being blinded and carried off into the howling winds. Of pain and loss for someone I loved dearly. It was like being in another one's thoughts, only I could not divest myself from it. I normally could stop any sort of mental intrusion, but this was quite unusual for I could not block it."

"We have encountered no storms in this hunt," Nyx said. "Perhaps you accidentally intruded on the dreams of one of the hunters?"

"No, it was not a dream, more like an event that had recently happened…" Just as Miri said those words, a sudden sharp stab of pain forced its way to the back of her skull. She cried out and fell to her knees, clutching her head.

"Miri!" Nyx said as she knelt down beside the protector. The teen girl placed her hands on Miri's shoulders, hoping to try and comfort her.

For a long while, all Miri could do was moan as the agony pressed down into her mind. She began to chant mentally as she used all her disciplines to stabilize her thoughts and cancel out the pain. Another minute passed before she opened her eyes again. As her vision came back to normal, her mind was now clear. Miri stood up once more while she began to mentally probe the dunes ahead of her.

Nyx stood beside her. The young girl's face was still a mask of concern. "Miri? Are you alright? What happened?"

Miri immediately ran down the crest of the dune and raced towards the edge of the wadi. Nyx was briefly surprised, but she recovered her wits and took off after the protector. Miri jumped into the bottom of the sandy trench and ran down along its length. Nyx was slightly behind as she sprinted and kept up. Soon enough, both women made it to the edge of the gully, as Miri climbed up over the side and stared at a small mound in front of her.

"There," Miri said as she pointed to something on the nearby sand.

Nyx turned and looked to where she was pointing at. The moonlight wasn't too bright, but there was enough illumination to see what it was. Nyx doubled back and gasped.

Lying near a broken sand drift was a young boy. He looked to be around eleven or twelve cycles old and had pale hair like bright silver that caught the reflection of the moonlight. The child was unconscious and breathing heavily, a layer of dust covered his thin little body. Dressed only in a loincloth, the boy wore a single sandal while his other foot was bare.

## Chapter 4

By the second day of the hunting party's return, the young boy had regained consciousness. The tribe had been holding a feast since the first day and some food had been set aside for the child, while Elder Zedne needed to ask him some questions first. Nyx was told to head over to the protector's home and summon her back to the healer. The teen girl ran all the way. She was in a state of excitement these past few days, for so many new and interesting things had been experienced. Since they were within the familiar confines of the settlement, everyone tended to be dressed a bit more casual. The traveling cloaks were stored away and the females wore breast cloths in addition to their loincloths, while the men only wore the latter. Most of the adults wore simple leather sandals on their feet, and the dozen or so little children would run around naked in order to preserve clothing material for the tribe. It was customary when a child reached their tenth cycle to be given their first loincloth, as a sign of impending adulthood and all of its future responsibilities.

Nyx trotted past the main avenue of the gods, near the main gathering hall. She headed towards the house of the protector, situated near the outskirts of the settlement. Her mind had been filled with so many new sights lately, such as the wondrous feasting upon their return, the joyous singing, and the honors being bestowed upon her for the courageous use of her Vis. Even the hushed murmurs of what they had found in the stomach of the great dargon, and of the discovery of a mysterious foundling in the wastes did not dampen her eagerness. She had seen the protector in action, and she was fully confident that the entire village could more than handle anything that would come their way.

As she turned the corner and made it closer to the periphery, Nyx noticed her brother Jinn standing beside one of the huts along the alleyway, talking to his betrothed, the girl his age named Kere. Nyx remembered playing with the slightly older girl when they were small children. Her brother and his fiancé instantly noticed her and the couple quickly separated, Jinn moving away into the middle of the street while Kere ducked back inside her hut. Nyx placed a hand over her mouth to suppress a laugh. Her brother was not supposed to speak with his future bride at all until the marriage ceremony was over. For reasons she could not explain, Nyx wasn't envious of the other youths who would be married in this cycle. She knew her destiny would be that of a powerful Striga, and her allotment in that kind of life was never to be married, or to bear children. *Such is not the life for me*, she thought. *I prefer and accept the gift of Vis and all the obligations the position carries with it.*

Stopping in front of the protector's entryway, Nyx called out her own name and her intention to come inside, as was the custom. When she heard an acknowledgement, the girl pulled back the leather flap that covered the entrance and stepped into the abode. She had only been within the protector's house once before, when she was but a child of eight, to be scolded for doing childish things. Seizing her chance, she looked around to see if there was anything of interest. The protector's dwelling didn't seem any different from the other houses in the village. The walls were bricks of dried sand and silt, mixed in with the abundant black algae found just below the surface of the Silt Sea as a binding agent, and hardened by the sun. There was a large hole in the center of the roof, just above the fire pit. A crude stone table and two medium sized, flat-topped boulders that served as chairs were to the side. A bed made of soft sand, a fur pillow and a leather sleep sack lay at the far end of the single room hut. A tall rack made of bones held together with dried sinew string and leather strips held the black spear and a few other weapons.

Miri was sitting cross-legged by the unused fire pit. She was tying a leather strap around a polished dargon tooth spearhead, to further strengthen its grip to the bone shaft. "You have come about the boy?"

Nyx nodded. "Yes, Protector Miri. Elder Zedne has asked me to summon you. The boy is awake and she needs your help."

Miri placed the nearly completed spear on the ground and stood up. "Very well, let us proceed to the house of the healer."

As they came out of the hut, Nyx glanced at the protector as they started walking. "Protector Miri, I-I wanted to ask you a question."

Miri smiled at her. "Nyx, you do not have to be so formal all the time. You are now a Striga, a sister of the gift. The goddess Vis has strengthened your power and I consider you as an equal to me. Do not be shy."

Nyx blushed a little, but she quickly recovered. "I seem to have developed a problem with my brother, Jinn."

"What kind of problem?"

"We were very close growing up, not long after our parents died of the fever," Nyx said as they walked along the dusty alleyway. "Jinn always protected me, but now it seems he has become distant. When we were traveling during the hunt we became close again, but when we returned to the village it seems we once more go about our separate ways. All he can think about is his bride now."

Miri smirked. "He is of that age when his loins begin to dictate his actions. I sense he will be a great husband for that freckled girl. Are you jealous now that he has turned his attention to her and not to you?"

Nyx shook her head. "I would not call it jealousy. I am his sister, not his mate. It just feels a little sad we are drifting apart now that we are back in the village. This had led me to think, why are Strigas not allowed to marry and why do the Magi slice off their genitals? I know it is customary amongst all the tribes across the lands, but I do not understand the reasoning behind this tradition. I heard the teller say it is because the ones who do not interest themselves in building a family are the ones who become powerful users of the gift of Vis, but that explanation seems so … inadequate."

"There is another reason why Strigas and Magi do not have any children," Miri said. "It is quite an important justification as well, though few of us like to talk about it."

"Oh? What is the other reason then?"

"You remember the legends of the Gorgons?"

"Yes, of course," Nyx said. "The tales of the Gorgons were one of the first stories the teller told. Powerful beings that enslaved the world, and only a destructive war which lasted for thousands of cycles finally ended their reign. The blood of so many men, women, and children was spilt. It is said that the last of the plants and trees had died out at the end of that cataclysm."

"Do you remember hearing about the power of these creatures?"

Nyx nodded. "The Gorgons had the power of both Strigas and Magi, only magnified. I remembered hearing a tale that even said these Gorgons could do things that no one else could- they could disappear into thin air, or stop the sun from shining. Many people they enslaved worshipped them as gods who walked the land."

Miri stopped in front of the healer's house. She turned to look at the younger girl. "There is your answer. After the Gorgons were defeated, the Magi and Strigas were separated and commanded never to bear any children. The Grand Magus at that time went a step further and decreed all Magi were to be stripped of their loins to guarantee that they would bear no successors."

Nyx scratched the back of her head. "But why, though? What did that have to do with the Gorgons?"

"Think about it," Miri said softly. "There is a legend not many tellers know about. It was the story of the origins of the Gorgons. Long ago, there were many wars between Strigas and Magi. One day, the most powerful Magus in the world fell in love with the most powerful Striga. They had three children. These three were given all the gifts their parents had, including their Vis. Thus, the first three Gorgons were born. After that, the world was enslaved. Now you can understand why Strigas and Magi cannot bear children. For any child born to this union could once again become Gorgons."

Nyx gasped. She just stood there, without saying anything else. She had once thought that the prohibition of marriage to one with the gift of Vis was just tradition, yet now it had a very practical side to it. The thought of being able to sire a Gorgon just like that was quite shocking to hear.

Miri cupped her hand around her mouth so that the people inside the larger dwelling would hear her. "This is Miri and Nyx. We ask permission to enter the house of the healer."

The customary reply came almost immediately. "Enter and be welcome."

Miri pulled back the leather flap and gestured at Nyx to go inside first. The girl nodded and went in after. Elder Zedne's home was larger than the others, for the healer needed the space. The main room contained many bone and leather shelves that contained all sorts of different ingredients for healing poultices and other medicines. A large, rectangular stone slab was near the central fire pit, it was used for surgery to mend bones and sewing up of wounds. A stone table was at the far end and contained many instruments for the healing of the sick and injured. Rare and valuable glass bottles contained strange powders and medicine. Two other entryways led to Elder Zedne's private chamber and the other was for her patients.

One of the inner flaps parted and Elder Zedne came into the room with a gap toothed smile. She had once been a powerful Striga, but age had slowly waned her Vis. Matted silver hair hung limply down on her shoulders, but beneath her wrinkled cheeks, her ever sharp blue eyes still held great wisdom and power. She was dressed in a leather tunic, as was customary for all elders of the tribe. Elder Zedne extended her scrawny arms as she hugged Miri and kissed her cheek. "Welcome, welcome, my dears. It is so good to see you again, my child. You must come see me more often here."

It was Miri's turn to blush. Elder Zedne was considered to be her mother after Miri was found in the wastes by Zedne's older sibling Elipe. After her sister's death, Zedne continued to raise her and taught her the ways of the Striga. "Oh, Mother. We saw each other just yesterday, during the feast, do you not remember?"

Zedne winked at her. "Of course, I do. But that does not count. We should not be seeing each other only when it comes to our needed tasks, we ought to just have pleasant talks, like the times when we were both younger."

Miri laughed. "We did have a nice talk during yesterday's celebrations, that was not work, yes?"

Zedne just smiled while they clasped hands. "Even a feast these days is work for me, child. I can only rest when I have no worries about my children and everyone is well and good."

"You still keep calling me child these days," Miri said. "It is the one habit of you that I find slightly annoying. You can see that I am fully grown and have been for many cycles now."

Zedne tilted her head back and laughed. "I took care of you since you were just a baby. And since I am older than any of you, it is my right and privilege that I call you all my children."

Miri giggled. "I will give you that then, Mother."

Zedne moved over to Nyx and gave her a kiss on the cheek as well. The teen girl couldn't help but smile. Elder Zedne was respected throughout the entire tribe, and when one needed to be consoled for any sort of sadness or grief, she would always be the one everybody sought out. The time began to pass by so pleasantly, Miri had to focus back to the task at hand.

Miri finally placed her hand up. "Let us get back to work again. How is the boy?"

Zedne nodded. "He is somewhat malnourished, but his health is coming back to normal. The boy must have spent days out there in the wastes. A very resilient child."

"Can he communicate with us?" Miri asked.

"I asked him a few questions in the trade language, but he did not answer," Zedne said. "Though I suspect he does understand our language from the way his eyes dart around."

Miri rubbed her smooth, delicate chin. "Have you tried to use your mindsense on him yet?"

"I did a simple probe of his surface thoughts," Zedne said softly. "But I was unable to discern anything. That is why I summoned you both. It seems this boy might have some sort of mind blocks in place to prevent the scrying of his thoughts and intentions."

Nyx's eyes opened wide. "Are you saying he may be a Magus, Elder Zedne?"

"It may be possible since only Magi would have that kind of training," Zedne said. "But his loins are intact. If he is a Magus, then surely he would have been emasculated, yes?"

Miri looked away. "This is most peculiar. We found the remains of two men in the dargon's belly. Our skinner says at least one of them was a Magus. Now we have a boy who is not cut, yet exhibits the defensive mind techniques only taught by the Magi. No male user of the Vis has come anywhere close to our tribe in recent memory, so far all this to happen at near the same time cannot be a coincidence."

"Perhaps with the three of us working together, we might be able to determine who this boy truly is," Zedne said as she gestured towards the second entryway. "Come, let us speak to him."

All three women ventured into the healing room, a simple place with two fur beds on opposite sides facing each other. There was a clay pot near the side and a small window that let in a shaft of light. The other bed was unoccupied, while the other contained the boy. The child was awake while lying on the bed, his bottle green eyes darting back and forth. When he noticed the three women step into the room, he immediately closed his eyes and pretended to be asleep. Zedne smiled as she stood over him and placed a reassuring hand on his arm. Not sensing any danger, the boy once again opened his eyes.

Elder Zedne gently squeezed the boy's arm. "Do you wish to have some water, child?"

The boy looked up at her and shook his head. Miri suppressed a nod. So the boy could understand the trade language after all. Now they needed him to speak.

Zedne gestured at the other two women. "These are my friends. The woman with the red hair is our protector, Miri. She was the one who found you in the wastes. The other woman is Nyx, her apprentice. Do not fear, child. No one shall harm you."

The boy blinked a few times. "W-where am I?"

"You are in a settlement near the Great Silt Sea," Zedne said. "Our tribe is called the Arum Navar, it is the old name for the people of the wastes. As our custom, all guests who enter peacefully into our village are given the promise of sanctuary. This means that no harm is to come to you here, as we pledge it by the names of our gods, Duun and Karma. Since you are a foundling, you may be adopted into the tribe if your parents are lost. What is your name, child?"

"Rion," the boy said softly.

Zedne held her hand over her chest. "It is an honor to finally know your name, Rion. I need to ask- where are your parents?"

The boy looked away. "I-I do not have any parents."

"Were they lost out in the wastes with you?" Zedne asked.

The boy shook his head. "No."

Miri's eyebrows arched. "Rion, how did you find yourself out in the desert?"

"My friend Aertos," Rion said. "He took me into the wastes."

Miri rubbed her chin. "Your friend … do you know where is he now?"

The boy's lips began trembling. "He is dead."

"We were out in the wastes hunting and we killed a dargon not far from where we found you," Miri said. "Inside the beast's stomach, we found the remains of two men. Could one of them be your friend?"

Rion blinked rapidly. It looked like he was trying to hold back his tears. "I do not know. Perhaps."

"Was your friend traveling alone with you?" Miri asked.

"Yes," the boy said softly. "Two men were hunting us."

Miri glanced at the other two women. Both had surprised looks on their faces. She faced the boy once more. "These two men, why were they hunting you?"

"They wanted to bring me back to the citadel," the boy said.

Elder Zedne let out a deep breath. The abodes of the Magi were called citadels. "Rion, why were you in the citadel?"

"I-I do not know," Rion said. "My memories fail me. All I remember was being held in some cold, dark room where the lights would come from bright yellow spheres. Then it was the bloodletting, when they would use these sharp needles and thrust them into my arms. It was very painful. I was in constant agony."

"Do you remember anything before that? Where did you grow up?" Miri asked.

The boy shook his head once more. "I-I have no memories of my life before the dark room."

"But who taught you how to speak the trade language? Who brought you up? Surely every child knows that," Nyx said. Miri placed a hand at the younger girl's elbow, and Nyx instantly became quiet.

Rion's breathing became rapid. The boy was clearly uncomfortable at the line of questioning he was receiving. "I-I do not know. All I can remember is the pain of that horrid place."

"But you escaped," Miri said. "Do you remember how you got away?"

"One of the others who used to hurt me," Rion said. "His name was Aertos. He saw my sufferings for many moons. I think he took pity on me and took me away when the others left the dark room. He made me wear a cloak and we made for the desert. We journeyed for many days, then they caught up to us. Aertos told me to run and then he tried to fight them. I saw them kill him."

Miri leaned closer. "Rion, these other men. Were they Magi?"

The boy was weeping now. His words came out in slight gasps. "Y-yes."

"Do you know why you were being bled?" Miri asked.

The boy placed his hands over his tear filled eyes. "No! All I-I remember was the pain!"

Elder Zedne placed a hand on Miri's arm. "I think the boy needs to rest now," she said to the protector before placing a comforting hand on the boy's shivering shoulder. "Go back to sleep, child. I shall bring you some food. Do not worry, all is well."

The healer led the other two women back out into the main chamber. "I think that is enough questioning for now," Zedne said to them. "The child is clearly upset, and he cannot seem to remember anything other than his terrible experiences in that citadel, and of his flight across the wastes."

"Mother, this could have serious consequences for the entire tribe," Miri said. "We have given the boy the promise of sanctuary, and we are now pledged to protect him with all our lives. But what if the Magi come looking for him and we decide to keep him? This could be a start of a war."

Nyx was shocked. "The Magi will come here? But I thought they no longer send out patrols into the wastes. I was not even born before the last time they had come into this village."

"I was but a child myself when the last Magi patrol came into this village," Miri said. "I have not seen another since that time. Rumors in the tribe spoke about their kind dying out. There has been no Magus born in this tribe since Elder Rawn's son was sent away to the citadel. I was so small then, thus I could hardly remember it."

"Yet the boy's story proves that the Magi still exist," Zedne said. "It seems they have been doing things that we were not previously aware of."

Miri turned to look at the old woman "I was never sure as to how the ancient treaties worked when it came to determining the fate of a Striga or a Magus. How could the Magi know if any of the tribes produced Magus as offspring?"

"The patrols would regularly visit the tribes of this area, at least once per cycle," Zedne said. "Then the tribes were to give away any male child that had the potential power of the mindforce. Our people were allowed to keep girls who had the Vis. There was an old story about one tribe in the wastes, called the Dar'kar, who refused to hand over their male children, who had the Vis, over to the Magi."

"What happened to them?" Nyx asked.

"The Magi sent in an army of warriors, each one with great power in their skills of Vis, and they slaughtered the entire tribe," Zedne said. "Men, women, and children. Killed them all for violating the great pact. There were even rumors that the Magi employed a group of Strigas to help them in this most grisly task."

Nyx was shocked. "The other tribes never rose up against this?"

"All the tribes in the known world signed onto the great pact," Zedne said. "So they could not do anything since the Dar'kar had violated this most sacred treaty. Of course, there have also been wild rumors of renegade families living by themselves out in the wastes, siring both male and female Vis users. The Magi sent many patrols to root out those that did not sign the pact."

Nyx remembered Miri's earlier tale about the origins of the Gorgons. No wonder the Magi were trained as warriors. "But since the patrols stopped so long ago," Nyx said. "How do the Magi know if any child of the tribes would still exhibit the Vis now?"

"That is a question that I do not know," Zedne said softly. "Our tribe is fortunate, for no male child has been born a Magus since the patrols stopped. As for the other tribes, assuming they still exist, I am fearful of what has happened."

Nyx scratched the back of her head. "So if the Magi do not patrol the tribes anymore, what happens to the male children of Vis then?"

"According to the great pact, they must be taken to the nearest citadel if the Magi do not come for them," Miri said. "If that is not possible, then the child is put to death."

Nyx let out a deep breath. "By the gods! That is a horrible fate!"

Miri held out a hand and gestured at the younger woman to lower her voice. "We have had no contact with the other tribes since the patrols ceased as well. So perhaps the Magi stopped bothering with us simply because there have been no male children born with the Vis in our tribe."

"But how would they know that we do not have any?" Nyx asked.

"That is the question that has yet to be answered," Zedne said. "Though I think the other explanation is more likely- that we are the last remaining tribe out here, and the Magi have been corrupted."

"We may need to find out. If the boy is a Magus, I do not wish death upon him if the Magi no longer exist," Miri said. "Mother, where is the closest citadel that we could journey to?"

"The citadel of Doss, many days travel to the west of here," Zedne said. "I know of no one who has journeyed in that direction since the day we found you, child. Elder Devos the teller probably has an old map to guide you, should you decide to travel there."

"The hunting party was ranging out in the western area when we encountered the dargon," Miri said. "It is entirely possible that the boy and those that were seeking him might have come from that place."

Nyx had been listening intently. All these tales were new to her. This was something that wasn't taught by the tellers and the elders. "Pardon me, but what lies beyond that citadel?"

"Barren hills and the remnants of the city of Ceorath," Zedne said. "I was quite young when I visited that city, and it was already decaying. So few inhabitants were left in there. I would imagine that the entire settlement would have been a ruin by now, unless the gods somehow blessed it and it would thrive again."

"Do you think it would be worthwhile if we investigate that citadel? Perhaps the answers that we are looking for might lie in there," Miri said.

Zedne smiled as she placed a wrinkled hand on Miri's cheek. "You are the protector of this tribe, child. It is up to you if you feel that such a place needs to be explored. But if the boy's story is true, then it seems the Magi of that place are doing strange, evil things to children in there. If you were to ask for my counsel, I would say be very cautious. We do not know what the Magi are up to these days, and you may be heading into a trap you cannot escape from."

Miri smiled. Elder Zedne was always a fountain of wisdom. "Then let us err on the side of caution for now. What I would like to do is to try and probe the boy's thoughts and gleam any additional information on this enigma."

Zedne nodded as she turned and headed for the healing room. "Wait here, I will see if the boy has gone to sleep."

While the elder went into the other room, Nyx stood beside the protector. Her excitement was at a fever pitch. "Miri, if you will travel to that citadel, can I come with you? I have never been out more than two weeks away from this village."

"If I do make the journey to that place," Miri said. "Then it will be a dangerous one. It is best that you remain here, your Vis is not yet strong enough to withstand the rigors of battle, should it come to that."

Nyx was crushed. "Miri, please! I have never made a long journey, it will be an adventure for me. I am tired of sitting around in this village, it is the same thing over and over again. This last hunt was the greatest thing that ever happened in my entire life!"

Mir held her hand up again. "Calm down and lower your voice. The village is safe, we have sentries guarding the outer perimeter so there has never been an attack against us since I became protector. If you go out there without any experience, you will be easy prey for the beasts and men who wish to do you harm. Have patience and do not be so brash. Your time will come, just focus on getting better with your Vis."

Nyx turned around and walked to the other side of the room as she began to sulk. Zedne came back out into the main chamber and walked over to Miri. "The boy is asleep now. Our questioning must have placed a lot of strain on him," the elder said.

"Alright, I shall attempt a mind probe on him," Miri said as she walked towards the other entryway. "You might want to console Nyx, she is pouting again."

As Zedne went over to the teen girl in order to cheer her up, Miri opened the leather flap and stepped into the healing room. She could see the boy sleeping on the bed. Standing over him, Miri began to refocus her Vis. Although she believed the boy was telling the truth about what had happened to him, she wanted to see if he might have withheld any crucial information that could shed some light on how he escaped and what the situation was with the Magi.

Closing her eyes, Miri began to expand her mental presence. Her senses became highly acute as she became aware of the slightest pressure in the air, the subtle changes in temperature and the smells of oil, fermented algae, and dried urine. She could soon hear the boy's light breathing as her mind hovered over him. Soon enough, her Vis began embedding itself into the boy's head. At first, Rion's thoughts were merely blank since his mind was resting in a deep sleep. Miri went past his dormant surface cognizance and began to enter Rion's subconscious, the place where he stored his memories.

The images that began to flow through her mind were in fragments. It was like brief snippets of flashback, short recollections that had branded themselves into the boy's memory. Miri refocused as she began to sort through the cascade of images, sounds, smells, and past feelings. She needed to carefully arrange them into a coherent set of senses in order to understand any of it. The discipline required intense concentration as any lapse in her Vis would throw the whole thing into a jumbled, incomprehensible mess that would take a long time to sort out.

The first reminiscences were of Rion crying in the dark. The boy was held down tightly, unable to move his arms and legs. He was bound naked on a slab of cold stone. Then a blinding light hovered over him, like a small sun. The boy blinked as he tried to turn away from the intense radiance that was practically blinding. Then she saw shadows looming over him. Hushed whispers, even an occasional laugh was heard. Rion cried out, begging to be let go, but they ignored his pleas. Miri felt the boy's pain as metal needles were inserted into his arms. Rion's screams intensified when his limbs began to feel numb. He turned his head, and Miri saw a strange sight: all along the boy's arms were transparent, ropy material, like crystal worms that snaked around his arm. The needles embedded in his limbs were drawing crimson liquid from his body. Miri gasped. The end of the glass tendrils led to a strange contraption, a box made of dark metal with strange, glowing symbols that was draining Rion's blood. Just as the boy began to pass out, the painful needles were removed, leaving a red welt along his thin arms. The boy began to whimper, the pain and the weakness continued. Another shadow stood over the child. One set of eyes looked at him, only this time it showed a modicum of pity and sadness.

"No one will hurt you any longer," the voice whispered in Rion's ear. Then the boy felt the straps being removed from his arms and legs. Rion moaned as his rescuer threw a cloak over his bare body and lifted him up. More darkness. The sensation of being carried through a twilit corridor. Then the sudden gust of wind in the night air as the man who carried him ventured into the outside.

Miri opened her eyes. As she adjusted back into her own thoughts, she nearly lost her balance. Reacting quickly, she held onto the side of the wall at the last minute, which stopped her from falling onto the floor. She was breathing heavily. Refocusing her own mind back into place took longer than usual. The horrific memories of the boy being tortured like that were still quite vivid in her mind. She silently chanted her meditation mantras while the foreign memories bled out.

As she ventured out into the main chamber, Elder Zedne walked over to her. "I sent Nyx back to her home, there was no point in her brooding around here," the old woman said. "Did you glean anything useful?"

Miri nodded. She was exhausted. "He has been through a terrible ordeal. I think it is best that we go slowly with whatever needs to be done. The Magi were doing some sort of ritual on him. He spent most of his time lying on a stone slab as they would drain his blood. Those evil men only stopped because he was near death, then they would wait and do it all over again as soon as he had sufficient strength for another bloodletting. To what kind of nefarious end all that torture was about, I have no knowledge. Much of his memories seemed to have been burned away, or suppressed so deep that not even I could fathom them. He must have learned how to speak the trade language from somewhere, but all his recollections are about the agony he endured and escaped from."

"Better we wait," Zedne said. "If his pursuers were both killed, then we are reasonably safe here. I would suggest we treat the boy as a foundling for now. We can have Elder Devos instruct him in the tales of our people. Perhaps with a stable life with the tribe, his full memories will reveal themselves in time, and then we could act on it."

"Agreed," Miri said. There was something else about the boy. Rion didn't seem to be just any sort of Magus, for there was nothing special about a Magi's blood. She sensed that the boy might be someone even more special, but she needed to know more before deciding on anything else.

## Chapter 5

Once the day's teachings were over, the other children got up and left the teller's hut. The younger ones were on their way home to their mothers, while the older ones would go out and play. Rion wanted to learn more about the stories the teller told, so he volunteered to stay behind and help clean the teaching room. It had been days since he recovered from his ordeal in the desert and his fear and suspicions were replaced by an innate curiosity, a trait common with every child. His mental sessions with Elder Zedne and Miri were of great benefit to him, since it helped to lock away his bad memories, though he would still sometimes wake up in the middle of the night, drenched in sweat, when the dark recollections entered his dreamstate.

Elder Devos placed the stone tablets back into the bone shelf. He glanced at the boy who was sweeping the floor with a hair broom. Rion had only started the teachings quite recently, but he was a fast learner. The boy had a quick mind, and seemed to be able to learn the chants and songs after just listening to them but once. Devos had been looking for such a child with a talent like that, for he needed to train a successor soon.

Rion stood to the side and looked at the results of his handiwork. The floor was smooth once more, the loose dust finally swept into the depressed entryway. He placed the broom to the side of the wall, near the shoe rack, then turned to face the teller. "Elder Devos, I have finished cleaning the learning area. Do you have another task for me?"

Devos looked at the boy and smiled. Unlike the other men in the village, he had a full growth of beard on his chin and it extended down to the middle of his neck. However, since his only child had passed away from the great fever of forty cycles ago, Devos's unique gift would soon be lost once the wastes reclaimed him. "Come over here, child. Would you like to eat something?"

"No, thank you," Rion said as he walked over and sat down on the floor beside the teller. "Elder Zedne makes a very thick soup, full of green algae and shrooms. She forces me to eat it every morning before coming here."

Devos laughed as he sat down in front of the boy. "Do you reside with Elder Zedne for now?"

The boy nodded. "I sometimes stay at the protector's house if the healer needs to treat anyone. Elder Zedne says that it is best to keep away from the sick, lest I catch whatever it is that ails them."

"Protector Miri must also be kind to you," Devos said. "In all my cycles of life here, I feel that she is our most powerful protector. The only one that comes close to her was a male protector named Lakajan. He was a Magus who completed his training at the citadel and returned to us, for he was once born here. Of course, all this was many cycles ago, I was but a boy your age back then."

Rion's blond eyebrows shot up. "Oh? I thought only Strigas could become protectors."

Devos shook his head. "No, child. Anyone can be a protector. Even those that are not blessed with the gift of Vis can be elected by the council of elders to defend the tribe. The protector is usually the best fighter. Many hunters have been elected to the title."

"I see," the boy said. "I have another question. You and the others sometimes remark about Vis as a goddess, while other times you use the word to describe the power of the mind. Are there two meanings to it?"

"You are very perceptive," Devos said. "We consider Vis as a deity, and yet we also call the gift that she bestows in her own name as well. The power of the mindsense and the mindforce are but manifestations of Vis. Other children have a slight difficulty in grasping this, but you seem to have understood it at once."

Rion listened intently. "The one thing that confuses me is that some in the village call Vis a man, yet others refer to him as a goddess. Which is it?"

"An astute observation," Devos said. "You see, the Magi consider Vis as a male god, for their powers are derived from the aspect of the god's manly side- his loins. Strigas consider Vis as a goddess, they believe that she is not a man, but is in fact, a woman."

"So which is the correct belief?" the boy asked.

"They are both right. The tales tell of Vis being part man and part woman. He or she can assume a different form, depending on who channels her power. If a man uses her gifts, then he receives the male aspect of the god. If it is a woman with the power, then Vis shall also become female to accommodate her."

"It somewhat makes sense," Rion said. "So the gods can change their gender?"

Devos smirked. "It depends on who you ask. The Magi believes that Vis is exclusively male, while some Strigas consider her wholly female."

"What do you believe?"

"I do not believe in absolutes," Devos said. "No one is truly right or wrong. The gods are mysterious and their goals are hard to understand. The best we can do is not to displease them."

"So does the tribe worship Vis then?"

"We venerate Vis, but she is not our primary god," Devos said. "Our tribe primarily worships two other gods. Duun is the god of the wastes, and his wife, the goddess Karma, she who controls fate."

The boy nodded. "I have heard some of the hunters whisper a prayer to Duun as they stand guard on the outskirts. Is he a kind god?"

"He can be," Devos said. "Though he can also be harsh if the situation demands it. We must respect Duun and his ways. He provides us with the sun to grow our algae for food, yet his gift of heat and light can also spell the doom of the unprepared who venture out into the wastes. If one is without proper tools or is lacking knowledge on how to navigate the harsh lands around us, then Duun will take their lives. To acknowledge Duun is to respect the land, we hunt only to provide enough food to feed the tribe, never for trade. If we were to hunt as many beasts as we wanted to, then Duun will punish us by no longer providing any animals for the people to hunt and we will ultimately die. If we disrespect his gifts, then we will incur his wrath, it is as simple as that."

"What about the goddess Karma?"

Devos laughed a little. "Karma is very much like her husband. She decides the destinies of men. Like Duun, her ways must be respected. Karma teaches us we must value each other, and our words must all be promises and always the truth. If one disrespects the goddess of fate by becoming destructive with such acts as stealing another's possessions, lying, or murder, then the offender shall incur her wrath. When Karma gets angry, she sends curses and a dark fate awaits those who have offended her. Karma's way is that of divine retribution upon those that break their vows and murder one another. Her justice is implacable, and it is best to stay clear of those that have violated her commands."

"I somewhat understand why they are husband and wife now," Rion said. "One compliments the other. Duun teaches us the way to survive the wastes while Karma teaches us the proper ways to interact with one another. If either god gets disrespected, then the cosmic order goes awry. Did I get that right?"

Devos beamed as he leaned forward and ruffled the boy's blond hair. "You are very perceptive! You have completely understood what has been taught to you right away. I foresee a great future ahead for you, Rion."

The boy blushed. "Thank you, teller. I still have much to learn though."

"Feel free to ask me," Devos said. "I will tell you everything I know."

"Is there any other gods that the tribe worships?"

"There are a multitude of gods," Devos said. "The primary ones you now know about. Though there is one other god that is as powerful as all of the others combined."

"Oh, which god is that?"

"Death," Devos said softly. "In the end, when all is said and done, death will come for us all. We try and follow the ways of Duun and Karma for as long as we can, but soon enough, not even their blessings can halt the inevitable. Once somebody dies, their essence travels to the spirit lands. If they had led a life that respected the gods, then Karma may grant them a blessing by being reborn back into the world once more. Those that violated the pact of the gods on the other hand, would face unimaginable torments."

Rion looked down on the floor. The words struck him hard. He hoped that his friend Aertos would find peace and be reborn someday. The jumble of harsh memories in his mind threatened to overwhelm him, but he used the mental techniques taught to him by Miri and Zedne to hold back the tide of dark thoughts. After a short minute, he succeeded in pushing the nightmares back into the recesses of his mind, but just barely.

Devos sensed the boy's melancholy. The old man stood up and patted Rion on his shoulder. "I know you have been through a lot, but you are among friends now. I will brew some brown tea, give me a minute."

Rion's face brightened once tea was served. He drank the steaming liquid slowly, the bitter taste was rejuvenating to him. Devos felt that he had been subjected to enough teachings that day, so the boy left once he had finished his cup. Rion wandered the dusty streets for the next hour. Several of the younger boys invited him to play with them, but he declined. He noticed a couple of the older boys just sitting by the side of a hut, staring at him silently. Elder Zedne had told him that he would be getting a lot of curious looks, since the color of his hair and pale skin would be considered as an exotic novelty.

The boy slowly made his way towards the eastern edge of town where the algae farms were. This part of the village stood on the banks of the Silt Sea, the sand in front of him had taken a darker, more grayish hue. Looking around, Rion quickly noticed Miri standing on a high bluff, overlooking several teams of algae farmers. The boy grinned as he ran up to her.

Miri gave him a slight smile as soon as he saw him getting close. She held her spear on her other hand while she waved at him. "Welcome, Rion. How was your day with the teller?"

The boy squinted in the bright sunlight. "I learned a great many things today, protector."

Miri giggled as she kept her eyes on the men and women dredging the silt below. "More tales about the gods and even more songs, I bet. And you do not have to keep addressing me as protector. Just Miri is fine."

"Alright, Miri. What are they doing below?"

"They are breaking the upper crust of the silt bed. That is usually the place where they would find the green algae, the primary foodstuff we use for our soups," Miri said as she glanced back at the boy.

"Is the algae abundant over there?"

"Here," she took off her cloak and wrapped it over the boy's bare shoulders to help shield him from the sun's rays. "As for your question, the answer is sometimes." She pointed to one of the men who was leading the others. "Elder Etul over there is an experienced farmer. He usually knows where the green algae are hidden just by looking at the topsoil."

The boy held a hand above his eyes as he peered out towards the others. "How much of that stuff do they find?"

"On a good day, each of them will return with a couple of handfuls each," Miri said. "On a bad day, considerably less. If one finds only a small patch of the algae, they will mark it down and return to it in the future when it has had a chance to grow."

"If there are enough algae lying around, why not just keep eating them? Why hunt for beasts?"

Miri couldn't help but smile. While many children would usually ask silly questions, this boy always asked the right ones. She liked that. "The algae will keep us alive, but it is not enough. Meat provides far more nourishment, especially for the very young and the very old."

"I see. What about the black algae?"

"There are a lot more black algae that will be found when our farmers forage like this," Miri said. "But the black colored kind cannot be eaten. They do make great building material when you combine them with silt, though. We also coat our leather with the stuff, for it helps to bind the material together."

"Are there other kinds of algae?"

"Well, there is the red algae," Miri said. "Very rare in finding that one, though. Zedne considers the red kind to be an effective medicine when treating wounds or the fever, for it kills infected flesh. Then there's the yellow and purple algae, but I would not ingest those either, for they are very deadly poisons to us."

Rion nodded as he kept staring at the farmers doing their work. "Why are you keeping watch over them?"

"The poisoned norpions inhabit this part of the land, they are asleep beneath the silt at this time of the day," Miri said. "These beasts usually do not bother with us, but since our algae farmers scrape off the topsoil, they may inadvertently disturb those slumbering creatures. Most of the norpions we encounter are quite small, so their sting leaves nothing more than a red, painful welt on one's skin. On rare occasions though, the group may sometimes end up disturbing one of the larger ones, or maybe even an octapede. If that happens, then I will need to react quickly by using my Vis to tame the animal, to give time for the farmers to move away, or if failing that, take its life with my spear."

The boy understood. "Why not just use your mindsense to detect the beasts before the farmers encounter them?"

Miri giggled as she shook her head. "Because that would be too taxing for me. Using one's Vis requires great concentration and effort, and after prolonged use I am exhausted. If I keep using my power on every patch of sand, I will end up as an old crone, older than Elder Zedne, and I may not be able to use my gifts when they will be most needed."

Rion started laughing. "Elder Zedne, a crone?"

Miri blushed. She shouldn't have said that. "Please do not repeat what I have said to her."

The boy was still chuckling. "Do not worry, Miri. Your secret is safe with me."

"Good," Miri said. Despite her duties and her vows to stay aloof from being too attached to anyone, she was really starting to like the boy. When they first met, Rion was guarded and fearful to all of them. But with their loving care, the boy was opening up as a bright and cheerful lad, highly intelligent, and he returned their kindness back twofold. Nevertheless, she sensed a trove of secrets still lay behind Rion's suppressed memories, and she was innately curious to find out more. But the boy needed time to learn the ways of the tribe, Elder Zedne decreed. It was not the right time to pry yet. When the time came for the whole truth to be revealed, Miri hoped that the boy would be strong enough to face it.

As the group of algae farmers began to make their way back towards the village, Nyx came running over towards Miri and the boy. "Miri," the teen girl said. "I have sad news."

Miri turned to look at her. "What is it?"

"After a long illness, Elder Neris has passed away," Nyx said slowly. "Her body is on the healer's slab, and is being prepared for the ritual of the dead."

Miri nodded. Rion was about to learn something new again.

# Chapter 6

Administrator Odrin pursed his lips while holding up the final vial of the boy's distilled essence in front of him. Shafts of slanted red sunlight beamed diagonally across the great chamber from the tall, narrow windows, irradiating the motes of dust in the air. The red crimson liquid in the small glass tube was nothing more than a few drops, and he silently cursed that traitorous worm Aertos for stealing the child away from them. Even now, he could feel his own weakness steadily taking control over his old, frail body. He was nearing the end of his time, and he grew more fearful as the days went on.

Removing the small stopper from the ampoule, Odrin tilted his head upwards as he placed the end of the tiny container to his lips and drank the last of the crimson liquid. As the rejuvenating effect began to flow through his veins, he experienced a mild sensation of lightheadedness, before he finally opened his eyes once more. He was feeling a lot better now. The constant aches from his creaking limbs had dissipated, at least for awhile. Odrin's lungs felt more robust, there was no longer a shortage of breath either. Even his blurry vision began to coalesce, putting the entire room back into focus. He would not need to use his reading crystal for the next few days.

Odrin rose from his tall chair and walked over to a long table near the center of the room. Lying on the smooth stone slab was a map of the nearby regions. The citadel of Doss lay in the center of the leather diagram. To the west was the dead city of Ceorath, now nothing more than a scattering of ruins. Over to the east lay the wastelands, a vast stretch of desert all the way round the Great Silt Sea. The northern and southern reaches had been unexplored for over a thousand cycles and were deemed to be deathlands, places of nothingness. Odrin placed a crooked finger from the citadel's location and traced an invisible line eastwards. *Aertos must have taken the boy to the few tribes that are still out there,* he thought. *The two men I had sent after them had clearly failed, lest they would have returned by now.*

Turning away from the map, Odrin frowned as he slowly walked back to his chair. If the boy was not recovered, then he would soon meet the gods. He ran his bony hand along his shoulder-length, silvery mane before he carefully placed his scrawny buttocks on the stiff throne. He had done everything he could, now it was just a matter of time. The old man closed his eyes and tried to enjoy a short rest without the customary aches and pains. If the soreness was to become too great, then he wondered if he had enough courage to kill himself.

He was not aware of how much time had passed the moment he closed his eyes. When Odrin opened them again, it was because he was suddenly jolted awake by the sounds of distant doors slamming and the angry shouts coming from the nearby corridors. Odrin refocused his mind while storing a short spurt of Vis in case he needed it. His hands clutched the sides of the chair as he used all his strength to lift himself up. Odrin's legs felt weak, but he needed to reach the long table in order to get his steel dagger lying at the far side of it. The old man concentrated as he used part of his Vis to power his legs when he began to take a few steps forward.

Just as he started to limp towards the table, the double doors at the far end of the room were suddenly swung open with such a terrific force that a harsh current of air nearly blew the huge map from the table and staggered him. Odrin grabbed onto the side of the counter to steady himself while a man walked into the chamber.

The stranger seemed to be on the short side, the cross-hilted bastard sword he carried at his waist looked almost as tall as he was. The man had pale skin, like ivory, though Odrin could see occasional blue veins along the stranger's neck and forehead as he got closer. A mop of curly black hair on top of the head seemed natural enough, but what truly set him apart were the pointed ears along the man's sides. He looked young, probably around thirty cycles or thereabouts. The stranger wore a steel cuirass over his chest, along with knee-high plated greaves down to his boots and a furred cloak was draped over his shoulders. When he got to within twenty feet of him, Odrin could see the stranger's eyes were a set of bright crimson.

Odrin steeled himself. Even though the other man radiated an aura of dread, he was still master of this citadel. He held up a bony finger and pointed to the intruder. "Who are you? What are you doing here?"

The short man's eyes darted around back and forth, scanning and noticing the little things around him. He didn't even seem to notice Odrin standing there. It was as if he was the only living person in the hall. He was either delusional, or deliberately ignoring Odrin's presence. The man walked over to where the map was, leaned over to carefully look at the areas indicated on it. After studying a part near the indicated markings of the wastes, the man rubbed his chin with a gauntleted hand, revealing the metal bracers over his forearms.

Odrin's anger began to overcome his fear. He started to mentally gather his remaining reserves of Vis. If this interloper wanted a battle, then he would have it. "You are standing in front of the Administrator of Doss. To ignore me is an insult I will not endure. I will ask you one more time, who are you? I demand you respond to me!"

The stranger suddenly jerked his head up as if he saw something up in the high-domed ceiling. Then his eyes once again began to skim through the room, before finally staring right at Odrin. "Oh, there you are," the young man said. "Did you not get the message?"

Odrin's rage turned to momentary confusion. "Message? What message?"

"The message that was sent to you of my impending arrival," the man said.

"I have received no message," Odrin said curtly.

The man instantly began to run his gauntlets along the folds of his cloak. A few moments later, he produced a small stone tablet, holding it up in front of him. "Oh, it seems I have been carrying the message with me all this time. Here," he said as he tossed the stone towards Odrin.

The old man shrieked as he used his frail legs to get into position to catch the small piece of carved rock. Odrin managed to snag it in his right palm, but he had leaned too far ahead and he started to fall. Just as his face was about to connect with the smooth stone floor of the chamber, some invisible force suddenly stopped him so he lay almost horizontal just a few feet off the ground. Odrin looked up, and he saw the stranger had his hand out and had used his own Vis to stop his fall.

Odrin quickly recovered from his surprise as he regained his balance and stood upright. While the stranger withdrew his hand back within the folds of his cloak, Odrin looked at the engraving on the stone tablet. He read the runes, then looked up in awe. "Y-you are Lord Slane? Executor of the Grand Magus?"

Slane grinned. His mouth was filled with small, razor sharp teeth. "There, now that our proper introductions have been made, it is time to get down to the task at hand, Administrator Odrin."

Odrin's face was still a mask of bewilderment. "Task? What task?"

"The Grand Magus sent a message to all the citadels in the last ten cycles with orders to eliminate the children," Slane said. "All but one of the citadels acknowledged that the task had been done. I am now standing in the very one that did not."

"Y-yes of course, we did what the Grand Magus had ordered," Odrin said. "We sent the message to signify it was done as well. Did you not get it?"

Slane smirked. "You are lying to me."

Odrin frowned. "I am telling you the truth! Search the citadel. You will not find one of the children here. The orders were carried out!"

Slane turned and made a low whistle. A four legged creature came out from the open doorway and started to sniff around the room. Odrin gasped the moment he saw it. The beast was the size of a small boulder and was hairless, the purple veins on its pink flesh pulsated as it moved rapidly around the chamber. Large, pointy ears covered the sides of the head, with a snout protruding from underneath its eye slits. It had short, stubby legs that ended in claws. The beast growled the moment Odrin tried to move backwards.

"I would suggest you do not move lest you anger my pet canis," Slane said. "You see, when it hunts, it expects the prey to run. So unless you wish to be killed, then it is best to be as still as a slab of rock."

Beads of sweat began to form on Odrin's forehead as the beast moved past him. The old man twisted his head slightly as he observed the canis jump up on top of his chair. The creature started poking around the leather cushion and the sides using its bulbous nose. Odrin's eyes opened wide as the animal found the empty glass ampoule. The canis gently gripped the glass tube with its dagger like teeth before jumping off the chair and ran back towards Slane. The moment it got in front of the executor, the canis sat on its hind legs and opened its maw to reveal the vial.

Slane picked up the ampoule from the animal's mouth and examined it. Then he stuck out his forked tongue and licked the edge of the container. He looked back at Odrin with a wicked smile on his face.

Odrin was breathing heavily now. "Th-that vial was taken a long time ago! I had been keeping it for over a cycle in order to preserve its vitae!"

The canis started to growl once more. Slane bent down and platted the top of its head and it quickly fell silent. Then executor stood fully upright again, this time with a menacing stare. "That is the second lie you have told me," he said softly. "I must warn you, I will not tolerate a third."

Odrin placed a hand on the table to prop himself up. The dagger was only a few feet away. "I-I am sorry. Yes, I admit it. We kept the child alive so we could drain his essence regularly. It was only done with the best intentions. As you can see, there are less than a dozen Magi left in this outpost by the wastes. The city we have been guarding has died out and we could no longer provide patrols to venture out to the tribal wastelands. We have sent numerous messages over the last fifty cycles begging for new recruits, yet the Grand Magus stayed silent all this time. Our members have grown old and weak. The boy's vitae was the only way we could revitalize ourselves. Surely you can see the reasons for it."

"A noble dialectic," Slane mused. "Yet a violation, nonetheless. The Grand Magus believes that only strict discipline and adherence to his commands is what keeps the order of Magi from descending into chaos. As the chief administrator of this outpost, you were chosen because we felt we could trust you to do the will of Vis. While the Magi under you are scum for going along with this mad scheme, your betrayal is the cruelest one of all."

Odrin scoffed. "We had to do something! Our order is dying out. Without the child's vitae, myself and at least half of the others would have died long ago! Can you not see? There are less than a dozen of us left here. How can we follow the commands of the Grand Magus when we are all dead?"

"Your words make sense," Slane said softly. "Where is the boy now?"

Odrin put his head down in shame. "He escaped, out into the wastes."

"Escaped? But you said there were almost a dozen of you here. How could a child get away from so many Magi?"

"There was a traitor among us," Odrin hissed. "A Magus named Aertos. I am not sure as to what his reasons were, but he took the boy with him. Perhaps he wanted the vitae all to himself, or he may have developed a fondness for the child. I dispatched my two youngest Magi to go after them and bring the boy back, but none have returned."

Slane nodded. "How long ago was this?"

"Almost two moons," Odrin said. "After the first moon, I instructed my best seeker to find their trail. His orders were to either bring back the boy, or his remains."

"Why did you not dispatch your seeker first instead of two fools?"

"I underestimated Aertos," Odrin said wistfully. "I thought his two friends would be enough to bring him back or maybe kill him, but it seems they have become lost as well. The seeker will succeed though. He is the best warrior among all of us. He will find the boy, of that I am sure."

"I do not share your confidence," Slane said. "For it seems that I will have to travel the wastes to make sure that the Grand Magus's orders are to be carried out. It has been a long time since I have been to the Great Silt Sea. Perhaps this will be a memorable journey."

"The citadel is at your disposal, Lord," Odrin said while gesturing at the map on the table. "I have a smaller copy of this chart in my private chambers, and we still have some supplies to equip you and your men. Let me know what you need, and I will make sure to provide it for you."

"What I need," Slane said, "is for you and your men to die."

Odrin knew the game was up. He turned and looked at the dagger on the table while holding up his palm. The dagger lifted itself into the air as it headed towards him, hilt first. But just before it got near his outstretched hand, the dagger suddenly flew higher up, turned until its point faced him and instantly flew downwards, heading towards the top of his own head. The old man cried out in terror as he fell on the floor. His body lay sideways as he looked up and used all of his Vis to try and stop the dagger from striking him. The blade hovered just beyond his reach while it darted back and forth, as if an invisible hand was wielding it, trying to force its way through his mindforce and into his quivering body.

Slane was laughing maniacally while the canis made loud barking noises. His own right hand was gesturing as he used his powerful Vis to keep the dagger in the air, just beyond the reach of the struggling administrator. He would aim the point of the dagger right at the old man and send it towards him at a terrific velocity, only to hold it back at the last minute before choosing another angle of attack. Then he would attempt to fling it at the old man using another approach, only to once again pull it back just before it stabbed him.

Odrin had had enough. He used his hands to shield his face as he started screaming. "Stop! Stop it! I beg you!"

Slane continued to chuckle as the dagger flew near him and hovered over his hand. He took the blade and examined it. "My, my. Very fine workmanship. This is no doubt an artifact from a bygone time. If I am not mistaken, this dagger was probably made during the Rylth Empire, right before the last age of the Gorgons. If that is accurate, then this very weapon is thousands of cycles old."

Odrin was weeping. "Yes, y-you are right! Please, have mercy on me!"

Slane pondered on the weapon for a bit before continuing. "But, if it is over several thousand cycles old, then it surely cannot be steel nor iron, for those kinds of metals rusts away into nothing but red dust. Tell me, what kind of metal is this blade made out of?"

Odrin gritted his teeth. He was on his knees. "It is bronze! The weapon is made of bronze!"

Slane nodded. "Ah, but of course. Bronze. A kind of metal that does not rust. Though, I have heard that bronze deteriorates as well. I think it is called the green sickness, yes? Tell me, how did you preserve this weapon against such a rot?"

Odrin wiped away his tears with his tunic sleeve. "T-there is a special salve in my chambers. Rub the metal with it once every cycle a-and it will prevent the green rot."

Slane placed the dagger on the side of the table. "Good to know. I shall ask you a few more questions and this time I want the truth. No more lies, or this blade will once again take to the air and come down upon you."

Odrin let out a deep breath. It was all over for him unless he could somehow make himself useful. "Yes. I shall answer with the truth as to whatever query you make."

Slane bent down and pored over the map. "What do you know of the tribes in these wastelands?"

"Our last patrol was many, many cycles ago," Odrin said. "At that time there were only three tribes still living in the entire area that we cataloged. They were the Nartos, Arum Navar and the Silids. Of those, the Arum Navar were the most numerous. The Silids were down to only a few families left. The final six patrols had reported that no more male children had been born with the gift of Vis, so they were unable to recruit anyone. Perhaps the tribes had finally bred them out."

Slane's crimson eyes made a quick glance at the old man. "No more Magi perhaps, but what about Strigas?"

Odrin nodded. "There were Strigas, yes. They mostly served as guardians of their respective tribes."

Slane rubbed his chin as he continued to ponder the map. A Striga was a dangerous opponent for a Magus. While the Magi could use their Vis to move things with their minds, Strigas could delve into the thoughts of others, and use their mental powers to anticipate and defend against incoming attacks. His men needed to stay vigilant and focus on their thought defenses, lest any Striga overcome them. Of course, this was under the assumption the child had somehow found sanctuary among the tribes. "Are there any dangerous beasts I should be aware of out in the wastes?"

"Fifty cycles ago, the patrols always encountered large sand dargons," Odrin said. "But the final ten expeditions barely chanced upon any animal worth mentioning in their reports."

The executor looked up at the waning shafts of light coming from the windows. The Grand Magus was right. The land was in its final death throes. Within a few more generations, the whole world would be nothing but dust and rock. Mankind and all their ways would soon pass into the oblivion that awaited them. A part of him pondered as to why all this was even needed, when everything was at the edge of annihilation, anyway?

Slane smiled to himself. At least it would give him something to do. It was better than to just waste away like this pathetic old man. He twisted his neck and stared at the administrator. "When you ingested the boy's essence, how did it feel?"

Odrin looked back at him. "It was like a part of my youth had been restored. I felt young again."

Slane strode back over beside his canis and faced the old man. "I heard … stories. About these children. The tales that were told about them said they had …the power to bring the dead back to life. Have you witnessed such a feat?"

Odrin shook his head. "No, no. All I have seen was that the child could revitalize us, extend our lives."

Slane had a blank look on his face. "Do you know why the Grand Magus had decreed the deaths of these children?"

Odrin thought about it for a minute, trying to recall if there had been any reasons that were spelled out in both the correspondence and in the archives. "It was never stated as far as I know."

"Let me tell you a story," Slane said. "It happened two cycles ago. My men and I journeyed to the citadel at Tioch, thousands of leagues from here. We found that the entire fortress was but a ruin. Only one Magus was left, and he had one of these children with him. I dispatched the traitor rather easily, but the child was a very strange creature. A little girl, not more than twelve cycles of age, I believe. She didn't fight back when I drove my sword into her gut, but she did scream. Do you know what happened afterwards?"

Odrin shook his head and said nothing.

Slane gave a faint smile. "We were about to depart when a strange thing occurred. The child rose up from where I had gutted her and just stood there before us. We were all quite astonished. The girl had somehow survived a killing blow and not only that, she seemed to be none the worse off. I must tell you that a sense of panic swept over my group, we thought that we encountered some sort of god. One of my men, by the name of Baradine, came forward and cleaved her nearly in two with his axe. We all stood around her body while keeping vigil over it, just in case it attempted to rise from the dead once more. Do you know what happened then?"

Odrin's lips trembled, but he still didn't answer.

"The child suddenly opened her eyes once more," Slane said. "We soon realized that we had to resort to drastic measures. In the end, we used fire to incinerate her body and we scattered her ashes along the barren plain. It was a harrowing experience and it got me to think about what my task was and what it meant to be a Magus. If the world is about to die, then what did these children signify?"

Odrin's eyes were wide open. "I-I … do not know."

"My curiosity then got the better of me," Slane said. "I went over to where the body of that last Magus lay and I tore through his clothes. Do you know what I found?"

Odrin started holding his breath. He thought it only happened to him. "His … loins?"

Slane chuckled. "Yes! The dead man's loins had been intact. It had somehow grown back again! It was then that I realized that the child might have had something to do with it. At that very moment I understood why the Grand Magus had decreed to kill all of these children, for he knew what they were capable of! Imagine an endless sea of undying Magi, why it would threaten the order to its very core. That is why he could not allow the children to live."

At that moment, a tall, bald headed man walked into the room. He stood at almost eight feet in height, his red beard was like copper wires as they dangled down his chin. He wore a sort of armor made out of overlapping metal and leather scales, the ancients called it a coat of plates. Odrin could see the handle of a large axe strapped to his back. The man was carrying what looked like a bundle of hairy balls in a leathery net.

Slane turned to look at the man as he moved in closer. "Baradine, welcome to the citadel's main chamber! Show the administrator that your task has been done, please."

Baradine threw the net and it landed with a squishing noise in front of the old man. Odrin looked closer, then suddenly recoiled in horror. The mesh was full of bloody heads. All of the other Magi in the citadel had been killed. Odrin writhed on the floor as he clutched at his chest. His heart felt leaden and he was gasping for air.

Slane laughed as he brought his right hand up. Odrin shrieked when he was suddenly suspended up in the air once more. Slane's eyes twinkled while the old man's tunic was ripped away from his body. Using his mindforce, Slane tore away Odrin's loincloth, revealing a small, vestigial set of male genitalia. So it was true, the blood of the children could somehow regenerate that which had been stripped away from them.

Odrin screamed as he continued to dangle in the air, just a few feet off the ground. "No, please! Have mercy on me! Mercy!"

"Let me tell you another story," Slane said as he gestured at the old man to stay quiet. "Yours is actually the first inhabited citadel that we've chanced upon for many cycles. With the exception of our temple in the last city, the once great Order of Magi is no more. We are the last of us. The Grand Magus is a decrepit old man, one prone to delusions. He still believes that he somehow rules over a vast empire of citadels, with thousands upon thousands of Magi who follow his commands. What an old fool he is! As per my own calculations, I have reached the end of my task and with this final execution of your men in this, the final outpost, then we can say that we shall soon be all part of the dust. Since my mission is at an end, I am now free to indulge myself, and I have plans to be even greater than the Grand Magus ever was."

Odrin had become hysterical. He flailed his arms and legs in the air, but his body kept on spinning, like one of the motes of dust floating in the air. "If we are the remaining ones, then spare me, please!"

Slane's face was a mask of stone. "You know, many Magi worship Vis, the god of the mind. I worship death. He is the most powerful of the gods, more powerful than that god in the wastes which those barbarians ascribe to, at least. For all things ultimately come to death. In the end, there is no escaping him. Death claims all."

Odrin cried out as he was suddenly thrust into the stone floor, head first. The top of his head gave a loud thud as he landed with such force that it crushed his skull. Slane snapped his fingers as the canis ran forward and began tearing the old man's body apart using its jaws. Slane loved his pet, and he always made sure the beast was well fed.

Baradine turned and looked at his superior. "We have secured supplies for the journey across the wastes. What is your command, Lord Slane?"

"Let us rest a little first," Slane said as he walked over to the map and pointed to a few symbols that were marked with ink. "This administrator dispatched a seeker to track the boy. If he does not return in a few days, then we shall venture out there ourselves. In the meantime, this citadel has quite an extensive archive. I have much to read."

# Chapter 7

"Elder Neris had lived a long, fruitful life," Devos said. Almost the entire tribe had gathered in front of him. "She was an accomplished farmer, a master in the art of growing shrooms in our fungi garden. Along with her two daughters, she worked tirelessly to feed her people for over fifty cycles. Once she was too old to farm, she still continued to visit the gardens every single day without fail, to offer sound advice on how to grow shrooms and encouragement to any who were present with her. Neris never asked for special favors, and she always considered the good of the tribe ahead of any of her own goals. She was never selfish, always willing to share what little she had to those that needed it. Her skills and experience will be missed, as well as her cheerfulness and love."

Miri stood near the center of the crowd while the teller spoke. Devos was standing beside a flat slab of rock with the old woman's body lying in its center. As per the custom, Neris's innards had already been carefully removed and strewn about in the underground garden that she was so devoted to. Right behind the rock slab was an entrance to a subterranean cave. The underground cavern beneath was extensive, with many nooks and tunnels. Inside the cave were gardens of glowing phosphorescent mushrooms. These organisms were one of the primary food sources for the entire tribe. Along with the green algae, the shrooms provided much needed sustenance, but they needed waste material in order to grow. Consequently, the caverns also served as the tribe's burial grounds.

Devis continued. "So, let us not be saddened by her passing. For Neris shall not be forgotten, for her memory will live on with her children, and then with her grandchildren. The god of the wastes reclaims one of his own, just as he brought her forth when she was born. Neris rejoins her late husband Sor, and now they are together at last, and in peace."

Two bearers who stood by carefully placed the old woman's body in a leather stretcher and then carried it into the mouth of the cave. Within minutes, the two men disappeared as they hoisted the corpse into the cavern.

"It is now done," Devos said. "Neris's final gift to her children and to her people will be to nourish the farm that she had been so devoted to. While her essence is now in those other lands, the realm of the gods, her body returns to the people. Amen."

The crowd began to disperse. Rion had been standing beside Miri as he glanced at the people around him. The boy noticed Nyx whispering to her brother Jinn, before they separated and went off into different directions. Krag had not been present at the funeral oration, for he had been keeping watch at the outskirts of the settlement. Elder Zedne was also not there, she was back in her hut, taking care of a sick child. The other children soon started running off in different directions, trying to forget their sadness with play.

Miri placed a reassuring hand on the boy's bare shoulder. "Are you alright?"

Rion looked up at her and nodded. "Yes. I was curious and wanted to ask Elder Devos about this ritual, but now I can see what it was about."

Miri pursed her lips. It had been many days now. Rion was already accepted as part of the tribe. Perhaps it was time for more questions. "So was this the first time you had ever witnessed something like this."

"Yes," the boy said.

"Do you have any memories at all before your escape into the desert?"

Rion looked away. "Not … much. All I remember were brief flashes of pain. Of being held down on a cold slab of stone. Then of the journey in the wastes. With Aertos."

"This Aertos," Miri said. "Do you know what he was?"

"From my conversations with Elder Devos, it seems he was a Magus."

"Did Aertos ever say anything about why he rescued you?"

The boy shook his head. "Not directly. I remember once when I spent the first day out in the wastes. He wanted me to sleep so that we may wake up at eventide, because it was easier to journey at night. I could not sleep because of the pain in my arms from the previous bloodletting, so all I could do was close my eyes and moan. He held me in his arms for the entire day until I finally fell asleep. When I awoke, it was already night and he had been carrying me for a long time. He was exhausted, but I noticed a happy gleam in his eyes when I looked up at him. I think it was because he cared about me. In the end he saved my life."

Elder Devos came over to the two of them. He was somewhat tried, but he had a smile on his face. "Well, it seems my task as a teller is done for today. Would the both of you like some tea in my hut?"

Rion sat down on the teaching floor as Devos sat by the fire pit, brewing a pot of tea. Miri felt she was needed elsewhere, but Devos insisted that she have at least a cup before she resumed her sentry duties. The protector was sitting beside the boy as she tried to use her mindsense again in an attempt to probe Rion's memories, but she went up against a solid wall of mental blackness. After a few minutes of trying, she gave up as she shook her head slowly in order to free up her mental state back into a sense of normality.

Rion looked up at her. "You were trying to probe my mind, were you not?"

Miri smirked. She was now convinced that the boy was no ordinary Magus. "I am sorry, Rion. It was merely a reaction."

"A reaction to what? Because I am not telling you more about my life?"

"Yes," Miri said softly. "As protector of the tribe, it is important that I would know of any potential threats to the settlement."

The boy looked down onto the smooth floor. "Do you think I am a threat to the tribe?"

Miri leaned forward and placed a warm hand on his knee. "No, Rion. Not you. I was thinking about those men who were hunting you."

"Do you think they might try to find me here?"

"There is a possibility," Miri said. "Do you have any idea why you would be so valuable to them?"

The boy said nothing as he just shook his head.

"Do you know if there were others like you in that place?"

Rion looked away. "I do not think so. But there were times when I would be asleep and I would dream about others. It was like they were calling out to me. One was a girl near my age, she was begging me to help her, yet I knew I could not."

Devos walked over and placed a steaming pot on the floor in between them. "Dreams, eh? There was a story that once said that the gods spoke to people using dreams. Another story told of a very powerful Striga, who could communicate with anyone across the entire world while she dreamed. You see, this Striga was always asleep, and the others were using her as a sort of machine with which to communicate with others from faraway lands. What they would do is to go into the resting place, and whisper into her ear while she slept. Then she would relay her thoughts as they traveled across the farthest reaches to their destination."

Miri looked up at the teller while she accepted a hot cup of tea. "Devos, do you know of any stories in which men could have the mindsense?"

Devos poured another cup and handed it over to the boy as he turned away to think. "None of the stories have told of men with that kind of power, except perhaps the male gods."

"So the power of thought only belongs to the women? Were there any male Gorgons?" Miri asked.

"From what I remember, the stories were not clear," Devos said. "It was said that the first Gorgons were women, but there were other stories of Gorgons being both male and female. It is said that they were able to mate with each other and bear offspring as both husband and wife. Why do you ask about this?"

Miri looked at the boy. "Perhaps there is another child like Rion, who can communicate across the land using his thoughts."

Devos stood up and walked over to a nearby bone shelf. He took out a small rock with intricate carvings on it. "The stories always told of children who grew up and became powerful users of Vis, but there was not a single tale of a child with the power of a god." He looked closely at the flat stone. "It is a pity that the ways of the tellers have been lost through time, for all stories are now passed from one mouth to another."

Rion noticed the rock that the teller was holding. "May I see that?"

Devos gave the small stone to the boy. "Of course, child."

Rion ran his index finger along the chiseled grooves of the stone. It was starting to make sense to him. "This stone tells a different tale. It says, 'inventory for the fourth ship in the dock is as follows: forty amphorae of wine, sixty baskets of gold.' I do not know what gold is. What does it mean?"

The teller's eyes opened wide. "By the gods! You know how to read the glyphs!"

Miri was shocked as well. "Gold is a kind of shiny metal. Rion, how did you learn that?"

The boy simply shrugged. "I thought it was natural for everyone to be able to read glyphs."

Devos shook his head. "No, child. The entire tribe has forgotten the art of reading and deciphering these glyphs for generations now. You are actually the first in known time to do this! Why have you not told us of this before?"

Rion looked somewhat confused. He thought that the teller had read all of the stones in his possession. "Uh, because you never asked me?"

The teller started laughing as he took out a leather basket from the shelf and placed it on the floor beside the pot of tea. It was full of stone tablets similar to what Rion was holding. "Rion, please go through all of these. They are called telling stones. If you find something of importance, I beg of you to tell me."

As Rion picked up several carvings and started reading them, Miri edged in closer. "Rion," she said. "Do you have any memories as to who taught you to read this?"

The boy didn't take his eyes off the telling stones as he shook his head. "No, all I remember was the bloodletting. Before that, my recollections were of nothing."

Devos was in an excitable mood as he crouched down beside the boy. "Do you know why tellers are so important to the tribe, Rion?"

The boy shrugged while he picked up another carving and kept on reading. "No."

"The teller of the tribe is a preserver of knowledge for the people," Devos said. "Through them, the tribe learns the will of the gods and the ways of the land. The teller is the one who teaches the children and counsels the elders on what paths the people should take. A teller must know a thousand stories by heart, the more legends he can tell, the more understanding the tribe has. Since you can read the glyphs on the stones, then surely you can unlock many areas of our knowledge that have been lost through time. Can you not teach me this gift, Rion?"

The boy looked at him and nodded. "I would, but I think you know far more than me when it comes to telling stories."

Devos chuckled. He had found his successor. "I am old. My memories fade with time. I have observed many people in the tribe, and none of them have your talents. Please teach me how to read the glyphs and I will tell you all the legends I know. When I am gone, you will be the tribe's new teller."

Rion stopped reading. "You will do all that? For me?"

The old man placed his arm around the boy's shoulders. "You have great gifts, Rion. I foresee that you will become the greatest teller of this tribe."

Miri smiled as she finished the last of her tea and stood up. "Well, I think the two of you working together will be of great benefit to the settlement. Now if you will excuse me, I have to return to my duties. Farewell."

Devos waved at the protector as she opened the flap in the entryway and stepped out. "Farewell, Miri, We shall see you later." Then he turned and saw the boy looking at a gold tablet. "Oh, so you have found my most prized possession. It is as Miri described, a golden rock, inscribed by many unknown and wondrous glyphs that I hope you will translate for me."

Rion didn't reply. He just kept reading the writing on the stone. The boy had a serious look on his face.

"Is everything alright, child?" Devos asked.

Rion let out a sigh. "Many of the glyphs in the others stones do not really tell any stories, they seem to be just lists of mundane possessions, or messages.

But this one tells a very strange tale."

"Could you say it aloud for me to hear?"

The boy nodded. "It says, 'the last child shall venture into the last city, and the new world will begin.' The rest of the glyphs seem indecipherable."

# Chapter 8

Erewn drew his cloak closer to his body while staring out at the settlement ahead. He spent nearly a moon out in the wastes, and all he found was a single sandal. Judging from the size of the shoe, it had to be the boy's. If the child had managed to survive the rigors of the desert, then he might have very well have made it into that village, he figured. Since Erewn had seen the bloodletting, he knew what the child looked like. What made the whole scheme risky was the possibility of the boy recognizing him even though he had worn a mask during the whole process of extracting the essence. If that were to happen then the alarm would be sounded, and he would have to fight his way to get the boy back. He needed to find a way to get inside, and take the boy while the others weren't looking. His pack of supplies was buried a few leagues away, near a small crop of boulders.

The seeker thought about it for a moment. He had read up on the tribes using the citadel's archives before he made the trek. This looked to be the only surviving tribe within a hundred leagues. If any of them still had the power of Vis, then there were chances Strigas resided within the tribe. Although he had trained for such an event for many cycles, Erewn had no previous experience when it came to actually fighting one in battle. The best way to defeat a woman with the mindsense would be to overwhelm her quickly- use all his Vis and strike a killing blow, he mused. Use your mental blocks and fight ferociously, or else they would ultimately cloud your thoughts, and reduce your mind into that of a helpless, docile beast: easy pickings for a slaughter in the worst of cases.

He continued to crouch down near the edge of a sand dune, the shade offering a nice, comfortable hiding place, while observing the events occurring within the settlement. There was a knee-high wall of bricks along the perimeter. The opposite side of the village seemed to border the banks of the Silt Sea, and that would be the place where they would scrounge for algae to feed themselves. Man-sized boulders were strategically positioned behind the perimeter, with a single man watching out into the desert beyond. It looked to be less than four men who were serving as lookouts. Erewn had expected more. Either this village was also on the decline, or the main group of guards was somewhere else.

The seeker squinted his eyes as he tried to focus on the weapons they were carrying. He could see that the sentries carried spears with bone shafts, the crudest weapons imaginable. Erewn couldn't look far enough as to discern what kind of spear tips they had, but it looked to be nothing more than chipped stone. That was a good sign, it meant the tribe was not well equipped when it came to war. Erewn himself did not have much metal either, so anything that would give him an advantage was welcome.

When the sun began to dip closer to the horizon, Erewn lay on his back while he thought up a plan on how to succeed in this most delicate of tasks. If they still clung to the old ways, then they would surely offer him the promise of sanctuary. If they did so, it would give him the edge to succeed. He would take advantage of that sacred trust, locate the boy and kill him during the dead of night. Once the task was completed, he would slip away before anyone would detect him. The wastes were vast, and he was supremely confident he could lose them out here should they be foolish enough to pursue him. This was it then. The task was set, time to cast the die. He stood up, patted away the grains of sand that still clung on his clothes, and began walking towards the village.

The moment he made it to within visual distance, he noticed one of the sentries sitting on a boulder quickly see him and stand up, while uttering a loud, indecipherable yell. He made it to half the distance from the perimeter walls when a small group of five men and a woman began walking towards him. Erewn concentrated on his Vis to put up as many thought blocks in his mind as possible. The woman who was approaching him with the rest of the guards was obviously a Striga, and he had to be ready for it.

Erewn stood still and broke out into a smile as the small group walked up and partially surrounded him. He raised his hand in the air, palm up in the universal gesture of peace. "Greetings. My name is Erewn, of the Silid tribe."

The woman had slightly paler skin than the others. She had fiery red hair and carried a black spear with an obsidian tip. "Greetings to you. I am Miri, protector of the Arum Navar tribe. If I may kindly ask, what brings you here to our humble settlement?"

Erewn sighed in relief. "I have been travelling across the wastes for many cycles. I would like to request some shelter in order to rest before continuing onward."

Miri was on guard. Less than two moons ago, they had found Rion out in the desert and she had been expecting some trouble to find its way here. This man was the first outsider to chance upon the settlement since a mother and child of the Nartos tribe had come to the village, requesting sanctuary. But that had been over twenty cycles ago, when she was just a toddler. "I would like to ask some questions first," she said. "You say you are from the Silid tribe. We have not encountered any of their kind since I was but a child. Can you tell me where the rest of your people are?"

Erewn gestured towards the dunes out in the distance. "I am the last of my tribe. The Silid are no more. After my father had died, I have been wandering the wastes ever since."

Several hunters in the group gasped. Miri held out her hand, signaling the others to be silent. "That is a sad tale you tell. May the gods honor your tribe in the spirit world. From our old stories, we once traded with the Silid, and their memory will be missed. Tell me, have you had any strange encounters these past few moons?"

"Other than a small octapede I was able to hunt a few days ago, there is nothing but dust out there," Erewn said.

Miri nodded. She needed to know if this stranger was hostile. Looking away for a brief second, she concentrated her Vis, putting out some mental feelers to see if she could probe the thoughts of the man standing in front of her. Her mindsense began to cast mental waves to his skull, checking what his surface thoughts were. Almost immediately, she could picture endless dunes of sand and the bright, reddish rays of the sun. Slightly altering her mental frequency, Miri tired to go for a deeper probe, but all she could sense was an intensely bright light that quickly blinded her thoughts. The feedback was so acute that she staggered backwards for a bit, nearly losing her balance.

Krag caught her by the elbow and propped her up. "Protector Miri, are you alright?"

Miri quickly regained her sense of balance. "Yes, thank you, chief hunter." She turned and looked back at Erewn. "I cannot seem to sense your deeper thoughts, have you had training in mind defenses?"

Erewn shook his head. "No, not at all."

Miri was caught in a bind. The stranger was not hostile and he asked for sanctuary. According to the tribe's traditions, they could not refuse to help a peaceful outsider who asked for assistance. She knew he was lying, for only those trained to resist the Vis could put up a powerful thought defense like he did, but she was bound by honor to give him the benefit of the doubt. "Know this, Erewn of the Silid. I am inclined to reject your request, but the tribe must obey the old laws, for without the mercy of Karma, our ways will be lost. Do you make the sacred oath of peace, of pledging not to do violence within our abode?"

Erewn made a short bow. "I do. I swear to the gods that I shall abide with the pledge of peace."

Miri nodded. "As per the old ways, you must declare to us should you possess any weapons of any kind. Please show them now."

Erewn untied the collar around his cloak and let it slip onto the sandy ground. As he turned around everyone else let out a gasp. Strapped to his back was a bone sword. The base of the blade itself was made from the spine of a long dead beast, and it narrowed towards its tip while it got thicker towards the sword guard. The edges of the blade were serrated with razor sharp chips of obsidian embedded into the sides of the bone. There were strips of leather tied around the sword grip, while the pommel was made from heavy bronze. The point of the weapon was blunt, for it was clearly used for slashing. Erewn placed his hands behind his back as he unhooked the sword from the leather scabbard on his back and placed it on the ground.

Of the others, only Miri was somewhat unfazed. "Do you have any other weapons?"

Erewn smiled and nodded. He pulled out an iron dagger from the small sheath in his waist and placed it on the ground beside the sword. "These are all the weapons I have, Protector."

Krag crouched down as he ran a finger along the base of the dagger's blade. "This weapon seems to be of some very fine workmanship. Where did you get it?"

"I found the dagger while out in the wastes," Erewn said. "From a dried corpse half buried in the sand many cycles ago. It was still intact so I took it for myself."

"And your sword?" Miri asked.

"That belonged to my father," the outsider said. "He was my tribe's protector. Before he died, that is."

Miri nodded. He was lying about the dagger, it looked to be too well-maintained to have been found out in the desert. She had to find a way to get the elders to reject his pledge. "Very well. If you wish to enter then you come with us. We shall escort you to our gathering hall and you will speak with the elders of our tribe. We will carry your weapon with us and it may be returned to you, depending on what our elders decree. Do you accept these conditions?"

Erewn let out a deep breath. "What choice do I have? I am tired and in need of rest. Yes, I do accept."

"Very well, follow me."

Miri led the way into the village, followed by Erewn. Krag and two hunters were at the rear while holding onto the stranger's weapons. The elders had already been notified and they were already inside the hall, waiting for them. Miri deliberately chose a longer route towards the center of the settlement, going through a side street while passing close to the teller's hut, so that the children could see the stranger walking through. Miri wanted to make sure Rion would at least catch a glimpse of the outsider in case he recognized him. But as they passed by a group of children playing near the well, Rion gave a short glance at the stranger before turning back and chasing after a smaller boy who had playfully taunted him. A few adults noticed the outsider, and stared at him while pausing from performing their daily routines. After sensing that Rion didn't recognize him, Miri turned and tried to decipher any possible reaction from Erewn, but the outsider didn't betray any emotion as they arrived at the entrance of the hall. Opening a large leather flap for him, Miri bade the stranger to step inside. After Erewn entered the hall, she quickly followed.

The gathering hall was a circular structure, with a large central fire pit and a leather tarp that served as a roof. Near the far side of the chamber was a slightly upraised floor where the elders would usually sit. During assembly, the majority of the tribe would sit on the hard floor, some of them even bringing their own furs during cold nights. Most of the tribe was out by the Silt Sea gathering algae for food and for building bricks, while a few others were busy tending the fungus garden. Therefore, only the elders and a few adults were present at that moment.

Miri led the outsider to face the raised platform. After gesturing at him to face the elders, she walked over and stood beside him. "Honorable elders of the Arum Navar, I hereby present to you Erewn, last of the Silid tribe. He comes to us requesting the promise of sanctuary."

The six current elders of the tribe were all sitting cross-legged on the platform. Elder Etul's hands were still caked with sand, for he had been out with the other farmers before he was quickly recalled. Elder Zedne the healer sat at the center, Miri could sense that she was tired due to staying up with a sick child all night. Beside Zedne sat Elder Devos the teller. Sitting across from Devos was Elder Oro and Elder Pir, both former hunters. Elder Brar the teether sat on the far end, for he was also serving as the master builder for the settlement. Since Elder Neris had recently passed away, Zedne was the only female elder currently on the council.

Elder Brar was the current head of the conclave, so he held up his hand in the gesture of peace. "Peace and be welcome to you, Erewn, last of the Silid. We mourn the passing of one of the great tribes of the waste, and we shall hold a feast in their honor."

Erewn bowed. "I thank you, elders. But there is no need to gather up such a huge amount of food for a feast. I have been wandering the wastes for many cycles, and I know how hard it is these days to find proper game. I believe it is better that you save your food for another day."

Elder Oro smiled. "Do not fear, wanderer. We have been blessed by the gods, and we had a great hunt two moons ago. It was an expedition in which our protector slew the largest dargon that has been encountered in a long time. We have enough reserves for a small, humble feast. That is the very least we can do to honor the last of our brother tribes."

"I am at a loss for words," Erewn said as he bowed again. "I cannot possibly repay you for this sort of adulation."

Elder Brar nodded. "No payment is to be asked from you. Our tribe does this freely. You have been the first outsider to venture into our humble settlement in a very long time. According to Karma's wishes, any tribe who is kind to strangers shall be blessed by her twofold. We still follow the old gods here, and it is through their will and their grace that we have continued to survive."

Miri raised her hand. "Before we begin, I must speak."

The other elders gestured at her to proceed. She sensed that Zedne and Devos would take her side, but when it came to the others, she wasn't so sure. Zedne sent her a thought message, telling her that she could not read the memories of the wanderer as well. Miri immediately replied to her using telepathy, telling the healer to vote her way, should it come to that. Devos gave her a slight wink as he sensed what was going on. Nevertheless, it would be an uphill battle. In the tribe's entire history, there had not been a single instance when the oath of sanctuary was denied.

Miri sighed before she talked. This was going to be tough. "As protector of this tribe, I must explain my misgivings if we are to decide in invoking the promise of sanctuary. I have tried to ascertain the stranger's thoughts, but I sensed that he is trained to resist the mindsense. I was therefore unable to know what his true intentions are."

Elder Etul looked at the stranger intently. "What do you have to say about this, Erewn of the Silid?"

Erewn looked down. "I have not been trained by anyone. I have no knowledge on the use of the Vis."

Devos looked at his colleagues. "Then we are at an impasse. It is possible that one of them is lying."

Erewn held his hand up. "It seems I have come by at a sensitive time. I appreciate the effort in extending your kindness. I do not wish to create strife amongst you, and I will therefore leave and continue my wanderings in the wastelands. With this, I shall go in peace." He quickly turned around and started walking towards the entrance flap.

"Wait!" Brar said. He held out his hand while Erewn stopped and turned back to face them. "I must apologize for our rudeness towards you. You have indeed come at a sensitive time for us here. Strange things have been happening, and some of our people have been feeling uneasy, for interesting times means that the gods themselves are agitated, and a period of great change is about to occur. Your promise of peace has been noticed, and by the old traditions, we cannot turn away a stranger like this. The gods compel us to help."

Miri grimaced. "I must protest, elders. I have sworn a sacred oath to protect the people, and I feel that we cannot abide and must make an exemption. I understand that this has never been done in all the annals of the tribe, but recent events call for new ways to do things. We can provide the outsider with food and water, but he must leave before eventide."

Elder Oro shook his head. "Protector Miri, you have blasphemed the gods with your outright rejection of one of our sacred principles. The promise of sanctuary enabled many to survive and was instrumental in the continued existence of the people in the wastes. I may not be a master teller like Elder Devos here, but there have been many instances in the past when one of our own was given sanctuary by another tribe after being lost out in the desert. In my younger days, I myself was given that very promise when I was found wounded and near death after a failed hunt by the Viir, a tribe that died out a long time ago. If they had not given me sanctuary, I would not be alive to tell you this."

Devos raised his hand. "While we know that the will of the gods is sacred, we must also trust in the words of our protector. If she says she cannot trust this stranger, then we all must take her advice seriously. We cannot just reject it merely because of tradition."

Brar twisted his head and looked at Devos. "Our traditions are what has kept us alive, we cannot discard the old teachings because of mere suspicions," he said, before turning back to face Miri. "Do you have any proof that this man is hiding something from you? While I do not have the gift of Vis, surely it is possible that some men are naturally attuned to resist your mindsense?"

"There have been instances in which the untrained can resist, yes," Miri said. "But that only happens on very rare occurrences."

"Perhaps only once in our distant history, as I recall," Devos said. "And these old tales could merely be legends."

Oro pointed his finger at Krag, who had been standing behind the stranger. "Chief Hunter Krag, do you sense anything out of the ordinary?"

Krag knew he had to tell the truth. He hated politics and these kinds of situations. "No, I have not seen anything that strikes me as peculiar just by looking at the wanderer's appearance. The timing of the stranger's arrival may seem to add to our recent plethora of interesting events, but unless any oaths were violated, then I cannot agree with rejecting his plea for sanctuary."

Brar looked over to Zedne. "Elder Zedne, can you use your mindsense on the outsider?"

Zedne closed her eyes for a brief minute, then opened them again. "I tried, but I cannot sense any surface thoughts."

Elder Pir nodded at her. "You have not had much rest, healer. Perhaps your fatigue is making your Vis weak."

Miri stole a glance at the stranger, but he remained totally opaque to her. The council of elders was divided, and unless she could come up with a compelling reason, then her pleas would certainly be rejected. She held out her hand so that the others would notice her. "If I could make a suggestion? I would like to ask the outsider remove his loincloth."

Everyone stared back at her in shock as the hall suddenly fell silent. Even though their tribe was more modest than the other people in the wastes, to force an adult to go naked in public for all to see was a dire insult. The only sound that came from within the chamber was when Nyx opened the flap of the entryway and walked inside. Although she was confused for a minute, the teen girl soon realized something important had just happened, and she wisely stayed near the entrance in mute observance.

Several minutes passed. Etul looked at the protector. His tan, wrinkled face was twisted in a mixture of bewilderment and outrage. "Miri, have you gone mad?"

Brar slapped his hand on the stone stage. "Protector Miri, you have committed a grave insult at a guest, and in front of the elders, no less! I demand you apologize to him!"

"Wait," Devos said while the rising cacophony of voices threatened to drown everything out. He wanted to congratulate Miri for being so shrewd, but protocol needed to be followed even in a case like this. "Let us know the reason why our protector is requesting this."

Miri held her hand up so that they could allow her to speak. "I meant no offense, but if our guest is a Magus, then the surest way for us to know is if he shows us his loins."

Pir shook his head, his long wisps of silver hair was almost floating in the breeze. "Oh, Miri. You have gone too far. You have no right to ask such a thing, especially when our guest has pledged the oath of peace. To even suggest this, just because you deem it so- is a desecration of our laws of hospitality. We extend our kindness to strangers and we will give up our lives if necessary to defend him, for that is the way of the gods. Our people have continued their existence because we have been helped by others in the past using the same sacred oaths and promises that we have to this day."

Brar was visibly angry. "Protector, are you accusing the stranger of being a Magus? Because that is what your insult implies. You have effectively called him a liar without any proof, or without any precedent to do so."

Miri looked at Erewn. "I meant no offense or insult. If I have offended you, then I am truly sorry."

Erewn seemed to take it in stride. His face continued to be a mask of stone. He stared back at the protector. "I am curious, why would you think I am a Magus? Because your mind probe would not work on me? What reason would a Magus try to hide himself to go here?"

Miri bit her lip. He had her in a bind. If this man was here because of Rion, then she couldn't very well tell the truth about the boy. "I am sorry, but I cannot tell you the reason why we are on guard against the Magi."

Oro made a shrill whistle, which signified extreme disapproval. "Enough, protector! If you wish to accuse our guest, then state a reason why, or withdraw your request."

Devos wanted to help Miri out, but he could find no legitimate reason to speak up, so he stayed silent on the matter. Zedne rubbed her temples as she fought off a headache. The protector's allies within the council were now powerless to support her.

Miri knew she was at a disadvantage. But her own beliefs held firm. "I cannot withdraw my request. I swore an oath to protect the tribe."

Etul made an audible sigh. "Then we are at an impasse."

Erewn took two steps forward and laughed. "I understand the protector's wariness, even though I do not know the cause of it. When my father was protector, he acted in the same way- his oaths to protect the people would sometimes clash with the old laws and he stood his ground, just like your protector has. Since I do not wish any further animosity with her, I shall accede to her request willingly."

Brar had a surprised look as he held his hand up. "That will not be necessary."

Erewn faced the elders and pulled down his loincloth. The council could see that he had an intact set of genitalia, though they seemed quite small for a man his age. Nevertheless, they were visibly pleased while Erewn pulled his loincloth back on. The rest of the crowd in the hall did not bother to look since the expressions of the elders had already told them what the result was. Miri felt the whole thing was some sort of trick, but she couldn't explain how or why, so she just kept silent.

Pir nodded. "Even though it was not required of you, you have indeed proven that you are not a Magus. Therefore, we extend our invitation to Erewn, last of the Silid," he said before turning to face the others in the council. "Elders, what is your vote. If you wish to bind our guest in the sacred oath of sanctuary, please raise your hand."

Almost everyone started to raise their hands. Devos could so no reason to oppose the vote, but as soon as he turned and looked at Zedne, he realized that she wasn't raising her own hand. Devos gave a curt nod to her and kept his hands on his lap.

Brar looked disappointed that the vote was even close to a tie. He turned and faced Erewn. "By a vote of four to two, the oath of sanctuary is approved. Erewn of the Silid, we of the Arum Navar extend this sacred promise to you. As of this time, our water is your water, our food is your food, our house is your house, our lives are with you. You may stay for as long as you want, and no harm shall come to you. We swear this, by the laws brought down to us by the goddess Karma and by the god Duun. We are pledged to defend against anyone who opposes you or attempts to do you wrong. May the gods curse us if we break this vow. Amen."

Erewn knelt down. "I humbly thank you. I shall stay no more than a few days at the most. For I have a long journey ahead of me. Amen."

Brar stood up. "There is to be feasting tonight. We still have some dried meat and plenty of algae and shrooms. Let us celebrate the arrival of our honored guest. Let us forget the arguments that took place today. Break out the wine stores. This is a time to celebrate the arrival of a brother, and in memory of an allied tribe."

As the crowd began to break up, Miri walked over to Zedne and knelt down beside her. "Are you okay, Mother?"

Zedne smiled as she was helped up by the protector. "Oh, I am fine. I just did not get much sleep lately. But it is all worth it for the sick child is now on her way to recovery. It makes me feel so good when I know I have done my duty."

Devos stood beside them both. "His loins looked small, but they were intact. There was no chance of us winning that vote."

Miri nodded. "This will be a long night. We need to be vigilant- keep the boy in our sight at all times. I have a feeling this Erewn might try something against him."

Devos frowned. "Do you really think that he is a danger? If he is not a Magus, then how can he be a threat?"

"I cannot be wholly certain," Miri said. "But I believe there is more to him than what meets the eye. Even though I cannot sense his thoughts, there is something wrong about all of this."

"I am with you," Zedne said. "What do you need for us to do?"

Miri looked at the both of them. "Can Rion stay in either of your huts tonight?"

"Yes, of course," Zedne said before she suddenly felt light headed and had to be held up by Miri.

"Mother," Miri said. "I think you need to go take some rest."

"I shall take the boy in my hut tonight," Devos said. He turned around and headed for the exit.

Nyx walked over to Miri as the protector was helping Zedne towards the entryway. "I am so sorry for being late, Miri," Nyx said softly. "What just happened?"

Miri saw Erewn being led out of the hall by a smiling Brar. "I am assigning you to watch the outsider. If you see him do anything suspicious, use your mindsense to alert me at once. I will be watching the outskirts of the settlement, just in case he has any allies waiting for him outside."

Nyx bit her lip. She had been hoping to hang out with her brother Jinn during the feast that evening. "Do I have to watch him all evening?"

Miri nodded. "Yes, where is your bone axe?"

"In my hut," Nyx said. "Do you want me to carry it?"

Miri shook her head. "No, it would arouse too much suspicion. Keep it close by so you can retrieve it quickly, though. You do have a knife with a dargon tooth blade, keep that with you at all times."

Nyx nodded. She had a feeling her growing collection of weapons would be put to use sooner rather than later.

## Chapter 9

Erewn carried the wineskin as he walked towards the perimeter. The feasting had been going on for several hours now, and a large number of the tribe had already gone back to their homes to turn in for the night. The stew was quite good, and he had eaten heartily. Since he was the guest of honor, Erewn was toasted several times by his hosts, but he merely took small sips of the wine that was offered to him. He needed to remain alert for the upcoming task. Using his sleight of hand skills, Erewn was able to sprinkle some of the white powder he had been carrying with him into all the wine and water containers in the hall. Just before venturing out into the wastes, he took a satchel of the sleeping powder from the citadel's store rooms, expecting to use it for just this very occasion.

A young couple held out their hands in greeting out to him while he walked along a narrow path in between the huts. He smiled and returned the gesture before moving on. Erewn knew that the boy was sleeping somewhere very close by. Once the tribe was fast asleep, he would do a very quick search for the child, then use any sort of weapon to kill him. There were still a few complications that might upset his plans, though. This protector of theirs was a very cautious woman who happened to be quite powerful with her mindsense. Erewn had to use most of his Vis just to stay focused to prevent her mind probe from sensing anything suspicious. The fact that the protector was nowhere to be seen during the feast, made him doubly worried she was on to him. He sensed there were at least three Strigas in the settlement, and he needed to account for them all if he had any chance to succeed.

When he got to the edge of the low wall, he came upon a young man sitting on one of the boulders, looking out into the darkness beyond. The youth was accompanied by a teen girl and they were both talking with each other. Erewn started dragging his feet so they could hear him coming. When they both turned in his direction, he held out a hand in a gesture of peace.

"Hail and pleasant eventides to you," Erewn said as he got closer.

Jinn got off the boulder and stood fully upright as he held out his open palm. "Hail honored guest, what brings you out here at this time of the night?"

Erewn grinned as he held out the wineskin so they both could see it. "Your name is Jinn, is it not?"

Jinn nodded. "Yes, honored guest. This is my sister, Nyx."

Nyx made a slight bow. She had been observing the outsider during the feast, but decided to pay her brother a visit, thinking that Erewn would still be in the hall when she got back. She was somewhat surprised to find him out here, and was glad that she didn't lose sight of him after all. "A pleasant eventide to you, honored guest."

Erewn bowed in return. He immediately sensed that the girl was a Striga. "I wanted to see what the village would look out here in the evening. To be honest, sitting around feasting and everyone staring at you makes me uncomfortable, so I had to venture out, if only for just a short while."

Jinn nodded. "You have been given the promise of sanctuary, so that is your right. But since you have traveled the wastes for a long time, can I ask you a question?"

Erewn smiled. "Of course, young one. I will attempt to answer to the best of my ability."

Jinn turned and stared out into the twilit dunes out in the distance. "Have you come across other settlements like this one? Other tribes?"

Erewn shook his head. "I am afraid not. Yours is the first tribe that I have found during my wanderings after my own. I was but a child when my father took me away from our village, for it was already abandoned and we were the last ones to leave."

Nyx wasn't sure why Miri distrusted this man, but she found him to be friendly and fascinating. She soon forgot about her task as an innate curiosity overcame her wariness. "Honored guest, have you encountered ruins and such? The teller tells us many stories about how the land was before the wastelands consumed everything. I have heard that there are villages filled with thousands of people and they were called cities. Are any such places still in existence?"

Erewn looked down. "I am afraid to say this, but I think all the cities are now dead. Many ruins have I stumbled upon in my wanderings, and all were either devoid of life or inhabited by fell creatures that would have killed me had I lingered. Yours may very well be the last village out here. If there is another part of the world that might still have thriving cities, I do not know, but it is always good to hope."

Nyx frowned. Perhaps Miri was wrong about this man. He seemed forthcoming and friendly enough. "I have to tell you about our protector. I must apologize on her behalf. Her behavior to you earlier during the day was rude and it is so unlike her to be this wary of outsiders who come in peace."

Erewn grinned once more. "That is all in the past now. But it seems that I missed her during the feasting, was she not there?"

Nyx blushed with shame. "She is near the edge of the Silt Sea…checking on things there."

"Well, I hope that she does return to at least partake of the feast before all the food and wine is gone," Erewn said while holding up the bloated wineskin in front of him. "Speaking of which, I had not seen you at the feast, Jinn, so I brought along this ration of wine for you."

Jinn shrugged. "I have been assigned as sentry for this evening. Your offer to drink wine is very enticing, thank you. But I must decline, for the chief hunter will be angry with me if he sees me drinking any of that."

Nyx elbowed her brother. "Oh come now, Jinn! Just a few sips will not get you drunk. I know you cannot take more than a thimbleful anyway before you're fast asleep!"

"Silence!" Jinn hissed. "Must you tell everyone about me?"

Erewn laughed as he held out the wineskin. "Do not worry, your secrets are safe with me. For when I wander out there, I shall have no one to tell it to. But your sister is right, just a few sips will not hurt. As guest of honor, I must insist."

Jinn was in a bind. As part of his oath as a tribal sentry, he wasn't supposed to drink wine while on duty. At the same time, the honored guest might be offended if he didn't. He took the wineskin in his hands, opened the stopper and drank a little bit of it. The warm liquid was soothing, a good remedy for the chilly night air. "I am honored you allowed me to partake of this wine that was offered to you."

Erewn chuckled as he handed the wineskin to Nyx. "And now you, girl."

Nyx took a step back and shook her head. "Oh no, I could not. Like my brother, I also have tasks to do this evening."

"Have a drink and I shall accept your apology on behalf of your protector," Erewn said as he held out the wineskin once more.

It was Jinn's turn to chide his sister. "Go on. No one is looking."

Nyx sighed as she took the wineskin in her hands. "Oh, very well." She titled her head up and took a long swallow. It was only the second time that she had drunk the potent brew and she quickly started to gag. Nyx almost dropped the wineskin as she staggered backwards, drops of wine dribbling down her neck.

Jinn laughed and quickly took the wineskin away from her. "Look what you have done, sister. You have spilled wine onto the sand!"

Erewn was grinning from ear to ear as he took back the wineskin. "You did well, Nyx. Was this your first time to drink such a beverage?"

Nyx wiped the remaining drops of wine from her chin with her arm. "My second. Please do not tell anyone of this."

Erewn nodded. "Of course. I am honored to have met you both this evening. I have not yet learned everyone's name, but I hope to remedy that soon."

"With the impression you have made," a voice in the darkness said. "It would seem that you will know the names of the others soon enough."

All three turned. Stepping out of the shadows was Krag, his long cloak fluttering in the night breeze. Jinn immediately looked away in shame, but

Krag walked over to him and placed a calloused hand on his shoulder. Erewn walked up to the chief hunter and offered the wineskin to him. Krag gladly took the leather pouch and drank several long draughts of the wine.

Jinn hung his head in shame. "I-I am sorry, chief hunter. I partook of the wine even though it was against my duty."

Krag let out a big, throaty laugh. "Have no fear, Jinn. I will not punish you for your indiscretion. This is a feast after all, and I will not let the other sentries know as long as we keep what had occurred within this group, yes?"

They all laughed. Krag offered the wineskin back to Erewn, but the other man declined. "I have had plenty already," the honored guest said. "You may go ahead and finish the rest of it."

Krag passed it to the siblings and each took another sip before handing it back to him. Krag took another long draught of the intoxicating liquid. The wineskin was now almost empty. "There. Now honored guest, I can escort you back to the feast or to your guest quarters and sleep off the rest of the evening. What shall it be?"

"I have been on my feet since the day began, so I believe I shall retire for the evening," Erewn said before glancing at a now tipsy looking Nyx. "I wanted to ask you if my weapons have been stored properly?"

Nyx grinned sheepishly. Only a few sips and she was seeing double already. "My apologies once again, honored guest. Your weapons are in my hut, the fourth one to the left of our central well." She pointed over to a row of houses nearby. "As the future protector, it was my duty to safeguard them. Have no fear, for they shall be returned to you once you venture forth into the wastes."

Erewn bowed once again. "I thank you and take my leave now. Enjoy the rest of the eventide."

Nyx tried to bow and almost fell face down into the ground. Jinn was able to catch her in time and they both started laughing. Krag just shook his head while he gestured at Erewn to follow him. Erewn nodded and walked alongside of him as they both headed towards the center of the settlement. So far so good, everything was going according to plan. When Erewn needed to escape back to the wastes, he knew which course to take.

While walking close to the main footpath, Krag suddenly stopped as he looked down on the ground while holding onto the side of walled house. "It seems that I had far too much to drink this evening. My senses have been dulled into a haze-filled oblivion."

Erewn took him by the arm. The chief hunter had drank the most, so it meant that he got a concentrated dose of the sleeping powder that was mixed into it. "Let me help you. Which is the way to your hut?"

Krag pointed with a shaky finger at a house just ahead of them. "T-there."

Erewn supported him as they both made their way to the front of the mud brick hut. Erewn used one hand to move the leather flap from the entryway as he peered inside. Krag's wife lay on the floor, already passed out. The chief hunter suddenly slumped on his shoulder, so Erewn had to drag him inside the place before placing the now unconscious man onto the floor beside his wife.

The sounds of revelry had already ceased and an eerie silence settled over the village. The sleeping powder had done its work and now almost everyone was in a deep slumber. The time to act was now. Erewn wore a heavy tunic made of thick leather, so his upper body was somewhat armored. He looked around the chief hunter's abode, looking for any weapons. There was a rack that contained Krag's bone spear. Erewn looked over the weapon closely. It had a metal spearhead, but bringing a large weapon like that might arouse suspicions on those that had not been exposed to the sleeping powder, so it was better for him to use a smaller weapon, one that he could conceal among his person.

Erewn quickly noticed a dagger lying on top of a low stone table. He picked it up and noticed that its serrated edges meant it was made from dargon teeth. *A good weapon*, he thought as he stowed it away beneath the folds of his cloak. He made his way back to the entryway, took a look outside to make sure no one was watching, then ventured out.

Most of the village was bathed in twilight as the full moon above gave enough illumination for anyone to make their way around the area. The distant fire from nearby huts and the assembly hall gave the streets a washed out, flickering orange hue, but there were still enough shadows to conceal one's self. Erewn dashed from one hut to the next, opening flaps and peering inside. Two of the huts were empty, their occupants may have passed out at the feast in the assembly hall. The third hut had a family of four, but neither of the sleeping two children was the blond boy.

Just as he made it to the western edge of the settlement, he soon remembered that the apprentice Striga's hut was nearby. Using the nearby shadows as cover, he dashed across one of the larger streets as he got to the entryway. Peering inside, he noticed that the place was totally in the dark. From the reflected light of the open entryway, he could barely make out the outline of the weapon rack. Slipping inside the hut, Erewn extended his arms so he could use his sense of touch to locate his bone sword. Just as his right hand ran along what he felt was a shaft of a bone spear, his first two fingers inadvertently touched the razor sharp obsidian edge of his blade, cutting right through the skin. Erewn gasped as he pulled his hand back and licked the cut on his fingers. *What a foolish way to find my own blade*, he thought as his other hand found the grip and he lifted it from the rack.

Putting on his leather gloves, Erewn gripped the sword with one hand while he slowly began to make his way towards the main well. He had made a head count ever since he started observing the village the past few days. Erewn figured that there were no more than a dozen hunters and perhaps another thirty men of fighting age at the most. The entire tribe's population didn't seem to be more than three hundred, with many of them old men and women representing a higher proportion of the population. With most of the tribe fast asleep, he now stood a very good chance of pulling this task off.

The next street ahead was located in the main thoroughfare, and a slightly large hut signified that it was the abode of someone important to the village, possibly an elder. Erewn silently made his way over until he was able to crouch down beside the entryway, using his senses to detect anyone present. He could feel a wave of heat and see the light coming from the gaps in the leather flap, meaning someone had lit a fire inside. Readying his sword, Erewn mustered up his full reserve of Vis, then flipped open the leather flap before thrusting his body inside.

The interior of the hut was larger than most. There was a smoldering fire pit at the far end and Erewn saw an old man tending it, his back turned away from him. Glancing around quickly, he noticed a small figure lying on a bed of furs near the far side of the wall. Recognizing Devos, Erewn knew that the old man was one of the elders in that council he had attended just a few hours before. This was the teller's house, and the boy was right there, asleep.

Devos immediately sensed someone behind him as he turned and saw that the stranger had come inside. His eyes opened wide when he saw that Erewn was fully clothed and armed. As Devos got up, he reached for the knife that was lying on a nearby table, but his hand suddenly froze in midair. He couldn't move as the outsider held out his free hand, as if signaling him to stop.

Erewn gestured with his open hand as he used his Vis. The old man was now floating in the air a few inches from the floor, unable to move. "Do not make me kill you, Elder."

No matter how hard he tried, Devos could not act. He tried to cry out, but his voice was barely a hoarse whisper. Then his lungs began to feel heavy while he floated helplessly just a few feet off the ground. Erewn gestured once more, and his mindforce pushed the old man straight into the wall. Devos collided into a rack full of carved stones before his back was driven into a wall of bricks. The force of the invisible push had stunned him, and the old man closed his eyes and groaned. The Magus noticed the old man's knife and used his mindforce to pull the blade back into the air and into his waiting hand. Now he had two backup weapons.

Erewn turned as he noticed the boy beginning to stir. The noise must have awakened him. It was the moment he realized that if he killed the boy within the settlement, then he would be in violation of the oath of peace. What he needed to do was to take the child and kill him somewhere out in the dunes and bury the body in the sand. Erewn placed his free hand over the boy's mouth, just as the child suddenly opened his eyes. "If you utter a sound, I will kill you."

Grabbing the child by his elbow, he pulled the boy up and pushed him through the entrance flap. The moment they were both outside of the teller's hut, he kept a tight grip on the boy's arm as he pulled Rion alongside of him while proceeding towards the perimeter.

"Stop," a voice behind them said.

Erewn turned around. Standing twenty feet away from him was Miri. She was holding her black spear with one hand. It looked like he was in for a battle after all.

Miri had been watching the edges near the Silt Sea during most of the evening. She was concerned that the outsider might have had allies who were waiting for the right moment to strike. When nobody turned up, she came back into the village center just to check up on the others and was shocked to see the entire tribe was mostly fast asleep. Miri tried her mindsense to see if she could warn Nyx, but her mental feelers soon told her that her protégé was also in a deep slumber. Then she proceeded towards the teller's hut, just in the nick of time.

Erewn smiled as he pushed the boy to the side. "This child is mine, thank you for finding him out there in the wastes."

Rion was thrown to the ground but he tilted his head up. "I do not belong to you!"

Miri's face was a mask of stone. "You have just told another lie. So I was correct, you are a Magus. What did you do to the teller?"

"Your teller is merely stunned," Erewn said. "He tried to keep me from the child I was tasked to retrieve and return to the citadel."

"I will not go back to that place!" Rion said.

Erewn gave the boy a backhanded slap which sent the child into the side of the dirt pathway. Miri started to advance, but she stopped when she noticed Erewn brandishing his bone sword. Miri glanced over to the boy. "Get away," she said.

Rion took off running. The two of them began to circle each other. Miri held her spear at chest level with both hands, keeping its point centered on her opponent. Erewn held his sword pointed up while keeping it close to his body, but his left hand remained free and at his side. They were both maneuvering in the middle of the main pathway, so there was at least ten feet in between them. A few of the older people who did not drink the spiked wine had come out of their huts and formed a small crowd near the intersection, silently watching the event.

"By the right of possession, I am merely claiming the boy for the citadel," Erewn said. "Your hostile actions are in violation of the promise of sanctuary."

"Prove that he belongs to the Magi," Miri said tersely.

"His name is Rion and he is eleven cycles old," Erewn said. "The boy is a Magus. I have been dispatched by the administrator of Doss to bring him back."

"So this proves that you are indeed a Magus," Miri said. "You are the one who violated the promise when you lied during the questioning."

"If you remember the exact words that I spoke, you will note I never denied I was a Magus, I merely asked why you suspected I was one," Erewn said. "By those very words, I did not lie to you, and therefore, I have not violated the sacred promise."

"Enough!' Miri hissed. "Your deceptions and your actions against the boy and the teller are as clear as the coming day. Drop your weapon and surrender peacefully."

"No, I claim the boy and I shall leave under the promise of sanctuary," Erewn said. "You cannot stop me."

Miri was in a wide stance, ready for battle. She moved a step forward and thrust her spear at the Magus, but Erewn sidestepped away as he brought up his sword in a blocking position. Miri circled again, keeping some distance since she had the advantage of reach, by virtue of wielding a longer weapon. Erewn was staying on the defensive, he needed to know just how much Vis she still had while keeping his mental defenses at their maximum strength. Just as he shifted towards his right side, Miri lunged at him and her spear tip was able to scratch his upper leg. Several people in the crowd gasped. It was a known law that the first to spill blood under the promise of sanctuary was the violator.

Erewn grimaced. "You wounded me! You have violated the promise of sanctuary!"

"No more words," Miri said as she stepped forward again, pushing her spear towards his neck.

This time, Erewn sidestepped to the other way as he used a bit of his mindforce to push his opponent. Miri was unprepared for it since she had lunged too far ahead, so her body was off balance. The force of the Vis caught her left side and she tumbled sideways into the dirt. The crowd made a collective gasp as the Magus ran at her, using both hands to swing his sword downwards for the killing blow.

Miri reacted in time as she rolled sideways, the sharp edges of the sword missing her torso by a scant few inches. She tuck rolled back into an upright position, and was able to block another swing as the shaft of her weapon tore off a few bits of obsidian from the edges of Erewn's sword. Miri quickly stepped backwards so she could gain some distance. At close range, the sword wielder had the advantage, but if she could put a little bit more space in between them, then her longer weapon would be in a superior position.

Erewn knew her intentions and he was having none of it. He gestured with his left hand as he used his mindforce to pull Miri in closer to him, right within range of his next swing. Just as Miri was suddenly thrust forward, she concentrated and used her mindsense to break through her opponent's lowered mental defenses in an effort to overload the pain receptors in his mind. Now that she was in close, Erewn tried to swing his sword at Miri, but was suddenly overcome by a terrible, mind-numbing headache. With his eyes losing focus due to the flashes of pain, Miri was able to pull away from his half blind swing, as the edges of the sword ripped the upper part of her leather bodice away.

The Magus screamed in agony while Miri retreated to a safe distance. Blood dripped down his nostrils, and it was obvious another successful mental attack would incapacitate him. Erewn was angry at himself for concentrating too much of his Vis for attacking rather than for defense. Miri continued to use her mindsense to instill pain in her opponent's head while Erewn started to rebuild his shattered thought blocks, channeling his entire Vis for protection this time.

As Miri started to advance on him with her spear, Erewn took out the dagger he had placed in his waist. When Miri prepared for another lunge and strike, he threw the dagger at her, using just a little of his mindforce to dramatically increase its velocity, hoping that she would not have the time to react. Miri immediately sensed the missile heading straight for her and she tried to dodge it, but she misjudged its speed. As the dagger flew past her, it made a long gash on the side of her right arm. Momentarily losing her concentration, Miri cried out as she got to one knee, blood pouring down her arm.

With the mental attacks against him temporarily subsiding, Erewn knew he was running out of time. He needed to end this now. Gathering up his remaining reserves of Vis, he used his mindforce, coalescing it into a huge, invisible wave of power and hurled it at the Striga. Miri screamed as the cascading, invisible wall of energy struck her and sent her up into the air, body tumbling sideways. The concussive shockwave hurled her into the side of a nearby hut, just near the top edge of its roof. The force of her fall ripped through the leather tarpaulin and her back landed just at the edge of an unused fire pit in the hut's deserted interior, her spear falling down by her side.

Erewn saw the Striga crash into the roof of a nearby hut. Now that he had her stunned, he rechanneled his Vis, filling up his mental reserves away from the defensive thought blocks and back into a final attack. Erewn then took a running leap and used his mindforce to jump up thirty feet into the air above the ruined hut. He held his sword over his head for the killing blow. As soon as he landed on top of his victim, he would cleave her head in two.

Miri blinked herself awake and looked up to see the Magus bearing down in a diving attack. Her opponent had leapt up into the air and was now about to bring death upon her. With less than a second, Miri's hands felt the shaft of her spear lying nearby. There was no time left and her instincts took over. Miri's left hand gripped the spear shaft while she brought its point up, just as Erewn landed on top of her.

The blade of the Magus ended up just inches from the side of her head as the weapon quivered for a bit before falling down on the ground right next to her. Blood poured out of Erewn's mouth as he realized that he had been impaled on the spear, its point having penetrated right through his ribcage and past his spine. It looked like he was leaning over her, though the spear kept him from falling down. He tried to move, but his arms and legs didn't react to his commands. He could barely breathe and his chest was numb. Miri's face was only a few feet away from his own and it was the last thing he saw. After a minute, Erewn closed his eyes and died.

Miri groaned as she rolled sideways and got up. Rion came through the flap in the entryway and saw what had happened. The boy ran over to her and hugged Miri tightly. A slight breeze came though the exposed roof, and it was enough to tilt the body of the Magus when it suddenly shifted sideways and the still warm corpse fell into the wreckage around it.

# Chapter 10

The angle of the sun indicated it was midmorning, and the assembly hall was in an uproar. People were shouting at each other to the point where any kind of intelligent conversation could no longer be understood. Miri was sitting down near the center of the fire pit. There was a foul smelling poultice that had been salved over the wound in her right arm. Devos and Zedne were beside her, offering support. The other elders faced her and their expressions ranged from bewilderment to outrage. The crowd around them were most of the adults, while the children were not present. Rion was back resting in the teller's hut, being watched over by Nyx and Jinn.

Elder Brar stood up and clapped his hands in an effort to restore order. "Enough! We cannot have all this shouting and talking at the same time! We must have silence! Please!"

The crowd had quieted down to slight whispers and murmuring. Miri looked around and all she could see were faces that belied concern for the future of the tribe. Zedne placed a reassuring hand on her knee which gave her a slight feeling of confidence. This emergency assembly had been called the moment that everyone had finally recovered from their stupor. There was debate as to whether it was Miri who had initially violated the oath of sanctuary by spilling first blood, as well as the possible recriminations the Magi would seek once word that one of their own had been killed.

Now that a sense of calm had pervaded the hall, Brar looked around to read everyone's faces before he started talking. "Let us begin. People of the

Arum Navar, we have gathered here in order to find out what had happened the night before. The sacred oath of sanctuary was violated last eventide, and now a man is dead. We mourn the passing of Erewn, a suspected Magus and last of the Silid."

Devos grimaced. "Suspected Magus? By the gods! I and the others who witnessed last night's battle know for a fact that he was indeed part of the Magi. As to whether his name really was Erewn, or if he really was part of the Silid- well, that kind of information cannot be trusted! He was a wanton liar and he nearly murdered our protector!"

The crowd erupted into shouting and recriminations once more. This time, Krag stepped forward and pounded on the floor with the shaft of his bone spear. The throng quickly became silent again.

Brar gave a menacing look at Devos. "There will be order! Only one shall speak at a time. Chief Hunter Krag, if anyone interrupts another, you will escort the offender out of this hall."

Krag said nothing and merely nodded. He had three other hunters ready by his side.

Brar nodded as he glanced at the elders sitting beside him. "Let us get to the heart of the matter. As to the exact identity of this Erewn, we may never know. But what is clear is that we gave him the oath of sanctuary, a sacred promise that was never violated once in the history of our people." He pointed a thick finger at Devos. "You are the teller of this tribe, I would like to ask you, have there been others in our distant past that were given this oath and were later proved to have been lying to us?"

Devos sighed. He was bound by oath to tell the truth, just like everyone else. "Yes, there have been several instances in which the people have given sanctuary to someone who was not who he claimed he was."

Brar kept his eyes on the teller. He already knew about this tale, but wanted the others to know. "Please recount the last time this has happened, teller."

"Close to a hundred cycles ago, a man came out of the wastes and requested sanctuary," Devos said. "He gave his name as Ulseig, of the Khezni. We accepted him into the tribe and he remained with us peacefully until the final cycles of his life. When we asked him what he had been doing before he came to our settlement, he claimed that he was a hunter with another tribe."

Brar crossed his arms. "Go on, tell us who he really was."

"On his deathbed, he told us that his real name was Eizg," Devos said. "And he was not a hunter, but a Magus who had fled from the Citadel of Doss to live out his life in peace."

Several loud gasps were heard from the crowd. Krag glared at a few others who were murmuring too loudly.

Elder Pir raised his hand. "So as you can see, we have given the oath of sanctuary to others who did not speak the truth before, and we never violated that promise."

One of the women in the crowd put up her hand. "But the people only found out that he was a liar upon his deathbed. Surely if he had told the tribe what the actual truth was before he died, then they would have surely cast him out."

Brar shook his head. "Never. There was a time when a hunter from the Nartos sought refuge with us when he had killed one of his own over a dispute with the man's wife. He told us of this the moment he requested sanctuary. Our elders at that time accepted him and even defended his life when the Nartos came to our settlement, seeking his return. That was the one time when we nearly went to war with another tribe, but cooler heads prevailed. We gave the Nartos a cycle's supply of meat, while that hunter stayed with us and lived a life of peace until his death of old age. Our people refused to violate the promise then, even if it meant going to war with our neighbors."

The murmurings started again. Elder Zedne raised her hand. When the crowd quieted down, she spoke. "Yes, I do not begrudge the ones in this assembly who speak about our sacred oaths. We know we cannot violate them. But that stranger who came before us, he already broke the bond when he used a kind of potion to put us into a forced sleep. Miri was one of the few who had not trusted him, and she saved the boy from being abducted."

Elder Oro raised his hand. "How do you know of this type of venom? We looked at the wine after we woke up, and you yourself admitted you could not find a trace of the poison in it."

Zedne sighed. "I am the healer of this tribe, I know about poisons. The venom in question is called the powder of dreams. I found traces of the white dust in a pouch on the stranger's corpse. Once dissolved in liquid, this fine grain induces a long slumber. It is potent but soon dissipates once liquefied. That is why I could not find a trace of it in the wine that was not drunk."

Elder Etul raised his bony hand. "You know I respect your words, healer, but even if the outsider was guilty of this, he still did not violate the oath of peace. Nowhere in the sacred words did it say anything about lulling his hosts to sleep would lead to the breaking of the pledge."

Devos frowned as he raised his hand to counter what was just said. "When you have been made unconscious against your will or without your knowledge, does that not constitute an offense?"

"Yet there was no violence done until Erewn was wounded by the protector," Brar said.

Devos was trembling with palpable anger. This time he raised a fist. "This assembly is but a mockery! It was I who the outsider first attacked. I was in my own hut when he came in and used his mindforce to hurl me into the air and throw me to the wall!"

"There were no witnesses to that event," Oro said softly.

"Then I suppose he gave the bruise on his head to himself?" Miri asked. "What about the wreckage on the side of his hut, did he do all that too?"

"Silence!' Brar said. "Miri, you are the accused. You may not speak unless you are asked a question by one of the elders here. Obey our ways or be cast out!"

"If what you said is true, Elder Devos," Etul said. "Then did you not also state that when the moment you saw him, you reached for a weapon? Could the outsider's response have been nothing more than a reaction to your threatening moves? You yourself said that you were stunned by the mindforce, and you could have easily been dispatched, yet he left you alone."

Devos exhaled loudly. "He left me alone because he was after the boy. Since I was knocked out senseless like the rest of you, there was no reason to kill me then."

"It is good that you brought up the boy, for that was Erewn's stated reason for coming here," Brar said. "The outsider claimed that the boy who had been found two moons ago is a Magus, and that he was merely reclaiming the child in order to return him back to the citadel. According to Elder Zedne's own words, she along with the protector and her apprentice, was unable to use their mindsense on the boy when he first arrived. This supports the notion that the boy is indeed a Magus."

Miri raised her hand but the elders ignored her. She turned and whispered into Devos's ear. Then the teller raised his hand since he was free to speak. "If you evoked the oath of sanctuary on the stranger who attacked us, then surely you remember pledging that very same promise to the boy?"

Etul glanced at Brar, who shook his head. "We never gave the promise of sanctuary to the boy. As a child of the desert, his true parents are fit to claim him once they find out he is here. That is our way," Brar said.

Loud murmurings erupted from the crowd once more. Krag pounded the blunt end of his spear on the ground to silence them.

Devos shook his head slowly as he raised his hand once more. "This whole proceeding is outrageous! We have clear evidence that the outsider lied and used venom to put most of you to sleep, then he attacked me and nearly killed our protector. Surely you can see this!"

A middle aged farmer in the crowd raised his hand. "I may not have the wisdom of the elders, but I am afraid for my family. If the Magi hear of what has happened, they will come and slaughter us all!"

The rest of the crowd immediately erupted. Loud curses and protests were thrown about, with multiple arguments for and against the actions of the protector. Some of the women screamed out loud, protesting their innocence in all of this and their unwillingness to support what had happened. Another man shouted at the top of his lungs that the best way to remedy the crisis was to execute Miri and send her remains to the citadel. Brar stood up and clapped his hands for a long minute, but the crowd would not be silenced.

Oro cupped his hands and shouted at Krag. "Chief Hunter, send them away!"

Krag nodded as he and his men began to push the wailing crowd out of the hall. There were a few protests, but on the whole the congregation filled out peacefully. After a few minutes, only Miri and the elders were left as the hunters stood guard outside to prevent anyone from entering.

Pir smiled faintly at Miri. "As you can see, protector, the life of an elder is not an easy one. Even though we no longer toil with our bodies, the people look at us to make these hard decisions. We had to show everyone that we respect the traditions, or else the whole tribe would descend into chaos. You may speak freely now that we are by ourselves."

Miri nodded. She needed to stay calm and try to reason with them, even though she felt it was pointless. "I am not happy at what I did, but I had to fight that Magus. He was trying to abduct Rion, and I could not let it happen."

Etul's age was at eighty-six cycles, it made him the oldest of them all. "This boy, why are you so fond of him?"

"He is intelligent and knows how to read the glyphs," Miri said. The four other elders gasped in surprise. "Rion can be of great value to our people," she said.

It was Brar who recovered from the surprising revelation first. "I am sorry for being so harsh on you this day, Miri. But you must understand our predicament here. There are less than three hundred of us now. We have few children and our tribe is slowly dying out. The people are afraid of what had just occurred last eventide. The moment the hunting party brought back that child, there were already murmurings. I heard many whispers myself that proclaimed the end times for us. There are many in the village who believe the boy is cursed. With this last incident, it could be the final stone that gets placed above our tombs."

"We can hide the corpse. Once we place the separate pieces in the fungi gardens, the shrooms will cover the outsider's bones so that it will be indistinguishable from the others," Devos said. "Even if the Magi do come, they will find nothing if we act now."

Etul shook his head. "What about the boy? If they sent one of their own here, then the others will surely follow. If they know that the boy is in this settlement, then he will be found and we will all be punished for hiding him. Even though Miri is formidable, one Striga and her apprentice will not be able to withstand the might of a Magi war party."

"Let us not forget that the boy is also a Magus," Brar said. "The ancient treaties we have with the Magi clearly state that if they do not come here to claim him, the child must be put to death. That is the one treaty we cannot ignore, for it will mean the annihilation of our entire tribe if we do so."

Miri pursed her lips. "Let me suggest this. Give Rion the oath of sanctuary, and I will protect him. We can use the black algae to darken his hair and alter the rest of his appearance. We can also hide him if more of the Magi do come."

"Have you not been listening, Miri?" Oro said. "Many of the people here do not want the boy. If we are to defend him, then we might all as well go to the tombs right now."

Zedne was appalled. "So what are your plans then? You wish to murder the boy?"

"The child must be put down, or he is to be given back to the citadel," Brar said. "We must abide by our ancient treaties. We live in precarious times. What the gods have given us, they can easily take away. We have to do what we can in order to ensure the continued existence of this tribe, or we will go by the way of the others that have been lost in the dust."

"I cannot believe I am hearing this," Devos said. "He is a boy, and he was subjected to untold horrors that the Magi inflicted upon him. We cannot send him back to them!"

Miri looked into the eyes of the other elders. She didn't even need to use her mindsense to know what they were thinking. She stood up. "If this is the wish of the tribe, then I will do my duty. I will be the one to bring Rion back to the citadel."

Brar conferred with the others, then he looked up at her and nodded. "You must take the boy and leave at first light by morrow."

The pain in Miri's arm had settled into a dull, but constant ache while she walked towards the healer's house. Devos and Zedne were by her side. All three remained silent until they entered the main room. Rion was sitting near the unused firepit as he was playing a game of rocks with Nyx. Jinn sat by the doorway rubbing his bone spear and he instantly stood up as soon as Miri stepped inside. Nyx and the boy looked up at them.

Miri looked at the youth. "You may go, Jinn."

Jinn nodded and opened the entrance flap once more. "I will see you later, Nyx," he said before exiting the hut.

Zedne smiled as she crouched down beside the boy. "Do the bruises on your arms and legs still hurt?"

Rion smiled and shook his head. "Not anymore, healer, thanks."

Zedne helped the boy up. "You may go ahead and play outside, Rion. I shall prepare something for us to eat."

As the boy happily ran towards the exit, Miri glanced over to Nyx. "Stay by his side at all times."

Nyx nodded as she got up and followed Rion outside. She wanted desperately to know what had occurred during the assembly, but she felt that it was better to speak about it later.

The three of them sat by the fire pit as Zedne took out some dried manure from a leather sack and used some flint to ignite it. The healer then placed two pots near the glowing flames while a pungent smell from the burning wafted through the air.

Devos looked at the protector, but Miri's face was a mask of stone. "Surely you do not intend to deliver the boy back to those beasts in that accursed citadel."

Miri stared into the fire for a long minute before she answered. "No, I do not. I am merely thinking of the consequences when my decision is known to all."

Zedne said nothing while she continued to stroke the fire. Her own mindsense was communicating mentally with Miri and she already knew what the protector's intentions were. The hard choices that would now be made saddened her greatly, for she knew that this was the last time she would be with the daughter that she considered as her own. Her lips trembled a little bit as she silently kept her emotions in check.

Devos could tell that the two women were communicating telepathically. "If there is any way I could help you," he said to Miri. "Just say the word."

Miri looked back at him. "There is. Can you tell me about the stories of the lands beyond the Great Silt Sea?"

Devos let out a deep breath while trying to recall some of the more obscure tales he had committed to memory. "Let me see. Ah, you have to realize that it has been ages since I have been required to recall these stories. Most of them are but legends now, for no one has travelled across the Silt Sea for hundreds of cycles."

"I remember some of the stories told to me when I was but a child. The most vivid that I can recall was the tale of the last great city," Miri said.

"Yes, the tales of Lethe, the city of sanctuary," Devos said. "It is said that all men who seek true refuge must face a long journey of temptation across the Great Silt Sea. The spires of Lethe are said to be so tall, they reach up into the sky, and if one walks up the steps for days and days, then they may reach out and touch the burning sun above us."

"Did the tales give any specific directions on where this city was?" Miri asked.

"There was one tale that I distinctly remember that tells of a Magus who had fought the Gorgons for many cycles until he had tired of all the blood and killing. While wandering in the wastes, he had a dream of the goddess Karma, and it was she who led him to the city. It took many cycles, but when he finally reached the gates of Lethe, he dropped dead with but a smile on his face."

"So he was guided merely by dreams?" Miri asked.

Zedne smiled as she sat beside them. "Did I not tell you once that our mindsense sometimes takes the forms of dreams, child?"

Miri had a quizzical look on her face as she turned and stared at the healer. "Are you telling me that the Magus in that tale was led there by a Striga?"

Devos nodded. "These tales that are told are passed down from generation to generation. For the past several hundred cycles our traditions have been an oral one, that is why tellers like me are the ones who have been chosen by the people to teach the young. As each tale is told, some tellers begin to add their own views into them and these stories soon become even more extravagant. Now these fables may have a basis in the truth, but you must sort through the more fantastical of the tales until you arrive at the facts."

"If it was a Striga that leads people using dreams from across the wastes, then it must be a very powerful one," Miri mused. "If it was that long ago, it most probably would be dead by now."

Devos rubbed his shoulder. Last night's battle left some bruises on his back. "I may need Rion's help, but there may be some glyphs about the last city in my collection of telling stones. Are you planning what I think you are doing?"

Miri bit her lip. "I cannot take the boy back to the citadel. The only other path is to the Silt Sea. I need to know what lies beyond, even if what will guide me will be mere legends."

Devos scratched his beard. "But if you disobey the direct will of the elders, you will violate your oath as protector."

Miri looked down on the bare floor. "This is my last day as protector of this tribe. Someone else will take over. I cannot send that child back to the Magi."

"If you do not bring Rion back to the Magi, they may come here looking for him," Devos said. "Once the tribe knows the truth, they may hunt you down as well."

"It is a chance I will take," Miri said. "I can no longer be ruled by the politics of the elders."

Zedne placed a gentle hand on her arm. "I believe that the tribe lost any remaining honor in that last assembly. You have my full support. I will give you as much salves and medicines as you wish. You and the boy will need it for your long journey."

Miri gave her foster mother a sad look. "I was hoping that you would come with us."

Zedne smirked. "I am far too old for traveling, child. I will only slow you down."

Miri blinked a few times, trying to hold back the tears. "Are you sure? If you do not want me to do this, you just have to say the word. I will always abide with whatever you decide."

"No," Zedne said. "You must make this journey. Since the people here do not want the child, you have every right to reject them. Their selfishness has doomed them and you must look out to the safety of the boy. Even though I cannot fully sense Rion's memories, my feelings have indicated that there is something deeper within him, one that could give hope to this decaying world. As of this moment, you have ceased to be the protector of this tribe, you are now the protector of the boy- do all you can to keep him safe."

Miri stood up and hugged the old woman. A few tears came down her cheeks. "You have always been good to me. I cannot bear the thought of leaving you behind."

Zedne's forehead touched hers. "Worry not, child. There is nothing they could do to me. I still remember the time when my sister first found you as a baby out in the wastes. When I looked into your eyes, I knew there was something special about you. Elipe and I have taught you everything we knew, and you are far more powerful than I ever was. Let this goodbye not end in sadness, but in a hope for the future."

Miri wiped away her tears using her wrist. "I will never forget you or Elipe. I never had a father, but I had two great mothers. I will pass on your values to the boy, so that your memories will never be forgotten."

For a long minute, neither said anything. Finally, Zedne smiled and pulled away. "Now I need to make us dinner and prepare additional food for your journey. You will need to talk to Rion, but knowing the boy, I am sure he is willing to travel with you."

Miri smiled and sat back down while Zedne went over to the fireplace and tended the stew. Devos had closed his eyes while trying to remember the old legends. "Ah, I think I remember now," the teller said, opening his eyes. "The name of the Magus who travelled the wastes was Kaelr, and he was a formidable warrior. I do recall that the first place he had come upon was the Black Redoubt. Even though we do not know the location of the city of Lethe, I do recall that the Redoubt is a hundred leagues east of us. There is a tale in one of the stones that may give us a clue as to finding it."

"If you cannot give me directions to that Black Redoubt by this eventide, then I am afraid I shall have to wander blindly across the wastes until I stumble upon it," Miri said.

"You shall indeed have additional eyes out there," Devos said. "For I shall be accompanying you and the boy."

Zedne smiled while Miri was pleasantly surprised. "This is unprecedented, but a welcome opportunity," the protector said. "Can you survive the rigors of travelling out there in the wastes with us?"

Devos snorted as he leaned back and puffed his chest. "I may be sixty-three cycles of age, but I am sure I can at least keep up with the boy. Do not worry, I will not slow you down."

Miri nodded. "That makes three of us then. Good, we can carry more supplies."

"I am afraid that I cannot carry too much," Devos said. "My back gives me problems."

Miri rolled her eyes. "I guess that I will be doing most of the carrying then."

# Chapter 11

Night had fallen, and the settlement was calm once more. After they had eaten, Miri had taken Rion aside and spoke to him about their plans. The boy was saddened because the healer would not be accompanying them, but he understood the necessity of it. Devos spent the next few hours rummaging through his hut for any telling stones that gave a hint as to the whereabouts of the city of sanctuary. Since he could read the stones, Rion helped out the teller, but he ended up just glancing at the entries before falling asleep. Devos gathered up the most likely stones that might have the answers into his fur pouch so that they could decipher the writings during their journey.

When the moon was at its full height and with most of the tribe asleep, Miri walked over to Nyx's hut and stood just outside of the entrance. She had hoped that the teen girl was still awake. "This is Miri, I would ask to enter the house of Nyx."

There was a brief pause and then the reply came. "Yes, enter and be welcome."

Miri flipped open the leather flap in the entryway and went inside. There was a small fire in the pit and it looked like Nyx was just about to get ready for bed. The teen girl quickly stood up and bowed slightly before suddenly letting out a gasp as she realized what the protector was wearing. Nyx saw that Miri was fully dressed, wearing a leather breastplate with matching pauldrons, high boots and cloak. The protector had thick leather bracers on her forearms and the black spear was in her right hand.

Nyx's eyes were as large as the full moon. "Protector Miri, I-I was about to ask you what had occurred at the assembly earlier today until one of the elders told me. They said you were to take the boy back to the Magi, is that true?"

Miri let out a deep breath. It was better that she tell the truth to her protégé. "I am leaving with the boy now, but we will not be going to the Magi."

Nyx's mouth was wide open. "What? Why?"

"I cannot bring the child back to those monsters," Miri said. "As of right now, I am no longer protector of this tribe. That position will no doubt fall to you once he elders decide on it. Remember the things that I have taught you, and I am sure you will truly be well and good."

Nyx blinked rapidly as her mind was still trying to make sense of all the revelations. "Miri, if you disobey the orders of the elders, then y-you will bring dishonor to your name. You will never be allowed to return here!"

Miri looked down at the dying embers of the fire pit. "I will not be coming back here."

Nyx was so agitated that her whole body shook with nervous energy. "W-why are you doing this? You were the greatest protector that this tribe ever had!"

"I cannot willingly send a child back to the horrors from whence he escaped," Miri said softly. "My conscience and honor compels me to bring the boy to a place of safety."

"Where would that be?"

"Old legends tell of a city called Lethe, far out there in the forgotten wastes," Miri said. "It will be a long and dangerous journey, but I must try."

Nyx held her breath. Her own world was shattered as well. The one person she looked up to in the entire tribe was leaving. All that she had ever wanted was to become like Miri. When the elders told her that the protector was ordered to return the child to the Magi, she didn't like it, but she knew there was nothing that she, as an apprentice, could do to stop it. All day she had been wondering as to whether Miri would actually agree with the elders. Now she had her answer.

Miri placed a reassuring hand on her protégé's shoulder. "Keep training your Vis. Elder Zedne will help you with that. I sense that you will be as good a protector as I have been."

Nyx looked straight into her eyes. She quickly made her decision. "I am coming with you."

It was Miri's turn to be surprised. "What?"

Nyx nodded. "You are right, Miri. The elders have dishonored you, and the rest of the tribe are nothing but cowards. I do not feel I belong here anymore as well. You will need an additional Striga by your side if you are to get to that city."

Miri shook her head. "I do not think you should go with us. The tribe needs a protector."

Nyx frowned. "Why not? I could learn far more by traveling with you than by just staying here! I have always wanted to know what is really out there in the far wastelands and this is my best chance to do it! They can choose somebody else to be a protector here, any hunter can do the task."

Miri sighed. The girl was too young and naïve. "This is not a wondrous journey. It will be hard, and we may lose our lives doing it. Lethe may prove to be nothing but a legend, and it may not even exist anymore. We could all end up dead out there."

"It is a challenge that I accept," Nyx said. "If you do not take me with you then I shall murder myself at the edge of dawn."

"Nyx…"

The teen girl fell on her knees. "Please! I must go with you!"

Miri bit her lip. "You still have family here. What about your brother?"

"Jinn is now a man," Nyx said. "He will soon be married. We have already drifted apart these past few moons anyway. I need to move on and make my own way in life too."

"He has been very protective of you since you were both children. Are you sure you want to leave him behind like this?"

Nyx gave the protector a single, confident nod. "Yes. I want to travel with you. Wherever you go, I want to be by your side."

"Very well," Miri said. "Prepare your possessions. I will give you a little time while I head over to the house of the healer and get Rion. Bring what you brought in the last hunt and anything that you cannot leave behind. Make sure that you are light enough to be able to move quickly. We will meet you by the edge of the silt bank, beside the old well."

Nyx immediately turned around and brought out her fur pouches as she started picking through the items she would need. "Thank you Miri! I shall see you in a little while."

Miri gave her a nod of acknowledgment and then left the hut. The only ones that were awake would be the sentries near the perimeter, but she knew a gap existed close to the edge of the Silt Sea. That would be the place where they would make their escape from. She walked noiselessly as her soft boots treaded lightly on the sandy ground until she reached the healer's house. Opening the flap, she walked inside.

The three of them were waiting for her. Rion was wearing a new pair of leather boots and a cloak covered his body while Devos added a thick leather tunic to the one he was already wearing. The teller also had an old floppy leather hat that he wore over his bald head. Two backpacks, a war shield and numerous waterskins were laid out on a nearby stone table.

Zedne walked up to Miri and smiled. "Everything is prepared."

Devos sensed a final goodbye as he picked up one of the backpacks and slung several waterskins over his shoulders. "Come on, Rion, let us get to where the old well is."

The boy ran up the healer and hugged her tightly. "Goodbye, Elder Zedne. My thanks for everything that you have done for me," he said softly. "I-I will never forget your kindness."

Zedne kissed Rion's forehead while cradling him in her arms. "Take good care of them, Rion."

The boy let out a sob as Devos took him by the hand. The two of them walked out through the open flap and disappeared into the night. A tear slid down Miri's cheek as she once more stood in front of the healer and hugged her. The protector wanted to say something, but the words couldn't form in her mouth. Miri held her head down as she rested her cheek on the healer's shoulder.

Zedne kissed her on the forehead and tilted her chin up so their teary eyes met for one last time. "Let there be no more goodbyes. Only love."

Miri nodded as she finally let go of the old woman. She turned and picked up the remaining leather backpack and slung the war shield over her shoulder. The protector stood by the entryway while looking out into the cold evening. "I wish I could return someday and see you again. For just one more time."

"We will see each other again, perhaps in the next world. Then we will talk, be merry and sing songs for all eternity. Go now, lest my heart breaks," Zedne said.

By the time Miri had walked to where the old well was, she could see Nyx was already there, talking with Devos and the boy. Her protégé was carrying her own leather pack, and had been prudent enough to bring her own war shield as well. The sun would not rise over the horizon for another few hours at least, and all three of them huddled in their cloaks to fight off the eventide chill.

Despite being mostly in shadow, they all could see Devos flashing a toothy grin. "By the gods, I did not think we would have another companion with us, but Nyx has told me everything, Miri."

Nyx giggled as she placed an arm over Rion's shoulder. "How could I not be a part of this adventure? The four of us will be trekking into lands that are only recalled in legends. This is such an exciting time to be living in."

Miri could sense a mixture of apprehension and eagerness. "Then let us go forth. There is no time to…" Just as she said those words, Miri sensed an approaching presence. The protector turned and readied her spear while she used her Vis to send out mental feelers to try and identify who it was.

Jinn came out from the shadows of a nearby street. The young man had been on sentry duty for the evening and he was wearing his cloak and carrying a spear. "Nyx, what are you doing out here? I came by your hut and it was empty, then I heard some voices in this direction." Jinn immediately stopped talking when he noticed the large amount of equipment the three of them were carrying.

Miri looked at Nyx. This was an awkward moment since she had told the elders that she would be leaving at dawn, and it would be from the other side of the perimeter. She had hoped Jinn's sister would find the right words to alleviate this situation.

Nyx walked up to her brother. "Jinn, I am sorry, but I must tell you that I am leaving. Please do not tell the others you saw me."

Jinn took a step back. He was in shock. "What?"

Miri sensed that there would be no hostility, so it was better to let him know the truth. "I am taking the boy out into the Great Silt Sea. I realize that this is a surprise to you, but I cannot abide by the elder's wishes."

"I will be going with them," Nyx said. "They need the support and I wish to explore the places where men have not traveled in for eons. Please do not call out to the others, Jinn."

Jinn looked down into the ground. "You are all …leaving?"

"Yes," Devos said. "We cannot go along with what the elders have decreed."

"Please understand us," Nyx said to her brother. "I think Rion is a good lad, and I do not want to return him to those horrible Magi either."

Rion bit his lip. He could hardly believe they were going through all this trouble just for him. The boy held back his tears while gripping Miri's hand tightly.

Jinn's head twisted back and forth listlessly. "I did not like what the elders have said either. But we have to abide by their ruling, or else we are lost as a people. Anyone who disobeys their words is cast out of the tribe."

"I have lived a full life with this tribe," Devos said. "It is time for me to move on."

"There is nothing left for me here, and Rion needs my help," Miri said.

Nyx took her brother by the arm and held him close. "You have always looked out for me, and I am forever thankful for it. I would like to ask one last thing from you. Please keep this to yourself. The people will find out soon enough, but many will think that we have gone the other way. I am sorry that I will not be able to attend your marriage ritual, and I hope you find it in your heart to forgive me for that."

Jinn placed a trembling hand on her neck as he kissed her cheek. "There is nothing to forgive. I have always kept you safe. There were many times that I dreaded losing you, but I never imagined that it would be like this. Do not worry, I will not alert the other sentries."

Nyx's chin trembled. It was her turn to start crying. "Farewell, Jinn. I know you will have a happy life with your mate. Whatever happens, you will always be my brother."

Jinn turned around and started walking back into the alley. "Farewell, Nyx. Do not worry, the others will not be told."

Miri turned to look at Devos. "Take Rion and lead him down to the edge of the silt bank."

Devos nodded as he took the boy by the hand and started to lead him on a downward sloping path near the edge of the vast plains of sediment. Miri walked over to where Nyx was standing at. She could see the silver glint of tears on the girl's cheek. Just as she was about to say something, Nyx turned around and walked past her while heading towards the pathway. Miri stretched her legs for a few minutes before turning around and following her protégé.

When Miri got down near the edge of the grey silt flats, the others were waiting for her. She looked at each and everyone's faces. "Alright, we shall go forth at single file. I will lead. Nyx, you shall follow behind me, then Rion, and finally Devos. Try to step in my footsteps. The pace will be fast, for we must cover the edge of the horizon before daybreak. Are there any questions?"

Devos peered out across the sands. "What is our destination?"

"The farthest we have been in all my memories was the well at the land's end. It is a pile of rocks that marks a small covered basin of water a few leagues from that horizon." Miri said as she pointed eastwards. "Once we are past that, we venture forth into the vast unknown. I hope that the gods will at least give us a sign to where the Black Redoubt is in the coming days."

Devos nodded. "It is a good plan."

Miri turned around and walked onto the sandy silt. It was hard packed due to the black algae underneath it. "We really have no other."

For the next several hours, all four of them moved briskly across the barren plain. Miri would occasionally glance back to make sure everyone was keeping up. She could see that the boy was doing well while he moved rapidly wearing his new leather boots that Zedne had carefully sewn for him. Devos was the slowest due to his age, but he was so far able to stay in formation. The silted ground was hard and smooth, and their soft-soled footwear hardly made an impression on it. The only sounds that were heard were their rhythmic breathing and the slight squishing noise on the ground where their feet were hiking on. There was an occasional wheeze coming from Devos, but he didn't look distressed at all as he lagged behind by only a few steps.

Miri kept up a relentless pace. She could occasionally see dark veins on the grey ground beneath her and she always sidestepped away from the ones with the darkest patches. The black algae was known to clump together and stepping on a large bloom might mean getting one's foot stuck in a knee-high morass of black, sticky goo. The last thing they needed was an accident or a delay while they were still within visual sight of the settlement. It was a testament to their respect for that everybody else was closely following her footsteps, as they finally got to the edge of the silt flats.

Everyone was breathing hard while Miri paused for a minute, then she used her hands to traverse up the edge of a dusty slope. She had figured correctly as her hands grabbed the hard edge of the crusted sand and rock. Using the strength in her arms, she pulled herself up almost immediately, despite the heavy pack and waterskins that she carried over her shoulder. The moment she got to the top, Miri turned and crouched down as she helped Nyx to climb up. The teen girl thought the short climb was easy, until the heavy pack on her back made her lose her balance as she tilted backwards and was about to tumble back into the dried silt flats before Devos was able to push her forward into Miri's waiting arms.

"That was close," Nyx muttered under her breath as Miri pulled her up.

Devos shook his head silently while Rion made a short chuckle.

Nyx turned and glared at the boy. "You should try climbing with a heavy burden on your back, you troublesome child."

"Save your words, for you will need your breath again," Miri said while pulling the boy up. "There shall be another long walk ahead of us."

Now it was Devos's turn. The old man grunted as he tried to pull himself up, but his frail arms couldn't take the load. His pack was heavier than the others because of the telling stones that he carried with him. Miri and Nyx each took him by his arms and after a serious effort, managed to get him up and onto the gradient. Everyone was breathing heavily as the first light began to break out across the horizon. It meant that the settlement behind them was about to wake up and the sentries were going to be replaced by a fresh batch. They needed to hurry.

Miri readjusted her carrying packs so they were level with her shoulders. She pointed towards a small mound somewhere out in the far distance. "The next few hours will be difficult, for we shall have the sun in our eyes and the heat around us will increase. Wear the hoods over your cloaks and move as fast as you can. Once we have reached the well at the land's end, then we may rest until the next eventide."

Nobody said anything. Devos was still catching his breath while Nyx nodded eagerly. Rion's face was unreadable as he replaced the hood of his cloak to cover it. Miri turned around and started moving again, this time her pace was much quicker as she spurred them all to go faster. Devos made a brief sigh before continuing. There was no turning back now.

# Chapter 12

The well at the land's end was a flat piece of brown stone surrounded by an endless sea of flat sand. A pile of smaller rocks had been arranged into a man-sized mound in order to mark it as the outermost territory of the tribe. A jagged cleft near the center of the boulder had been dug deep into it, and there was a small pool of warm water near the bottom. When the tribe had first ventured into the area over a thousand cycles ago, the well was already there. Some of the oldest stories that were passed on by succeeding tellers stated that it was the god Duun who had placed a small spring of water at the bottom in order to aid his people as they wandered across the wastes, trying to find a place that would serve as their permanent home. When the Arum Navar came across the well, it was a sign from their deity that their new homeland would be founded nearby.

Miri sat near the edge of the well as she pulled up a second filled waterskin from the leather rope that was tied to the rocks. The others were resting by the western side of the boulder, away from the sun. A slight wind had come out from the north, and it carried particles of ash that had already begun to obscure their tracks. As she placed the bone stopper on the waterskin, Miri slung it over her back and stood up. Her spear was leaning along the side of the mound and she took it while making her down way to the others. She was still on guard, just in case the tribe was attempting to track them down here.

She found the others by the side of the boulder, underneath the shade of the overhang. Devos lay flat on his back, fast asleep. Rion had found a sand beetle, and he was crouched down while playing with it. The little four-legged bug was desperately trying to crawl away while the boy kept poking at it to make it move back towards him. Nyx was sitting cross-legged beside the old man with her eyes closed, her rhythmic breathing indicated that she was doing mental exercises to strengthen her Vis. Miri sat down beside her and placed her spear along the rock wall.

Nyx opened her eyes as she turned to look at her. "I know what you are thinking. Jinn would never tell the others about the direction where we went to."

Miri gave a faint smile while looking out towards the west. Their vantage point was excellent since it allowed them to notice any incoming intruders from the settlement, while at the same time allowing them to stay hidden. "I trust your brother, Nyx. What concerns me the most is Krag. He is an experienced hunter, and if he finds our tracks near the silt farms, then he may very well surmise we have been going in this direction."

Nyx's demeanor instantly changed from an excited confidence into a palpable worry. She quickly reached over and grabbed a bone spear that was leaning on the rock wall beside her. "This is not good. Do you think the chief hunter will force my brother to come with him once they track us down?"

Despite her fatigue, Miri smirked. "Do not feel hopeless yet. Even if they knew our destination, they would think twice about going after us. If they were to mount a search party, having to move out here in the middle of the day will be enough to drain most of their strength. The sun's light upon the sands will make their journey quite slow and painful. By the time they get here, it will be late afternoon and we shall already be gone. Other than Zedne, we are the only two Strigas they had, so even if they had brought along three dozen men, the odds would still favor us, for the gift of Vis grants us an edge in battle."

"I am not worried about the others," Nyx said softly. "Only my brother."

"Calm yourself," Miri said. "Jinn is a capable young man. The elders will not do him any harm. They will soon realize that they need him more than ever now that you and I are gone."

"If they do come, then I hope I will not have to fight him," Nyx said.

"Please spare him if he tries to fight you."

Miri shook her head. "It will not come to that. Last eventide, I had already laid out some tracks just past the main perimeter that mimicked our own. I used Rion's sandals near the edge of the dune if any of them tried searching in that area. When Zedne made those new boots for him, she never showed it to anyone. I am also confident Jinn did not tell, so that is another point in our favor."

Rion had picked up the beetle by its back and it wriggled helplessly in his hand. The boy walked over to them and sat down. "My foot hurts."

Miri frowned as she gestured at him to sit closer to her. "Why have you not taken your boots off?"

"I liked the way they looked," the boy said softly as he threw the bug away and sat closer. He pointed to his left foot. "My ankle hurts here."

Miri pulled off Rion's boot and examined his feet. Right on the base of his left ankle was a blister. "You need to take your boots off whenever we rest, that way the skin on your feet can breathe." She leaned over to her side and took out a bone needle from the flap of her backpack.

Rion's eyes opened wide as he tried to wriggle away, just like the beetle he once had in his hand. "What are you doing? Please, do not hurt me!"

Nyx sighed. "Be calm, Rion. Miri is just going to pierce your blister."

Rion's breath became labored. There was terror in his eyes. "No! Please do not take my essence again!"

Miri frowned. The sight of the needle must have recalled terrible memories within him. "Rion, it is alright, I just want to prick the blister and drain out the fluid."

Tears flowed down the boy's cheeks. He curled up into a ball while lying on the sand. "The pain! The pain!"

Miri instantly concentrated, channeling her Vis and expanding them out into waves towards the whimpering boy. The mental feelers etched themselves into Rion's brain, as Miri began a soothing, telepathic song that calmed the boy's anxieties. In less than a minute, Rion opened his eyes and blinked slowly. Miri crouched down beside him as he gently took the boy's head in her lap. "Everything is well now," she said softly.

Rion took a deep breath. "I am sorry. I do not know what came over me."

Miri smiled down at him as she stroked his silvery blonde hair. "You had been through a rigorous ordeal in the past. The vicissitudes you endured has left scars in your mind that will take time to heal. I shall sing you a song of sleep so you can rest in peace for now."

Rion gave a faint smile and nodded. Miri used her Vis on him for a second time, only now she channeled a gentle, rolling wave of cerebrations that completely relaxed the boy's body and Rion was soon fast asleep. She took off the other boot before finally pricking Rion's blister with her needle. Then she laid him down beside the still snoring Devos.

Nyx had watched it all in mute amazement. Only when it was over did she say something. "That is one skill you have yet to teach me. All I know at this point is how to increase my pain threshold to withstand against wounds."

Miri grinned. "The technique is very similar to the mating thought ritual that we use for hunting large prey. You must be aware of the different kinds of emotions that men and beasts are capable of. Once you can comprehend one's distinct feelings, then you can work on controlling the mind that you choose. You already know what pain is like, and you know how you feel when you are weary. It is a matter of connecting the paths, so that you can guide your chosen mind towards the direction you wish for them to behave. There may be times when a forceful push is required, or there may be an opportunity for a gentle coaxing. The willing subject will always be easier of course, while a mind trained in thought defenses will be the toughest to overcome."

Nyx thought about it for a moment. "So the means to do it is to determine your host's feelings and then guide them to the state you want them to be in?"

"Exactly," Miri said. "You must remember that all feelings are but the sides of a sphere, all are intertwined. You can make things easier for yourself by knowing how each mood is related to the other. Fear is the twin brother of worry, while serenity and confidence are but distant cousins. Therefore, it is easier to mold one from sadness to grief, than it is to transfigure a mind of an enraged beast to one of docility. To go from one extreme of feeling to the other takes more effort, but all is possible."

"So far I have used this technique against that dargon we slew as well as the occasional octapede. I had done it a few times to my brother Jinn when I was growing up, even though I was unaware of it back then," Nyx said. "Can this be done with any beast?"

Miri pointed to Rion's bug that was still wriggling around nearby. "Anything is possible. There are some creatures like that crawling sand beetle over there, their minds are so tiny and alien that they resemble nothing more than simple machines, all they know is either to run away, to feed, or to mate. You can certainly try to project emotions into such a small beast, but it would be a waste of your Vis since there isn't much use for controlling one of them."

"I have heard the tales of the Gorgons controlling huge herds of dargons and swarms of flying bugs, just to distract their enemies," Nyx said. "Is it possible to control more than one mind at a time?"

Miri shrugged. "I have tried, but it seems impossible to do. I have to concentrate to my fullest just to prevent myself from completely abandoning my body to reside in another's. Just before I drove my spear into that sand dargon's heart, I had to take care so as not to linger in the beast's thoughts when it died. To do so would have brought me unimaginable pain. As a Striga, one of the first things that are taught to us is never to possess the mind of another for too long, lest you become trapped into your chosen target forever."

Nyx shook her head. "Oh no, I always make sure I withdraw my mental tendrils before I kill a beast. Last cycle, when I slew my first norpion, I stayed in its mind for too long and I felt my own spear pierce its heart. I was in pain for days afterwards. Do you remember that?"

"I do," Miri said. "Zedne and I had to hold daily visits to your dwelling in order to sooth your anguish. I hope it was an important lesson you learned about possessing another."

Nyx nodded. "It was as if my spear had pierced my own heart. I kept reliving the nightmare every few hours, I thought I was truly going mad. Other than timing your strike properly, are there any other safeguards to follow?"

"If you are to possess the mind of another, then always know your way out," Miri said. "Think of it as having one hand in your target's mind, while your other hand is holding onto your own. The moment you sense that something is amiss, you must withdraw back to your true self immediately. You must not tarry or linger for one moment longer. Zedne taught me a trick. What she said was that you should mentally build a rope made out of mindsense, tie it around your own spirit's body and be ready with it once you enter the mind of another. The moment anything goes wrong, the cord will instantly yank you back to your own true self. I thought she was fooling me when had she told me this for the first time, but it actually works. The key is to imagine such a strand exists in your mind when you empower your Vis. If your mind can fathom it as an actual object, then your subconscious will mentally reinforce your efforts when you need to pull yourself back from the abyss. The rope serves as both a tether point and a guide to bring you back."

Devos had awoken and propped his head up on one elbow, listening intently. "How I wish I too had been born with the gift of Vis. I would just like to know how powerful can one's mind be."

Miri glanced at him and smiled. "Every gift has a curse of its own. Many Strigas have become mad after listening to too many thoughts. The voices multiply and become ever louder. There are times the agony becomes unbearable and you cannot silence the screams in your head. Many of those with the Vis take their own lives when they become too old and they are unable to maintain their thought disciplines anymore."

Devos sighed as he sat up. "You are right, of course. So many stories about the children of Vis that tell of their rise and fall. The Gorgons were probably the most glaring example of them all."

"I did not realize just how important it was that every tribe had a teller until now," Nyx said wistfully. "Having listened to all the legends these past few days, it makes me realize that all these stories were not merely for amusement, they also act as important guides to explain why our laws and traditions are this way."

Devos nodded and smiled. "I remember when you were but a small child. Every time I would recite a story to the others, you would try to run off and play outside. I am glad you now know why the tribe required all the children to learn these tales."

Nyx laughed a little before she suddenly squinted and pointed towards the west. "I think I saw something."

Miri instantly got up as she too started scanning the horizon. "Are you sure?"

Nyx kept her eyes focused on the silt flats. The shimmering waves of heat were like ripples in the air which would sometimes cause mirages to appear before them. "I am quite sure I saw a dark object moving closer, but I cannot see it now."

Miri walked forward for a few steps to see if she could get a closer look. She noticed something at the far horizon, it was a distant black dot that would appear before suddenly vanishing like an optical illusion. After silently observing for a few more minutes, the object suddenly reappeared in her field of vision, only this time it was slightly bigger. Miri immediately turned around and ran back to where her pack was. "I see it too," she said tersely.

Nyx and Devos had both stood up. The teen girl ran over to where her weapons were and grabbed her spear. Devos looked down and saw that Miri was putting on a leather cuirass over her torso. He wasn't much of a fighter himself, so he just waited until the Striga attached the leather faulds underneath her armored torso before speaking. "What should I do?" he asked her.

Miri was busy tying the leather bracers to her forearms. "Just stay here for now. This part of the rock is still hidden from sight, so you and Rion will be safe here."

Devos crouched down beside the sleeping boy. "Should I wake him?"

Miri glanced down at them while readying her bone dagger. "Not yet, let him rest. If you see any fighting, then you may wake him."

Nyx was hiding by the edge of the rock wall as she continued to peer out into the west. "It is getting closer."

Miri ran over to where she was. The object out in the distance was clearly a man. He was wearing a large cloak that shielded him from the sun. The hood that drooped over his head made it hard to identify who it was. Miri was somewhat surprised and disappointed. She couldn't fathom why the tribe would be making such an effort to go after them. She figured it was probably

Krag since there wasn't anyone else around.

"I can only see that one," Nyx whispered. "Where do you suppose the others are? Could they be going around to get behind us?"

Miri shook her head. "Look around you, the sand tides are flat all over, it would take a great effort for them to move in a wide path to just to come up behind us. If there are many, then they would be following behind that first one."

Nyx was confused. "If they truly want us back, then why would they send out only one?"

Miri soon realized who it was. She started taking off her leather armor. "Help me slip out of these."

Nyx gave her a quizzical look. "Why? Do you not wish to fight?"

"I know who it is," Miri said.

"Your Vis must be very powerful indeed if you can project your mentality at such a distance," Nyx said as she untied the leather straps underneath the shoulder ailettes of Miri's armor.

Miri placed her spear down beside her abandoned cuirass. "I do not need to use my mindsense to know who that is up ahead."

Nyx frowned. "Who is it then?"

Miri smiled as she pulled the hood over her own cloak to cover her head. "Do not worry, you will know soon enough. Stay here, I shall go meet him." Ignoring her protégé's further queries, Miri drew her cloak around her and started running towards the figure in the distance.

After a brief sprint, Miri slowed down to a brisk walk as she got out of the shade and onto the hot, burning sand. The mid-afternoon heat was murderous, and her cloak soon became slick with sweat. The tough leather was heating up and it felt like she was being cooked alive. Her pacing was fast, and she covered half a league within the hour.

The figure just up ahead of her seemed to be walking slowly, it was as if each step forward was done in under the most extreme of effort. Miri could see that the man was probably dizzy from walking all day under the blazing sun. His gait was wobbly and it looked like he had been plagued by the curse of Duun. Miri shook her head as she quickened her pace, for it meant that the man ahead of her might just die before she could bring him to safety.

With less than two hundred yards to go, the man looked up and finally noticed her approach. It was at that moment that he gave out a hoarse cry and fell on his back. Miri broke out into a run and got to him within minutes. As she stood over the exhausted figure, she shook her head slowly. "You are the biggest fool I know. To venture out into the sands like this. It is only through the mercy of the gods that you could have possibly made it this far."

The man was lying on his back. He turned his head and the hood partially slipped away, revealing his face. "I-I am sorry, Protector," Jinn said in between his shallow breaths.

Miri tilted her head back and laughed. "Come on, get up. You cannot expect me to carry you for another league back to the shade."

Jinn took the cup of algae tea eagerly and started to sip, the nourishing liquid passing through his parched lips and down his throat. Miri had started a small fire using a little bit of the dried manure they carried, telling the others that instead of forging ahead that evening, they would spend another day to rest in the area. Nyx had mixed feelings for her brother, while she was overjoyed that he had joined up with them, she was also angry that he nearly died for being so foolhardy. Devos and Rion were both sitting closer to the fire, as they examined more of the telling stones in order to figure out a direction for them to take the following night. The old man was particularly happy for the extended break, for it would allow him to rest his tired legs for another full day.

Miri glanced up and saw the last glimpse of the sun dipping below the horizon. Eventide was upon them once more. She turned to look at the sunburned young man. "Are you sure they will not pursue us?"

Jinn nodded as he put down the cup of tea by his side and started rubbing his aching legs. "They all think that you went the other way- west, towards the citadel of the Magi. Brar and a few of the other elders were angry that Teller Devos and my sister had accompanied you, but that was the extent of their protests."

"And Zedne? How did she react to that?" Miri asked.

"Elder Zedne helped to support the deception that you had made," Jinn said. "Our healer had gone out of her way to inform the other elders that she had seen you venture forth from the main sentry area towards the western dunes. I strengthened her story by telling the others that all four of you passed through my part of the watch."

Nyx had been handing out hot tea to the others before walking back to where her brother was. "What about your bride? I cannot believe you decided to run away and join up with us just because of me."

Jinn shrugged sheepishly. "We had a disagreement."

His sister raised an eyebrow. "What do you mean?"

"She said she knew I was lying when I told the elders my story," Jinn said softly. "I do not know why, but Kere always seems to know when I was telling the truth or not, and she is not even a Striga like you."

Miri giggled. "It is difficult to hide your true feelings to your mate. What happened next?"

Jinn let out a deep breath. "We had an argument that raged for hours. Her parents banished me from their dwelling. As I gave her a final glance before leaving, I saw a look in her eyes. It told me that I would never be happy with her and that feeling persisted as time continued to progress. Finally I paid a visit to Elder Zedne and told her of my malady. That was when she made me realize that the most important thing in my life was not Kere."

Nyx crossed her arms and gave him a cynical look. "Oh? And what is the most important thing in your life then? Hunting?"

Jinn gave his sister a serious look. "You are. When our parents died, you were still quite young to know this, but I made a vow to Mother as she lay dying with the fever. I swore to her that I would always be there to protect you. I invoked the names of Duun and Karma to strike me down should I ever neglect that task. When I spoke with Elder Zedne, she told me to look inside myself and find the real reason as to why I was unhappy. That was when I had finally realized that being with you was more important than my betrothal to Kere."

For the first time since their sudden reunion, Nyx smiled. She leaned over and gave her brother a hug. "I am gladdened that you joined us. When you stayed behind at first, I thought a part of me was missing. Now I feel whole again."

Jinn smiled and kissed her cheek. "We are now five. So have no fear for you now have a mighty hunter by your side and we shall have plenty of food with which to make this journey."

Miri snorted as she tended the cooking pot. "When you made your escape, you could have brought more than just a pair of empty waterskins. For when we started this journey, we barely had enough provisions for the four of us. With you here, we now have insufficient food to make such a long journey."

Jinn turned to his side as he confidently brought out the weapons he had taken with him. "But Protector, I have brought along a bow in addition to my spear, this gives us a great ability to hunt prey. With two Strigas by my side, we can harvest meat every day."

Nyx rolled her eyes. "Miri is right. You make a lot of boasts, but you could have brought more provisions with you."

"But I was harried!" Jinn said. "I barely had time to make my escape. I hurriedly took what I could gather quickly and made off into the Silt Sea before the sentry watch would be coming to my hut this eventide. There was also a small sandstorm that blanketed the silt farms and greatly aided my flight."

Nyx turned to Miri. "Do you think they will truly come after us now that my brother joined up as well?"

Miri shook her head. "I do not think so. They would have to organize the entire tribe to do that, a major expedition would take days to prepare. I am confident that our ruse worked and they probably think that Jinn followed us to the west. Nevertheless, we will post a watch after we eat."

Devos gave a brief shout as he threw his hands up in the air. "I think we have found it!"

All eyes turned to look at him. Rion chuckled.

"What did you find?" Miri asked.

"Well, Rion has found that one of the telling stones actually contains a passage from the tale of Kaelr, the Magus who traveled to Lethe," Devos said proudly before turning to look at the boy. "Perhaps it is more fitting if you tell them the tale yourself, Rion."

Rion was in a merry mood. He shook his head. "I think it is better that you tell the story, Elder Devos, you are the teller after all."

Devos snorted. "Oh, very well. Kaelr was a Magus who had fought the dreaded Gorgons for many cycles and had slain a fair number of them. One of his most famous exploits was when he ventured into a forest of cedar to hunt down a powerful Gorgon named Huwa."

Nyx raised a hand as she listened intently. It was like being a child in the teller's hut back in the village all over again."What is a forest of cedar?"

"When the world was young, there were great towering beasts called trees," Devos said as he held his arms straight up into the twilit sky. "These beings did not move and just grew upwards until they reached out into the sky. Their bodies were cylindrical, like the spine of an animal, and instead of limbs, they had flat hands called leaves. They fed upon the soil and the sun and rain, for these trees did not need to eat other beasts. The lands were covered with them. A clump of trees growing together was called a forest, and many animals lived within these places to both feed on these things and each other."

Jinn closed his eyes and tried to imagine such a sight. He could picture large, tubular worms with the color of sand that reached out into the sky with their green tendrils. He always felt strange every time he listened to a teller's story.

"Kaelr had a trusted companion, a creature that was half-man, half-beast by the name of Idu. You see, Idu was said to have been created by the gods to find and murder Kaelr, but the half-man was defeated by the Magus, and instead of killing his opponent, Kaelr spared his life and the two became trusted friends. Anyway, both the Magus and the half-man ventured into this forest to destroy the Gorgon Huwa. They found her and defeated her. Huwa begged for her life, and Kaelr felt pity for the monster, such was his compassion for the ones he defeated. In the end, Kaelr refused to finish off the Gorgon, but his companion Idu slew her. The gods then cursed Idu and caused him to waste away and die while in the arms of his friend."

Miri looked at the teller. "A fascinating story, but what does that have to do with helping us find the city of Lethe?"

Devos was clearly irritated at the interruptions. "Alright, alright. I shall now get to the nub as to why I recited this tale to all of you. You see, this was the reason why Kaelr had finally decided that he would no longer do battle with the Gorgons. His grief over the loss of his companion Idu had changed him. He had heard about a city called Lethe, which was said to be the first and last city of man. Kaelr had been told by many elders during his travels that Lethe could offer him sanctuary, for the gods and the Gorgons held no power over its inhabitants. Whoever managed to make it past the gates of Lethe would be granted immortality and peace. Kaelr then had a new purpose in his life, he would travel across the ends of the world to find this fabled city. Once he passed through its gates, he would finally be at peace with himself."

This time, nobody interrupted the story. Devos took a sip from the waterskin before he continued. "Now, the passage in the telling stone that Rion had been able translate says that Kaelr wandered through the wastes for many cycles. During one particular journey, he had come across a wadi carved from solid rock. It was huge, twisting place in which the winds howled down the cliffs and crevasses to carve out pathways through stone using sand and air. The name of this place was called the Valley of Stone. After following a marked path through this wadi for many days, he soon found another desert and across that sea of sand, he could see the towers of the Black Redoubt out in the distance."

Miri was still skeptical. "I have traveled across the wastes many times, and I have been to many wadis. How can we tell if any of those places that we venture into is the actual Valley of Stone?"

"Ah, now here is a big inkling that our lad has found out about," Devos said as he looked at the boy once more. "Tell, them, Rion."

"The written passages on the telling stone described the wadi in great detail," Rion said. "The story told of rock walls with the color of bone."

Miri furrowed her brow. She had never heard of a valley composed of white stone. "So if we come across a wadi with walls of rock that are the color of bone, then this will be the sign that we are in that very place?"

"Yes," Devos said. "And there is also another mark that shall determine such a place. The glyphs on the telling stone told of Kaelr finding a number of black menhirs with carved inscriptions on them, telling him the direction to take in order to reach Lethe."

"Well, that is a start," Miri said. "Did the telling stones mention as to how tall these menhirs would be?"

Rion shook his head. "The glyphs only tell of the events, the descriptions do not seem to be exact in any way."

Miri frowned as she looked out into the night. With only vague descriptions from a bunch of old writings to guide them, they could easily get lost out in the wastes. Death would be slow and painful if there was but a slight error in the direction they were taking. All she could see out to the east was nothing but vast dunes of sand. But to turn back now would mean a death sentence for the boy, and she did not want that either. There was no choice but to move onwards. She turned to look back at the others. "Devos, you must discard any of the telling stones that have already been translated. As of this moment, we shall all only carry food, water and weapons. The cooking pot and our cups will be left here. That means we will no longer have any tea or hot food. I shall carry one sack of dried fuel for fire but leave the rest behind."

Nyx took out a small leather sack from her pack. "We still have plenty of fermented algae for tea. Do we leave all this behind too?"

"We will have to," Miri said. "We may as well drink all the tea now. Brew as many pots as you like, for we will not be having anymore of it for the foreseeable future."

Devos pulled out several waterskins from the mound of leather packs lying near the boulder. Jinn got up and poured the remaining tea from the pot into everyone's cups and refilled it with more water. It was going to be a long night of drinking.

# Chapter 13

Devos sighed as he sat down along the trough of the dune that was just enough to give a little shade. The straps of his backpack had dug into his shoulders and he painfully tugged them loose before placing the pack down beside him. It was their tenth day out in the endless sea of sand and he was feeling lightheaded. Glancing to his right, he saw that Rion was wrapped in his cloak, fast asleep. Devos had wanted to smile, but his lips were parched and he was no longer sweating. They had ran out of water a few days back, and nobody wanted to state the obvious. He knew the boy still had perhaps a few thimblefuls of the precious liquid in his waterskin, but he would never take the child's water ration away from him. Rion was simply too valuable, and he was the main reason they were out here.

He closed his eyes and tried to push away the headache that kept pounding his skull, but he could only rest for a bit before he had to climb up to the crest of the dune and keep a lookout. Miri and Nyx had gone ahead, braving the sweltering heat of the afternoon in order to use their Vis to try and detect any form of life out there. They had all gotten hopelessly lost, and Jinn was worried they would never find their way back, while the others knew there would be no returning at all. The night before, Miri had told them of her plan to use a hunting formation out in the daytime so they could cover more ground and try to locate some landmarks. Once again they were deployed in a V-shaped formation, with Devos and the boy at the base and the two Strigas along the wings. Jinn would act as a relay for either of them in case something useful was found.

It was not a good thing to travel during the heat of the day, but they no longer had any choice. Miri and Jinn had taken turns carrying Rion on their back when they moved at night. The lack of food and water for many days had made him weak and drowsy. Even though he couldn't read minds like the Striga, Devos could tell that Miri was already in a desperate mood when she outlined her plan last eventide. Death was lurking nearby, and one more mistake would doom them all.

Devos snapped awake when he suddenly heard a sound behind the dune. He turned and scrambled up the sandy slope. The angle of the sun was such that it was now late afternoon. He must have dozed off for a few hours at least. When he got to the crest of the sandbank, he looked back down at the trough to make sure the boy was okay. Rion was still lying where he was. Devos turned his gaze back to the drifts in front of him as he pulled his hood up to shade his eyes from the intense light.

He could see Jinn standing on top of another ridge a few hundred yards away. Devos stood up and waved. The younger man quickly noticed where he was and headed in his direction. After a long wait, Devos scrambled down the other side of the hill and met him halfway along another trough. Just as he was about to clasp the young man's hand, he stumbled forward, his weak knees finally giving way.

Jinn crouched down and made eye contact with him. The young man's eyes were glassy from exhaustion and his lips were flaky. "Are you alright, Devos?"

Devos took a few deep breaths before answering. "Yes, I can still move. Has there been any word from the others?"

Jinn sighed to catch his breath. Like the old man, he was exhausted as well, but his younger self gave him more energy. "I came to fetch you and the boy. Miri found something. She is on her way to meet up with my sister."

Devos slowly stood up. Every effort was agony. "Can we not rest? The boy is fast asleep and I can hardly keep my own eyes open."

Jinn shook his head slowly. "No, we cannot. Miri says we must move quickly to them. I will carry the boy. Can you bring the packs?"

"I-I do not think so," Devos said softly. "I am too …weak now."

"Stay here then," Jinn said as he turned and started walking away. "Let me get the boy, we can fetch the packs later."

Devos could no longer talk as his throat suddenly clamped shut. He just nodded. Jinn moved out towards the drift where Rion had been resting in. Devos sat down on the warm sand and decided to rest for a bit while waiting for them to come back his way. He closed his eyes and quickly fainted.

Miri grimaced as she gently placed Rion down beside her. Night had come once more, and the desert sands were beginning to cool. Jinn, Nyx and Devos were all lying on the ground nearby, asleep. It had been a long day and she figured a couple hours of rest would be alright for them. She was particularly impressed by Jinn, the young man not only carried Rion over to her forward position, but he also went back for Devos, and then a third time for the backpacks. Of all the people who deserved this brief respite, it was definitely him.

Like the others, her own mouth was dry and she could barely concentrate. She had heard tales of the ancient peoples who were so pampered with luxury, they could not survive a single day without water. By contrast, old tales of the tribes had painted them as a hardy breed of men, accustomed to days out in the wastes without taking a drop of water, for their bodies had been forged into tougher forms over the eons. Nevertheless, she envied the type of unimaginable wealth her distant ancestors might have possessed.

Miri stood up and scanned the twilit horizon. Up ahead of them was a canyon of some sort. During the heat of the afternoon, Miri was using her mindsense to feel around for any sort of life. Her instincts had told her that if she could just comprehend the thoughts of even the smallest creature within range, it would lead her to water. It was one of the first things taught to her when she was a young Striga. An old hunter of the tribe had told her that wherever there was life, then there would be water nearby, for both could only exist with each other. She took that advice literally to heart now.

Channeling her remaining reserves of Vis, Miri walked forward for a few hundred yards until she stood along a cliff. Ten feet down below her were what looked like bone white canyons of stone that must have been carved out of the rocks for untold cycles. The walls along the area looked strange. Unlike typical smooth stones, the sides of the canyon were pockmarked with rough, tiny holes. It was as if the gods had taken countless needles and punctured every single inch of the rock. Along the canyon floor were strange stones that resembled bones of some sort, but they seemed to have grown outwards, like a fungi bloom. She had used her spear to poke at the strange protrusions, but it was clear they were but lifeless stones. Whatever existed in this whole place must have died out long ago, their forms having petrified over time.

Miri sighed. Their ordeal wasn't over yet. While traveling on the canyon floor below would offer them much needed shade from the sun, they still needed to find a source of water very quickly. She believed that they could move around slowly for a few more days before their parched bodies would finally give out. It might take them forever to wander out here if they searched using their eyes, but Miri had other plans. All she had to do was to sense out any sort of animal, and that would lead them to that nourishing element.

As she crouched down at the top of the canyon wall, Miri closed her eyes and began to spread out her mental feelers. It was a known fact that animals of the waste were nocturnal, one either had to find them sleeping during the day or roving about at eventide, looking for food. With her mindsense in a weakened state due to her severe dehydration, Miri had to use all of her concentration just to cover a few feet in front of her. Sure enough, she began to sense the wind howling along the hollows of the crevasse as every grain of dust would float along its currents. Miri focused not on the noise of the wind, but rather on the breathing or movement of any sort of animal.

After what seemed like hours, she heard the distant clicking sounds of limbs crawling along the canyon floor. It was nothing more than a remote whisper at first, but as she refocused what was left of her mental reserves on it, the far noise of movement soon began to echo loudly in her skull. It was the sound of tiny claws scraping along the hard, stony floor. With the echo now reverberating in her mind, Miri began to use her mindsense to locate the animal. Her mental feelers soon tested the air around it, triangulating the vibrations of movement with the ambient flows of the wind. Little by little, a mental map of the twists and turns of the gulley had etched itself into her mind and then she knew where it was.

Miri opened her eyes and stood up. She walked slowly along the edges of the ravine until she found a spot where she could climb down. All she wore now were her boots, loincloth, bodice, and bracers. Having left her cloak with the others, she felt a slight pang of regret since the night was getting colder. But she needed to hunt now before she lost track of the beast. Miri held the spear in her right hand as she started moving along the canyon floor, her boots making crunching noises on the strange, stony ground underneath. Her mindsense was telling her that the creature was just up ahead.

When she rounded a curving passageway, she soon came face to face with it. The animal was but a little sand bug, its black, lozenge-shaped body was slowly moving along the floor of the canyon towards what looked like a crack along the side of the wall.

Miri felt a twinge of disappointment. The sand beetle looked to be the largest she had ever seen, for it was the size of her fist. Nevertheless, it was not a good beast to hunt for meat. Sand bugs had very little fluids, its body was mostly carapace. She would need to harvest at least two dozen of them in order to make a difference. Even if she found a whole hive of beetles, she did not relish the thought of having to pry and squeeze the fluids out of their bodies, for that would take hours. Since she hadn't seen any other animal nearby, Miri decided to follow it anyway, since sand bugs were the usual prey for bigger animals. If it led her to a larger beast or to its hive, then she figured it would be worth it.

The bug kept crawling along, using its front feelers to search for algae that it could feed on. When it got closer to the large crack, it paused for a bit. The bug reared its tiny head into the air, as if trying to sense any trouble. Miri followed until she was right behind it and crouched down. The bug was facing straight into the fissure and it didn't seem to notice her.

Without warning, something long and black whipped out from the shadows of the crack and its point landed on top of the sand bug, crushing it into a mass of pus and carapace. Miri had stopped using her Vis and was taken completely by surprise as she fell backwards, her buttocks landing onto the rough canyon floor, scraping some of its skin off. Miri looked up in horror as the long black tail whipped up into the air again, ready to strike her this time.

Just as the stinger drove down towards her, Miri quickly scrambled backwards and it missed her foot by only a few inches. As she got up, Miri held her spear forward, its shaft parrying the black tail to the side. Then she crouched down into a fighting stance, feeling a surge of adrenaline seeping through her body. The creature, sensing that its prey was just out of reach, crawled out from the narrow crack and out into the open.

It was a poison norpion, the largest she had ever seen. Miri figured it must have been at least six feet long. The beast had a flattened body that allowed it to pass through narrow cracks like the place it had just come from. The norpion had six segmented legs and was covered in a black, plated carapace, its long tail ending with a barbed stinger at its tip. The beast began to crawl towards her, its tail high up in the air, readying itself for another strike.

Miri concentrated as she began to use her mindsense to calm the beast down. The best way to defeat these creatures was with minimal physical effort. It was better to use a Striga's Vis to make the animal docile enough to approach it and strike a killing blow. Poison norpions also had large fluid sacs underneath its armored body, these were ideal for replenishment among those that had a desperate need for water. The one problem was that if the animal's stinger was damaged or cut off, then its poison sacs would burst, and the mingling of the body fluids with the toxin would make everything undrinkable. Her one chance to kill it intact was to drive the spear point into its tiny brain without damaging its tail. The one problem with that strategy was that it left her open to attack if the norpion would lash out for one final time the moment it died. Many a hunter had been killed in a foolish attempt to slay these creatures with a well-placed blow, only to be stung in return the moment the norpion was in its death throes. The poison would cause a paralysis that forced the afflicted one's heart to stop beating and their lungs to shut down, resulting in a slow, smothering death. Some of the better healers like Zedne knew how to treat poisons such as the one that was being brandished by the animal in front of her, but Miri knew she could never get back to the settlement in time even if she had wanted to.

The giant norpion paused for a brief second while Miri invaded its mind, making its tiny brain confused as to whether to attack or to run away. But just before the creature was about to enter into a state of hibernation, Miri's thoughts were suddenly jumbled as she momentarily lost her concentration. Her dehydration finally got the better of her, and Miri suddenly felt weak and all she herself could think of was to close her own eyes and rest. With the Striga's mental feelers having withdrawn, the norpion instantly sensed that an attack against it was imminent. The creature crawled forward, and lashed out with its stinger, just as Miri was still trying to shake away the fatigue inside her head.

Everything seemed like a blur as she saw the tail whipping towards her leg. Miri cried out and tried to parry the attack with the shaft of her spear, hoping to deflect the stinger before it could land on her vulnerable flesh. The norpion's tail was partly diverted as the spear shaft managed to connect with it. Miri could have easily grabbed the norpion by the tail and pin its thorax with her foot, but she was too slow as the creature withdrew its tail back behind it. Having no choice, Miri instinctively moved in reverse and her back suddenly collided with the side of the canyon wall, causing a few more scrapes on her bare shoulders. The norpion sensed that its prey had been cornered and it advanced once more, its spindly legs making scratching noises on the rough hewn floor.

Miri realized that she had no room to maneuver. Her own weakened state had caused her to misjudge the length of the canyon walls that surrounded them. Her Vis was spent, and she would be unable to use her mindsense without some water and a proper rest. She was nothing more than a glorified hunter now. She had to rely on her spear and physical abilities if she were to prevail in this. The norpion was now within range as it lashed out with its tail once more, this time it whipped upwards, right towards her head for a decisive attack.

Just as she saw the barbed stinger coming straight at her right eye, Miri's head suddenly shifted to the left. The sharp, needle-like organ struck the rough hewn rock and had quickly become embedded into it. The norpion tried to rear its tail back, but it wouldn't budge. Miri immediately held the creature's thorax down with her foot while she positioned the spear to strike it just behind one of its armored plates in order to land a clean killing blow. The norpion started thrashing about, trying desperately to pull out its embedded tail. Miri located the right spot and drove the spear downwards, its point passing in between the layers of carapace, through the chitin, until it penetrated the norpion's tiny, pulsing brain.

The creature suddenly became still, its raised tail still stuck along the chalky rock. Miri bent down while taking out the flint knife from her left boot. She quickly turned the creature on its belly and cut through where the base of the tail was. Sure enough, the poison sac was there as it pulsed a few drops of toxin that seeped out from the creature's stinger and down the canyon wall. Using the sharp edges of her knife, Miri deftly cut away the surrounding tissue until she could pull out the slimy cyst using her free hand. As she clutched at the sac, her fingers located the vein that attached it to the rest of the monster's circulatory system. Miri pulled it out, then she twisted the thin, ropy tube so the liquid inside it would not seep out. With the poison sac now safely separated from the other organs, she used her knife to slice the vesicle out and threw it onto the ground.

Miri then started using her knife to separate the upper and lower carapaces, being careful not to slice too deep into the chitin. Within a few minutes, she had a bulbous, slimy bag of assorted viscera, the warm liquid that sloshed inside ought to be enough to save their lives.

After squeezing the last of the fluids into her waterskin, Miri noticed that the boy had begun to stir. Dawn would breaking soon, and they would need to move down into the canyon for some shade. She walked over and sat down beside him. The boy slowly opened his eyes while she cradled his head and placed the leather bladder to his lips.

Rion tried to twist his head away. "I do not want any more, the taste is foul."

"I am aware that this liquid is not the best for drinking, but you need a few more sips or else you will stay weak," she said softly.

Rion grimaced as he took a few more sips. The boy looked like he was going to vomit, but he drew a deep breath and gulped a mouthful down. He let out a soft groan as the liquid began to settle in his stomach. "It is the vilest thing I have ever drunk."

Miri smiled a little. "You should be thanking Duun for saving your life. If it were not for that giant norpion, we would all be dead by now."

The boy drew in some deep breaths. While burping, his breath had a fetid smell and it disgusted him. "Please do not make me drink that anymore."

"Not for now," Miri said. "Though you will need to drink a little more of it later."

Rion growled.

Despite her fatigue and slight injuries, Miri giggled a little. She couldn't believe just how lucky they were. No one in the history of the tribe had made it this far out into the wastelands. The fact that they were all still alive was a miracle on its own. Rion closed his eyes once again and Miri placed his head on a folded cloak so the boy could rest a little more. A groan behind her made her turn around and she noticed that Nyx had sat up and was awake.

Miri held out the waterskin so the other girl could take it. "Would you like some more norpion juice?"

Nyx scowled while shaking her head. "No, thank you. Where are the others?"

Miri pointed down to the canyon below. "Jinn and Devos are exploring this place. They left but a few moments ago."

Nyx nodded. "I could have stayed up watch. After that hunt, you could use the rest more than myself."

Miri smiled as she placed the bladder on the ground beside her. "I am afraid that the moment I lay my head down, then I will not wake up for a whole cycle. There is a sandstorm in my head, but other than that, I feel fine."

"You surprised me when you woke me up earlier," Nyx said. "A part of me had thought that we were about to die. I must thank you again."

"For what?"

"I do not think we could have made it this far without you," Nyx said. "Just after we departed from the well at the land's end, a part of me had thought about returning to the settlement to face judgment. I was so fearful that we were going to die out here. I never bothered to tell you because I did not want you to look down on me. But now that we are on this place, I feel as though we will most certainly find this last city."

Miri looked away into the distance. "We are not out of this yet. What makes you so sure we would succeed?"

"I did not want to speak to you about this at first, though now I feel that I must," Nyx said. "You see, every time we lay in the shade and rested, I started having these strange dreams. I thought they were just jumbles of memories from a distant past at first, but I soon realized that I was envisioning things that I had never encountered before, and it made me feel strange."

Miri was intrigued, for she had similar dreams of her own. "These visions that you dreamt of, could you describe them for me?"

"Yes, in one dream, I was surrounded by the dunes, but instead of these hills being made of sand, they were made of water," Nyx said softly. "Never in my life had I ever had such a sight. It was as if the whole land around me was constantly shifting like the wind, only everything was made of transparent crystal that reflected the light all around me. I had never dreamed that such a place existed other than in the stories of our teller."

Miri placed a hand over her own mouth to stifle a gasp. She had dreamt of the very same thing, but she hadn't told them, for she was afraid of panic setting in amongst the group. Devos had told them about the stories of thoughts being transmitted into the air, where they would travel via the winds until they settled unto the minds of those that were sensitive enough to pick them up. Could someone out there be sending them messages through their dreams?

Nyx noticed her mentor's brooding silence. "Miri, are you alright?"

Miri looked away. This was all so troubling to her. "Yes. Was that splendid vision the only thing you remember?"

"There was one other dream that keeps returning to me," Nyx said. "I was standing alone in the middle of a flat desert. The sands beneath my feet were cracked and baked raw, revealing puddles of endless blood underneath. There was a stranger wearing a red robe and he stood near me. I called out to him but he did not answer. I tried to move, but my feet were stuck and I was suddenly being drawn into the bloody sand. Within moments I had sunk down to my chest. I cried out and held my hands out so that the stranger could save me and pull me out, but he barely moved. The last thing I saw before I was swallowed up by the blood red sand was when he started to pull down the hood over his robe. Just before I saw what his face looked like, the dream suddenly ended and I woke up. Then the next time I fell asleep, the same dream played out once again. Now I am actually reluctant to rest, for I fear I may end up dreaming the same thing once more."

Miri looked down unto the ground. "I... must tell you something."

Nyx leaned forward. "Yes?"

Suddenly, they both heard a bit of giggling and laughter coming from the gorge just below them. As both women turned, they saw that Devos had climbed back up to where they were, with a healthy boost from Jinn. After a few minutes, both men stood beside them, their smiling faces evident as the sunrise dawned over the horizon.

Miri momentarily forgot her worries as she looked up at the both of them. "Care to share with us why are you both so merry?"

Devos grinned and pointed to a pathway down the gulley. "We found something that shall give you joy."

Nyx's own curiosity made her forget about her nightmares as well. She looked up at her own brother. "Must you keep us waiting like this? Tell us!"

Jinn silently looked at Devos, who grinned. Then the old man held out his hand while looking down at Miri. "I think it is better if you see it for yourself."

Miri stood up on her own, without any assistance. "Rion is asleep, and I do not want to wake him unless it is of vital importance. Can you not just tell us what you found?"

Jinn sat down beside his sister, he was trying his best not to break out in laughter. "Perhaps it is better if you show the protector what it is, Elder Devos. I shall sit here with my sister and just tell it to her."

Nyx quickly stood up with a snort. "Let the gods take my life if I do not see what it is with my own eyes," she said, before pointing an accusing finger at her brother. "If this is but a trick, I shall run my spear through you."

Jinn shook his head, while he lay down flat on the ground. "Then the rest of you can go have a look and I shall watch over the boy. I need to rest now anyway."

Miri sighed. "Alright, let's get this over with."

It was a long walk that took many moments. By this time the sun was now suspended just above the horizon, indicating early morning. Devos led the way as the three of them trudged along the sandy bottom of the canyon. When they rounded the last bend, Miri and Nyx gasped at what they saw lying at the end of the passage. Embedded along the side of the rock wall was a chest-high stone of black carved onyx. There was a symbol of a grinning face with bulging eyes on it, the unmistakable emblem of the ancient Gorgons. Strange, unknown glyphs covered the menhir's marbled surface.

"The stories were indeed true after all," Devos said. "This black boulder and the white walls of this place affirm that we are indeed standing in the Valley of Stone."

# Chapter 14

Krag adjusted his cloak so there was a gap between the outer lining and his bare shoulders. He had been sitting on the boulder since dawn and the leather was practically burning to the touch by now. The currents of heated air streaming across the sands made it look like the dunes beyond were floating on top of a silvery, bluish sky. It was a mirage that played tricks with his eyes, but he was used to it. The chief hunter sighed while adjusting his sitting position. By early afternoon, he would be relieved by the next sentry, and he would get some sleep at last.

The night before, his wife had finally complained about his near constant sulking. Krag had been feeling uneasy ever since the old protector had fought and killed that Magus. He had spoken to Miri a few hours after the battle, and he was convinced she had done the right thing, even though he felt it was a violation of the oath of peace. When the assembly began and the elders commanded her to bring the boy back to the Magi, he hadn't protested, for he had felt that they were doing the right things as well. Less than half a moon ago, Miri had taken the boy and had gone in the middle of the night. The fact that nobody witnessed her leave meant that she had defied the elders, but they could see no proof of it, nor did they know where she had gone to. The very next day, one of his own had also disappeared and left behind a hysterical bride to be. So in the end, Krag realized that Jinn had known about Miri's flight, and he could have joined up with her in order to reunite with his sister, Nyx. Even the tribe's teller, Elder Devos, was no longer to be found either.

The other elders were greatly concerned, but they publicly stated to the great assembly that they themselves had ordered Nyx and Devos to accompany Miri to return the boy, and that they would be coming back soon. Only a select few outside of the elder council knew the real truth, and all had promised not to tell anyone else.

Krag frowned as he continued his lonely vigil. It was hot, uncomfortable days like this that made one think too much. He was already losing faith with the elders, even though he realized that they didn't have much of a choice. Could someone make the right decision, yet in the end it would prove to be wrong anyway? He surmised that the alternatives weren't any better. If the elders had decreed they would protect the child by keeping him in the tribe, then they would face future retribution if the Magi were to find out, so they forfeited their responsibilities. Had the elders known that Miri would betray their express command, would they have chosen him, the chief hunter, to lead the expedition to bring the boy back to the Magi instead? And if they had done that, would he have accepted the task?

The chief hunter shook his head as he tried to banish those dark thoughts from his mind. It was pointless to speculate any further. The deed had been done and both their most capable Strigas were gone, along with the boy in question. This meant that the tribe's greatest fears may very well come true nonetheless. The day after Jinn's disappearance, the elders summoned him for a secret meeting. As Krag sat back and listened, they told him that if the Magi were to come, he must act as the protector of the tribe. He could see the fear in most of their eyes. They told him to tell the Magi that the boy was being returned to them but had lost his life out in the wastes, along with the one who murdered their agent. So they were really telling him to lie in order to save the tribe. Even though he was told that the Magi could not read minds unlike the Strigas, would they still believe a far-fetched story like that?

Krag took out a waterskin from underneath his cloak and tilted his head upwards while he took a long draught. Curse all the things that had happened. He wished that the elders should have chosen someone else, for he hated politics. The only things that ever interested him were going out into the wastes to hunt down some beasts in order to feed the tribe. Now he had been entrusted with the people's very survival, and he feared that he was ill-equipped to deal with it. The settlement's protector had traditionally been a Striga, for it was they who had the power to fight against other men, notably Magi. All he had was his spear and little else. Krag thought of himself as a hunter of animals, not of men.

While strapping the waterskin back over his shoulder, he noticed something out in the distance. It seemed to be nothing more than a dark, greenish speck at first, then it quickly became bigger. The object was larger than the sand dargon they had hunted a few moons ago, and it was moving rapidly towards the perimeter. It looked like a vessel of some sort, with a set of gigantic leather sheets suspended on a long metal pole that jutted from the top of its hull to capture the winds and propel it forward. Along its bottom where what looked like enormous potter's wheels, only they had been laid onto their sides and were rolling along the sands. He could see men wearing black riding on its top, as they continually adjusted the tarpaulin in order to angle the wind in their favor. The men seemed to control the ship by leaning out along its sides while holding onto ropes when a turn was needed. For a long while, Krag just stared blankly in astonishment as it rumbled ever closer.

He was quickly brought back to reality when a young hunter came running up to him. "Krag! What is that thing?"

Letting out a deep breath, Krag knew that the time had come. "Alert the entire village. Tell them the Magi have arrived. And get me that bone sword."

The young man's name was Hrust, and he had been recently married, with a child on the way. "Do you mean the sword that was taken from the dead Magus?"

Krag leapt off the boulder as he checked the tip of his spear. The steel head might have to be used today. "Yes, that one. It is in the possession of Elder Pir. If he protests, tell him it could mean the difference between our survival, or our destruction."

Hrust nodded nervously before turning around and running back into the settlement. Krag removed his pouch along with the waterskin and placed them onto the ground beside him. In less than a minute, three more hunters came running over to him. The vessel had closed the distance and was now just moments away from reaching the perimeter. Just days before, he instructed all of the hunters to make sure that their spearheads were either metal or tipped with dargonteeth, for their flint heads would easily snap during a battle. He had also planned to hold a group drill to instruct them in the use of the war shield, but now it was too late. As he picked up the leather and bone shield by the base of the boulder and hefted it, another twenty-two men arrived, along with Elders Brar and Pir. They were carrying assorted weapons, from bone axes to daggers. A few carried war shields, but it was clear they weren't sure on how to use them. The remaining men in the village had been instructed ahead of time to herd the women and children into the assembly hall and guard them there.

Pir walked up to Krag. He carried the bone sword, its blade still wrapped in a fur scabbard. "The defense of this settlement is now in your hands," he said while giving the weapon to Krag. "As of now, you will be addressed as Protector Krag."

Krag took the sword while walking up to one of the other hunters. "Burd," he said, handing his own spear to the bigger man. "You are the best with the spear. Use mine, for it has a metal tip."

Burd nodded as he gripped Krag's spear. "You honor me."

Elder Brar had once been formidable in his youth, now he was paunchy and slow, but he still knew a few tricks in his sleeve. His most prized possession was his father's bronze dagger, and he kept it hidden beneath his tunic. "I will do the talking for the settlement," he said aloud, so that everyone could hear. "Nobody is to draw their weapons. Keep your spears pointed up."

The vessel began to slow the moment it reached the perimeter wall. Krag could see that there were four men that leapt down from the ship, all wearing black cloaks and armor. The smallest of them seemed to be the leader, since the three other men flanked him as they approached the anxious crowd. Krag kept the sword pointed downwards while hiding it underneath his cloak. Brar stepped forward from the crowd and held out his hand in the gesture of peace.

The smallish young man held out his hand in return before making a slight bow. "Greetings. I am Lord Slane, executor to his highness, the Grand Magus of the Order of Magi."

Brar bowed in return. "Greetings and welcome, Lord. I am Brar, chief elder of the Arum Navar tribe. I would like to welcome you to our humble settlement, it has been a long time since we have been honored by a Magi patrol. In fact, the last time this event occurred, I was but a young man myself."

Slane looked bored as he waved his gauntleted hand. "Yes, yes. The Magi have stopped their patrols, that is true."

Brar grinned. He needed to keep the conversation lively, and full of mirth. "That ship of yours, I have never yet seen such a wondrous machine. What do you call it?"

Slane's eyes kept darting around as he scanned the crowd of tribesmen. "It is called a sand sail, we use it to travel across the wastes. Much easier than just moving on foot, you see. It allows us to rapidly catch up with our prey."

The crowd suddenly fell silent. The tension in the air was heightened after Slane said those words. Krag bit his lip, it was apparent that the Magus had said those implied threats on purpose, just to intimidate everyone. His grip on the sword tightened. The large, bearded man who stood beside Slane turned and stared at Krag menacingly, the large axe in his hand ready for action.

Brar kept grinning. If he could keep them talking, then perhaps he could calm everyone down and they would be able to bargain for peace. "It is an honor to have you here, Lord Slane. Do the other Magi have their own sand sails, or is this miraculous vessel unique to yourselves?"

"I am bored with this line of conversation," Slane said. "This is an official visit. I have come to inquire about the whereabouts of a certain child. This boy had run away from the citadel and we would like him back, if you please."

Brar's chest heaved. Now he had to choose his words carefully. "Y-yes, there was such a child, but he is no longer here."

Slane's crimson eyes narrowed. "So he did come across this realm. Well, it seems we came to the right place after all. Where is the boy now?"

"I am afraid that the child is dead," Brar said. "You see, he ran away again, just before we were to return him to your citadel, Lord Slane. He ran out into the dunes and was stung by a poison norpion. He died before we could get him to the healer. I am so sorry that your journey here will end on this sad note."

Slane looked away again as he pondered silently for a minute. Then he suddenly turned and stared straight into Krag's eyes. "You, where is the child's body?"

Krag was shocked. He had not expected to be questioned abruptly like that. He thought about it for a short while before he answered. Karma was watching him, and he would be judged by what he uttered. "I-it was interred into the tombs in our fungi garden, Lord."

"What he meant was just the bones," Brar added. "You see, our tradition states that-"

Slane placed his hand up. "You will remain silent unless I ask you directly, is that clear?"

Brar nodded meekly. "Yes, my apologies, Lord."

Slane pointed to Krag. "You, I did not get your name. State it along with your profession as well."

Krag pursed his lips. "I am Krag, chief hunter and protector of the tribe."

Slane smiled. "Ah, that explains why you are wielding a sword. For a protector should always have the best weapon that the tribe possesses, yes?"

Krag threw a quick glance at Brar before nodding silently. He knew the goddess of fate was not happy with his lies, but he had to keep the ruse going.

"Tell me, Protector Krag," Slane said. "Are there any Strigas in your village?"

Krag nodded. "We have one, our elder healer."

Slane's left eyebrow twitched. "Just one? I had thought that every tribe out here in the wastes would have several Strigas, for tradition states that it is usually a Striga who holds the title of protector, is that not right?"

"We …have not had any Strigas born in our tribe for many cycles now, Lord," Krag said.

Slane titled his head back and laughed. "Do not take me for a fool! That bone sword you have in your hand is from the citadel, for we had dispatched a seeker to find the boy two moons ago. Did you murder him?"

Krag frowned. He was sick and tired of having to lie, but everyone was depending on him. "No, we found the seeker's body out in the wastes. I merely took this weapon since he no longer had any use for it."

Slane began to pace back and forth. "The image in my mind is becoming clearer now. First the boy makes it here, then runs away again, only to die by a norpion's sting. Then our seeker comes here but dies before he reaches your settlement? How could you have possibly found that sword, then?"

"During one of our hunts," Krag said tersely.

"And what did you do with his body? Placed his bones into your fungi tombs as well, I suppose. How convenient." Slane said. "I think you are lying to me."

"It is the truth, Lord Slane," Brar said. "Our protector has told you what really happened. We swear it upon the gods."

One of the men in the crowd made an audible gasp before he covered his mouth. Slane's eyes darted over to the others, some of whom held their heads down, while the others looked away. Brar turned and gave them an angry glare before looking back at the lord executor. By invoking the gods, he had twice cursed their fates.

Slane took several steps forward as his face was now only inches away from Brar's own. His crimson eyes glared at the old man like pools of fiery rubies. "I had instructed you to remain silent, and yet you opened your mouth anyway. What should I do about your insolence? During my time as an apprentice, if any Magi spoke out of turn, my master would use his Vis to rip out a tooth from the offender, and add it to his collection. He had a jar of say, ten thousand teeth, as I recall."

"Enough," Krag said. "I shall tell you the truth, for I will not be judged as a liar by the gods. Our first protector found the boy during a hunt, and had brought him back here. Your seeker came and violated the oath of peace when he tried to abduct the boy. Our protector was forced to slay him. The elders then ordered the protector to return the child back to your citadel. They left half a moon ago, and we have not heard from them since."

Slane nodded and smiled as he took a few steps backwards. "There you are! At last, the truth has finally come out. That was not so hard, was it?"

"W-we were reluctant to speak about it because our people are afraid,"

Brar said. "Surely you can see that we are but a small, humble tribe just trying to survive out here. Your seeker gave us no choice when the promise was violated. The protector who killed him is no longer here, but you are within your right to take her should she ever return."

"Miri did what she had to do!" Krag hissed. "You cannot fault her for that!"

Slane put both his hands up. "Enough, both of you. What a comical sight this is. The village elder and the acting protector arguing like two little children. I must say that I find this display to be completely pathetic. I was told that the tribes out here were hardy, honorable people. Imagine my disappointment when I can see that the truth tells me something else. All I see before me is a bunch of pitiful cowards who engage in obfuscation, even blaspheming the very gods that they claim to worship. You are a miserable lot indeed." He turned to look at Krag. "So this protector of yours, she was a Striga I take it?"

Krag nodded. "Yes."

"I can understand why she was able to slay the seeker then," Slane said to him. "She must be formidable, perhaps a challenge even for me. Her name is Miri, did you say?"

"Yes, Miri is her name," Brar said.

Slane turned and glared at the elder. "I told you to be quiet unless spoken to! That is twice you refused my order!"

Brar got down on his knees. "Please, Lord. Forgive me. We do not mean to offend you."

Slane snorted as he turned to look at his bearded companion. "Alright, I have had enough of this groveling. Can you see, Baradine? These people cannot be allowed to continue their miserable existence any longer. My canis is currently sick and still sleeping in the sand sail's cabin, his constant whimpering nearly brings me to tears. Why do you think it is sick, Baradine?"

Baradine continued to stare at the crowd. "Your pet has not had fresh meat for days now."

"Correct," Slane said as he held his hand out to Brar, who was still on his knees. "I need to feed my canis, or else it will waste away."

Brar gasped as his throat suddenly seized up. It was like an invisible vise had suddenly clamped around it, shutting off his airway. The old man struggled to get up, wheezing helplessly as Slane just stood there while gesturing at him with his hand.

Krag immediately realized what was happening. He drew back his cloak and raised the sword. "Stop! You are killing him, stop this at once!"

For the first time that day, Baradine's mask of stone was broken as he let out a big grin while hefting his battleaxe into position and looked at Krag. "Can I have this one?"

"You can have them all," Slane said. "Kill everyone in this village."

Baradine tilted his head sideways as he glanced at the other two Magi beside him. "Revok, Turru, clear the crowd."

The other two Magi were somewhat different in build. Revok had long black hair down to his shoulders, while Turru wore a gold mask that hid the upper part of his face. Both drew swords and used their Vis to advance upon the crowd of men. Their combined mindforce created an invisible wave of power that tore through the clump of people. Bodies flew sideways as most of the hunters were thrown into the ground, leaving a large number of them stunned. Hrust was somehow able to weather the shockwave and he slowly stood up before Revok stabbed him in the stomach. The young hunter spat out some blood as he clutched at the intestines hanging out from his torso and fell on his side.

"I do not need to use my Vis to fight you," Baradine said as he advanced upon Krag, swinging his large axe in a powerful arc towards his opponent.

Krag held up his war shield to stop the blow, but the layers of leather and bone shattered upon impact with the steel axe head. Krag staggered backwards as pieces of the shield fell away from his wounded arm. Baradine gave out a war cry as he brought back the axe over his shoulder and made another swing at Krag, but the chief hunter continued to move backwards, the axe blade narrowly missing his chest.

Krag knew he didn't stand much of a chance against an opponent wielding a steel weapon, so he bent his knees and tried to stay away from the axe's reach, waiting until the large Magus made another swing so he could close and get to within striking distance with the bone sword. Just as Baradine swung at him again, Krag leaned back and evaded the incoming blow, then quickly moved into range. The chief hunter swung the bone sword right at Baradine's torso, but the Magus was able to bring the axe back in time. The edge of the bone sword connected with the shaft of the battle axe, and more pieces of obsidian were chipped away. Baradine roared with rage as he headbutted Krag in the chin, momentarily stunning the chief hunter as Krag staggered backwards in a daze.

Baradine pressed his advantage as he swung the axe over his head before bringing it down towards Krag. The chief hunter could barely concentrate as he instinctively held the sword up to parry the attack, but the force of the axe was so great that it drove the flat part of his own blade onto his shoulder, ripping open a gaping wound in his flesh. Krag groaned as he fell onto the ground, the bone sword partly embedded on his chest. Baradine stood triumphantly over him as he prepared for the final blow.

The Magus swung the battleaxe on a downward arc, aiming for Krag's head. The chief hunter was wounded and he couldn't react in time. But just as the axe head was about to strike him, Krag was suddenly thrown sideways, Baradine's weapon missing him by a scant few inches when it struck the sandy ground instead. The Magus roared with rage while he shifted his stance and adjusted his next swing over to where Krag had somehow been displaced at. Baradine's eyes went wide as his attack was suddenly stopped in midair, there was some sort of invisible force holding him back.

Baradine turned his head and glared at the likely culprit. "Damn you, Slane! You are using your mindforce to toy with my fight!"

Slane held both his arms outwards, one hand gesturing to a choking Brar, while the other was clearly projecting in Krag's direction. The executor was chuckling. "Just having a bit of fun, you must admit that it is more exciting this way."

Krag knew he had his chance. He swung the bone sword at Baradine's left leg, hoping to strike at the unarmored part behind his knee. Baradine had seen the blade being flashed and quickly used his mindforce to tilt the attack upwards, to his torso. The bone sword connected with the armored plates that were sewn into Baradine's side. Given enough force, a steel blade might have penetrated in between the metal plates, but the edges of the bone sword used embedded slivers of obsidian, and the brittle rock failed to go through, as huge pieces of them were chipped away from the force of the blow.

Baradine had had enough. He used his mindforce to yank the broken bone sword from Krag's grip, sending it flying away towards the ground. Then he quickly recalibrated his Vis, using it as a powered leverage while bringing the axe down on Krag's chest. This time, Slane didn't interfere. The massive blow collapsed the bones in Krag's ribcage and the chief hunter lay sprawled on the ground as he began to bleed out.

With a gesture of his hand, Slane crushed Brar's windpipe using his mindforce before turning to look at his colleague. The chief elder twitched on the sandy ground for a few seconds, then lay still. "Well done, Baradine! See, you had to use your Vis after all."

Baradine briefly contemplated killing his superior, before turning to his side and joining in the carnage that was occurring in front of them. As his axe landed on top of a stunned hunter's head, Baradine knew that any attempt on Slane's life would mean his death. The executor was the most powerful mindforce user he had ever seen, and not even his mighty axe would have an advantage over Slane. Baradine kept his thoughts of revenge to himself. In the future, perhaps, when the time was right. All he had to do was wait.

Slane didn't even bother to draw his sword as he stood there, watching the other three use their Vis to stun and then execute their enemies. One man tried to hold them off with his spear, But Turru used his Vis to pick up a knife lying on the ground, then hurled it at the hapless victim's throat. The man collapsed onto the dirt floor, blood gushing from his open throat. Only two men were left standing, begging for mercy. Baradine used his mindforce to knock their heads together, and the two men fell stunned on the ground. Revok moved in and drove his sword into their bellies. One of the hunters backed away, and shot an arrow. Baradine gestured with his hand and the arrow veered off and struck another tribesman at the back of his neck instead.

Slane casually walked over and pointed towards the assembly hall. "Most of the women and children are in there, go get them."

Zedne had seen the butchery from afar. Women were screaming as they took their children inside the great hall in an apparent effort to stave off their deaths for a few moments longer. Two panicked old hunters were left guarding the entrance but it was clear they would not hold. Etul was the only elder left aside from her, and she saw him give a wave at her while she walked back into her dwelling. If she was going to die, then it would be in her own house, not in the hall with the others.

As she passed through the entryway of her house, the sounds of killing had begun. The healer had been a Striga once, before age had finally caught up with her. Tears streamed down her wrinkled cheeks as she could hear people begging for mercy, only to be replaced by an almost quiet death rattle, as their final breaths exited their dying bodies. She still had a little of the mindsense stirring within her, and it made the sounds she was hearing even more horrible. Walking over to where the stone slab was, she heard a noise. Zedne leaned over to see who it was and made an audible gasp.

A small girl lay huddled behind the slab. She was holding a crying baby in her arms. She looked up at the healer, her eyes bulging in desperation.

Zedne recognized her. She pointed at the corridor beyond. "Vida, take the baby and go. There is a loose set of bricks behind the bed in my quarters. You must go. Quickly."

The sounds of the leather flap being torn loose by the entryway made her turn around. One of the Magi walked inside. It was Revok. His sword and hands were all covered in blood. "So you are the last Striga? You do not look so formidable," he said.

Zedne straightened her shoulders. "This is the house of the healer. Leave this place, at once."

"You are not in any position to make demands, old woman," Revok said. He advanced further towards her while keeping his sword in a high guard position.

Zedne coalesced the full power of her mindsense into a shrieking ball of pain and hurled it towards the Magus. Revok's thought blocks were up, but he was completely unprepared for the ferociousness of her mental attack. Zedne's Vis bore through his defenses and his mind shut down. Revok blinked his eyes as he tried to form a coherent thought, but he couldn't even get past the lack of awareness in his senses. His sword arm became limp, and the blade fell from his hands. A small stream of blood dripped down from his left nostril.

The healer knew she didn't have much time. Her Vis was spent and her opponent would soon recover his wits. Zedne sidestepped over to the bone shelf, the rack where she kept her medicines. She quickly noticed one of the clay jars and picked it up, just as Revok's mind had begun to recover. She threw the small container at the face of the Magus, right while he was shaking his head, trying to remember what had just happened. The jar shattered on the bridge of his nose and the yellow powder spilled onto Revok's face. The Magus screamed as he fell on his knees, the substance burning through his skin and eyes. Revok began rolling on the floor, his cries mixing in with the sounds of the dying outside.

Zedne walked back behind the stone slab and took the little girl's hand. The healer led her past the squirming man on the ground and back out through the entryway. As the two of them got to the outside, they could see that the assailants had set fire to the assembly hall. The cacophony of wails was unnerving, but Zedne held onto the little girl's hand and they both started running towards the other side of the village. If they could just make it to the tall rocks situated near the fungi cave, they would be able to hide out until the Magi left.

Just as they rounded a corner, they came face to face with Slane. The chief executor was just standing there and smiled at them, his leering face a mixture of menace and delight. Zedne pulled the child behind her as she refocused what was left of her Vis.

Slane grinned at them. He was less than ten yards away and took a step closer. "Now where would you three be going? Can you not see that we are having a good time here?"

"I have met Magi in my younger days," Zedne said calmly. "None of them were ever such a creature like you. From what hell were you spawned from?"

Slane frowned. "You wound me with your insult. Apologize."

"I will not," Zedne said. "You have murdered my entire tribe and you expect me to play your game? I shall not."

Slane gave her a blank stare. "Murdered your entire tribe? No, not yet. After all, you are still alive. And that little girl behind you, as well as the baby she is carrying. That makes three."

Zedne continued to build up her Vis. Perhaps she had enough power for another mental strike. It was the one chance she had left, so she needed to keep him talking. "Why did you do this? By what right? The child you seek is not even here."

"Because your elder and your protector lied to me," Slane said. "Let us also consider that one of my own was killed, so that is more than enough grounds to condemn your entire people to death."

"It was your seeker who first violated the oath of peace! You did not even hold an inquest to see what the actual truth was!"

"I have the authority to do whatever I wish," Slane said tersely. "I have made my judgment, and I have the power to act on it. The strong will do whatever they wish, and the weak will suffer what they must."

"You are worse than the Gorgons of old," Zedne hissed. "May the gods curse you for what you have done!"

Slane titled his head back and laughed. Zedne knew it was time. She concentrated for a brief second before launching her mindsense towards the Magus. Her mental tendrils bore into his mind, trying to overcome his thought defenses by sheer force of will. Slane staggered backwards as she pressed her mental assault on him. Zedne scowled while using the last of her reserves, her Vis was now sucked dry. Her own head started to spin as she fought off the accompanying headache. Slane rolled his eyes and fell backwards to the ground.

"Come on," Zedne said as she turned and grabbed Vida's little hand. Just as they both ran past the stricken Magus, they heard a cackling laugh behind them. Zedne turned around.

Slane had suddenly gotten up. He dusted off his black cloak. "That was a very good attack, old woman. I have not been struck by a Striga for many cycles now. I have forgotten how it feels."

Zedne pushed the little girl away from her. She pointed towards the outskirts of the village. "Run, now!"

Vida started running. The little girl had to balance the baby on her thin arms, so her gait was somewhat wobbly as she ran past a house. Slane chuckled as he held out his right hand and gesticulated. The little girl was instantly launched into the air, as if an unseen force sent her flying up. Vida screamed as she was dangling more than twenty yards above them.

"Put her down!" Zedne pleaded.

Slane smirked. "As you wish."

The little girl screamed as she suddenly dropped like a stone thrown from a great height. Vida had let go of the baby and they both fell onto the boulders by the side of the fungi cave, the sickening sounds of flesh hitting rocks could be heard.

Zedne fell down on her knees. "Noo!"

Slane motioned his hand again and the healer was thrown up into the air. He used his mindforce to guide her landing towards the burning assembly hall. Zedne struck one of the old support pillars made out of bone, and her body was impaled as the rod punctured her back and exited from her right breast. The old healer shuddered for a few seconds, then lay still.

Baradine walked over to where Slade was standing at. "You better take a look at Revok," the bearded Magus said, pointing to the healer's house.

Slane shrugged as he walked into the dwelling. Lying near the entryway was Revok, and he was clutching at his horribly burned face. There was a sharp smell of brimstone in the air. "I am here, Revok," he said. "What happened?"

Revok's words were punctuated with pained shrieking. "Aah, that old hag! She burned me! She burned my eyes out! I cannot see!"

Slane looked down at the ground and noticed the broken pieces of pottery. "So she threw something at you. It looks like a corrosive substance. Why did you not use your mindforce to deflect her attack?"

"S-she used her Vis on me," Revok cried. "That old witch tore through m-my defenses. The pain! It burns still!"

Slane shrugged. "Ah, that is a pity. You should have been more prepared. Instead you were overconfident, and your hubris has made you blind and useless to me now."

Revok whimpered as he got on his knees. He wasn't sure where Slane was, so he faced in the opposite direction. "Lord S-Slane, I beg of you, take me t-to a healer."

Slane bent down and placed a reassuring hand on his shoulder. "Have no fear, I will help you."

"T-thank you, Lord," Revok sobbed. "Anything f-for the pain. Anything."

"Of course," Slane said as he stood upright and drew his blade from the scabbard. He made a downward swing and the sharpened steel instantly sliced through Revok's neck, chopping it in half. Revok's body slumped forward as his head rolled along the smooth stone flooring, before stopping by the side of the wall.

The flap by the entryway parted and Baradine stepped inside. He took a long look at what had happened before glancing over at his master. "We found a few of the children and some youths hiding out in that cave of theirs. What do we do with them?"

Slane wiped his blade with the folds of Revok's cloak before placing it back in the scabbard. "Do any of them appear to have the gift of Vis?"

"No."

Slane sighed. He was hoping to find a young Striga to add to his team. All he cared about now was to build an empire of his own to rival that of the order. In that regard, any child who had the gift of Vis would be raised as his personal foot soldier. Too bad there weren't any. "Kill them all then. From now on, anyone who is not a child of Vis is to be killed. The future race must be kept pure."

# Chapter 15

Rion stared carefully at the glyphs on the black menhir. He was tempted to run his fingers along the carved wording, but Devos had warned him about ancient curses to those that disturbed forgotten monoliths, so he dutifully kept his hands to his side. Crouching beside him was the teller while Miri stood nearby. Jinn and Nyx had gone exploring, hoping to find a source of water somewhere in the canyon, or if failing that, another norpion so they could extract the precious fluid sacs to drink.

"Take your time, boy," Devos said. "We have almost figured out the message, that I am sure."

Rion squinted to get a better look. Some of the words were easy to understand, yet others were completely alien to him. "It seems to tell a story in riddles that do not make any sense."

"Just say the ones that you can read," Miri said. "I am sure we can piece together the rest."

"One word is spelled e-on," the boy said as he turned to look at the old man. "What does that mean?"

"An eon means a long passing of time, too many cycles to count," Devos said. "It could mean that the monument we are looking at is far older than our tribe's history."

"It carries the symbol of the Gorgons," Miri said. "Might we be in one of their ancient territories?"

Devos nodded. "Our earliest legends state that the Gorgons ruled over the entire world for thousands of cycles. I am not surprised at all that they would leave monuments wherever they went."

"If the Gorgons were everywhere, why is it that we hardly find monuments such as this?" Miri asked.

"Not long after the great rebellion wiped out the Gorgons, many factions fought each other for control of their territories. A powerful group named the Avengers of Lem made a vow to destroy whatever memory the people had of the Gorgons, and their main attacks were directed at temples and monoliths such as this one," Devos said.

Miri looked at him. "They must have been full of rage to attempt the destruction of pieces of stone like that. I do not see what advantage they might have fulfilled with such tasks."

"They wanted to wipe the memory of the Gorgons from all existence, for such was their shame," Devos said. "The teachings of Karma state that to forget about someone means that you destroy their soul. To completely eradicate all memories of the Gorgons meant a form of revenge for them."

"I think I have understood the meaning," Rion said. "It says, 'oceans of water have turned to dust, fields of plenty have turned to ash. The Maker of Entropy sleeps for eons past and eons to come, and the Gorgons shall return when he awakens.' That is what one portion says."

Miri looked at Devos. "The Maker of Entropy? Return of the Gorgons? Do you know what to make of that?"

Devos shrugged. "I am not sure. Perhaps it is a prophecy of some sort. The age of the Gorgons lasted for eons. All sorts of legends and tales were lost through time."

Rion bit his lip. "What does entropy mean?"

"For your strength to wither away until you are nothing," Devos said. "Perhaps it refers to a specific person, or maybe a title."

"And what is an ocean?" Rion asked.

"Long before the wastes, the land we are standing on was covered by water. Many old tales once said that we would travel on the surface of this vast liquid sea on strange vessels. Many beasts once lived beneath the waters, I believe they were called fish. We used to harvest a lot of food in the water by hunting them," Devos said.

Rion shook his head slowly from side to side. "A land made of endless water? I-I cannot imagine such a sight."

Devos nodded. "Yes, we live in an age where such things are merely legends. I like to imagine it as a gigantic stew pot, before algae and shrooms are placed into it. Imagine yourself as a tiny creature sitting on the surface of the pot, surrounded by nothing but water."

Rion closed his eyes and nodded. "Yes, that I can imagine. So where did people live if there was nothing but water?"

Devos chuckled. "It was not all water, boy. There was still land in many parts of the world. That was where most of the people lived."

Miri and the others had somewhat recovered from their ordeal out in the wastes, but none were at full strength yet. While the old man and the boy were deciphering the menhir, she was constantly looking around, on guard for any potential surprise. She wasn't as superstitious as many others were in the tribe, but standing so close to a Gorgon monument gave her a feeling of dread even though her mindsense was unable to detect anything hostile. She was also worried that Nyx and Jinn might have encountered something they couldn't handle. She hoped that they would return soon.

Devos pointed at another symbol on the stone. "What about that one, boy? From what you taught me about reading glyphs I think that one says 'dark', yes?"

Rion looked closer. "It reads, 'to venture to the last city is to pass through the hollow of shadows.' I think you misread the final word for dark. It is a common mistake among early readers."

Devos smiled. "That is it! I think we are on to something."

Miri was confused. "What do you mean?"

"When Rion read out the last city, it must mean Lethe," Devos said. "So from here, we must venture to a place called the hollow of shadows."

"And where would that be?" Rion asked.

"If the description was written in this menhir, then it must be close by," Devos mused.

Miri sighed. "You are being far too sanguine, master teller. It could be at the far side of the world for all we know."

Devos nodded. "Perhaps I am. But I must tell you that I had not believed much in these legends that I have been telling all my life, until now. The journey we have had has opened my eyes and changed me. We are standing here, in front of an old monument that dates back to the Gorgons, and everything that has been described has been witnessed by us to be the truth. I had thought that these tales were just nothing but stories, but our experiences have proven them to be genuine."

Something stirred in Miri's head. She sensed someone approaching. "Both of you, get behind me," she said while holding her spear with both hands.

Rion and Devos immediately stood up and stayed behind her. At that moment, Nyx and Jinn rounded the bend in the canyon wall and walked over to them. They both had smiles on their faces as they held out a pair of bulging waterskins.

Miri relaxed while walking up to the younger Striga. "I was getting a little worried. Where did the two of you go?"

Nyx grinned as she handed out the waterskins. "We just kept on walking. This place is like a maze and trails branch out in many directions. I sensed a buzzing noise in my mind, so I used my Vis to try and find any sort of life. Jinn found a large hive of sand beetles, and we discovered a small pool of algae nearby where the bugs were feeding on. Jinn skimmed the top part of the algae off and underneath was some water."

Rion opened the waterskin's stopper and took a sip. "It is salty."

Jinn nodded. "Yes, but it is water. I drank as much as I could. There was enough to fill two skins, so we now have a day's supply between the five of us."

Miri was impressed. "Well, our situation has gotten better. The gods must be smiling upon us once more."

Jinn stole a mischievous glance at his sister before speaking again. "There is one other thing."

Miri sensed they were being playful, but she wasn't in the mood for it. "What?"

Jinn turned around and started walking down to another part of the gully. "I believe it is better to show you all. Follow me."

With a tired sigh, Miri motioned the others to go along with him. They all walked down several twisting spoors until the five of them came upon the algae pool. Just as Jinn had told them, most of the water had been drained and the scum still on the surface had begun to dry out. Rion noticed a few beetles scurrying to and fro. The boy kicked one of the bugs and sent it flying into the air until the hapless insect bounced off the petrified rock wall. The beetle landed on its back and wiggled helplessly.

Miri placed a hand on Rion's shoulder. "Stop it."

Jinn beckoned them to keep up with him. "Just around the next bend here."

The moment they all turned into another passage, Miri stood in shock while Nyx and her brother grinned triumphantly. Rion's eyes opened wide while Devos started laughing. At the far end of the gulch lay the entrance to what looked to be a large cave, its black maw open to them like some foreboding path of doom. Miri peered closer and she could see distant outlines of stalactites and a smooth, sloping tunnel leading down into the darkness. The cave ceiling looked to be around nine yards high. A slight breeze of cool air drifted out to them. There was a small, bubbling pool of black algae near the side of the entrance.

Nyx smirked as she turned to look at the old man. "Why are you laughing?"

Devos continued to chuckle. "This is the hollow of shadows."

Everyone else looked at him.

Devos pointed at the cavern entrance. "It is precisely what Rion had read about when he translated the glyphs in that Gorgon monument we had just came from. The writing mentioned a hollow of shadows. Another word for hollow is cave."

Jinn's demeanor changed from mild amusement into wary concern. "Surely you do not expect us to venture forth in there, do you?"

It was Nyx's turn to laugh. "What is wrong, brother? Are you afraid of the dark?"

Jinn frowned. "I am afraid of nothing! Look at what I went through just to find you."

"Silence, both of you," Miri said. "Let us think this through. While venturing into that cave will surely spare us from the harsh heat of the sun, we do not know where the passages would lead to. We could very well come upon nothing but solid rock and we may have to walk back out again."

"Or even worse, we might end up encountering something dangerous inside," Jinn added.

Nyx giggled. "Afraid of norpions and sand bugs, brother?"

Jinn growled. "There may be a whole nest of those beasts in there. When Miri brought those fluid sacs back, it must have come from the biggest norpion I had ever known about. If any of us gets stung by one of those creatures, it will be the end."

Nyx hissed. "Miri and I can easily handle a few norpions with our Vis. Now that we have water, I think we should explore what is in there."

"I agree," Devos said. "We have followed the old legends, and so far they have not let us down. If we are to get to Lethe, then this must be the way forward. The other choice is that we leave the canyon and try to make it across the surface once more. If we go by that route, we might face more vicissitude."

All eyes turned to Miri. As the undisputed leader of the group, she had the final say. This clearly was no easy decision. They had barely survived traveling on the surface, but the cave would be equally dangerous, for they would be stumbling into its vast, unknown reaches. Miri had only experienced the fungi caverns back in the settlement, but that was a small, benign place compared to the undiscovered hollow before them. They all depended on her, and Miri sensed that no one would dispute whatever choice she'd be making.

Miri let out a deep breath. She had a feeling that whatever happened, it would be her fault. "Alright, we shall venture into that cavern. Jinn, Nyx, bring all our packs here."

## Chapter 16

Night had fallen and they started their descent through the cave entrance. The remaining afternoon had been spent resting, while Miri fashioned three torches using leg bones, strips of leather and by smearing the tips with some black algae that they found nearby. Miri then used some flint to light the torches and she led the way, followed by Nyx, Rion and Devos. The old man carried the second torch while Jinn carried the third as he brought up the rear. The floor was smooth and quite damp, with small pools of salty water forming along the edges. A steady breeze of air wafted through the tunnels, occasionally bringing a strange, foul odor with it. They could mostly hear the dripping of water that would condense due to the humidity, and its high mineral content would slowly seep along the ceilings and walls, forming a smooth layer along the sides and the occasional stalactite. The other sounds seemed to be that of falling rock somewhere up ahead of them.

Miri used her mindsense sparingly, checking for any slight vibrations in the air that would indicate movement. Nyx kept her Vis in reserve, ready to use it against any potential hostility should they encounter any. Rion had never been in a cave before, and he did his best not to show his fear. There were times that the boy wanted to stay so close to Miri, he would inadvertently bump into Nyx who happened to be moving slowly just ahead of him. When Rion ended up kicking her ankle too many times, she made a quick turn and quietly pushed him away, prompting the boy to take a slower, less apprehensive pace. While Jinn had been in the tribe's fungi caves before, his fear of enclosed, dark spaces made him jittery, as he imagined endless, squirming swarms of norpions ready to pounce on him. Jinn's paranoia increased to the point as he would occasionally glance back and shine his torch down the passage that they had just passed through, hoping that there was nothing behind them, before hurrying along to catch up with the others.

Eventually, the cavern soon branched out into numerous tunnels ahead of them. Miri simply chose the largest passageway and they continued onwards. For several hours, no one said a word, hoping that their silence would not disturb whatever was residing in this lightless place. As they continued onwards, it was soon apparent that the caverns did indeed harbor life, but it was unlike anything they had ever seen. Strange, six-legged bugs were seen crawling along the floors. What made these lightless denizens odd was that many of them were pale, some were even translucent. Devos would sometimes hold his breath as he looked down and noticed strange, tiny water creatures that swam in the small pools along the floor, their pale skin glittering under the torchlight. The old man would sometimes spend far too long looking at something before Jinn tapped his shoulder in order to silently urge him to move along.

Another few hours passed as they kept on going. Miri noticed that the passageway up ahead seemed to expand. She looked up and saw that the cave ceiling was now over twelve yards tall and sloping higher. The wind also began to pick up, as the flames of her torchlight had begun to flicker. She turned to face Nyx, who was right behind her. "I think there is a large cavern up ahead. Be ready," she said softly.

Nyx just nodded before turning and whispering the message to Rion. Miri could see Devos walking up and peering over the boy's shoulder, his eyes expressing an eagerness to see what was ahead. With her other hand gripping the black spear, Miri held her breath and moved forward until she could see that the passageway led into a large, subterranean chamber. The moment she stepped through the entryway she made a slight gasp.

The cavern that stood before her had a high ceiling that stretched out into the darkness, well beyond the radius of her torchlight. Gigantic stalactites that resembled inverted sharp mountains loomed down on her. The entire chamber was like a gigantic cyst, a hollowed out space deep in the bowels of the world. Miri moved forward so that the rest of the group could enter. Miniature streams of flowing water formed tiny gorges along the smooth stone floor. An unclean odor assailed their nostrils as they fanned out and began to examine a place where no human had come upon for perhaps millions of cycles. Rion stayed close to Miri, while the Striga walked over to the base of a nearby stalactite in order to rest her tired feet. Jinn and Nyx stayed close to each other while Devos wandered over to what looked like a mound of white stones at the far side of the cavern.

As Devos got closer, he quickly saw a child sized black boulder jutting out of the smooth floor ahead of him. He turned to the others, his excitement at a fever pitch. "Look, over here!"

Miri quickly stood up as Devos's echo reverberated across the cavern and into the adjoining tunnels beyond. Gesturing at Rion to get up and follow her, she quickly moved over to where the old man was. "Devos, could you not shout out like that? Your words must have woken up whatever god sleeps down here," she whispered.

"I-I am sorry," Devos said sheepishly while Nyx and Jinn walked over to them as well. The old man pointed to the black boulder in the middle of the cavern. The stone was black onyx, and like the menhir they had found out in the canyon, this one had the unmistakable symbol of the Gorgon as well. "But I needed you all to look at this. The monument you see before you is also that of the Gorgons." He turned to look at the boy while bringing his torch closer so the carved glyphs on the rock were more evident. "Rion, can you read any of that?"

The boy could barely keep up as he studied the etched writings. "It says, 'Kaelr fought the many beasts in the dark when his light went dim, he killed so many that the caverns ran red with blood. He banished the rest to be forever in shadow, forever blind, and then he went back out into the world of the light.' That is all that is written on it."

While Devos conversed with the boy, Miri moved closer to the mound just ahead of them. As she used her torchlight to further illuminate the strange pile in front of her, she let out a muffled cry. What stood before her was not an accumulation of rocks, it was a mountain of bones. Everyone turned to her direction in mute shock. Miri put her spear down, then picked up a humanlike skull and held it close for a better look. Its forehead had somehow been elongated forward, and the bones had fused over what was once a pair of eye sockets. The jaw bones were larger, and filled with rows of triangular, sharp teeth. Large, protruding holes at its side seemed to indicate that whoever the skull belonged to had bigger ears than ordinary men. Miri threw the skull back into the pile and picked up her spear. "We need to go, now," she said tersely.

Suddenly, the shrill sounds of multiple wailings could be heard coming from every direction. Jinn pushed Nyx behind him as he tensed up, spear on the ready. Rion's heart began to beat faster as he got behind Miri, who was facing the tunnel that they had just came from. Devos stood beside them, while holding out his torch to try and determine a way out. Almost instinctively, Miri and Nyx quickly began to use their mindsense, sending out mental feelers to try and locate where the shrieks were coming from. Nyx was far too eager as she reached out with her thought probes, and was quickly met with an incoherent barrage of madness, fear and rage. The young Striga cried out as her knees buckled and she nearly fell over, but Jinn reacted and quickly grabbed her by the arm after dropping his torch onto the ground, where it soon fizzled out after getting dunked into the water of a nearby stream.

Miri had been able to keep her thought blocks in place, so she weathered the mental feedback better than Nyx did. She held out her torch to Rion. "Take this," she said. "Make sure you do not drop it."

The boy nervously took the torch from her as Miri pulled at her war shield that had been slung over her shoulder. Jinn also had a shield slung over his back and he quickly copied her as Nyx had recovered and was now standing on her own two feet. Devos was tempted to pull out his knife, but he just kept his other hand on the weapon's grip instead, ready to draw it out at a moment's notice.

Miri stole a glance at Nyx. "Are you alright?"

Nyx nodded as she held her spear with both hands. "I was unprepared for the mental reaction. I thought they were human, but it seems they have the minds of beasts. Their jumbled thoughts nearly overwhelmed me."

Miri turned to look at Devos as the shrieking seemed to get closer. "Can you think of a way out of here?"

Devos shined his torchlight close to the pile of bones. "If the legends state that Kaelr fought a battle here, then perhaps this mound of bones is his legacy." The old man started shifting through the large pile, he figured that there must have been hundreds of creatures that had been slain for a mass of this size. The one positive clue that he could deduce was there were no shrieking noises coming from this part of the cavern.

Rion's entire body began to tremble. The boy's hands shook as he feared for the worst. Miri nudged his elbow with her shield arm as a small token of reassurance. "Stay calm, Rion," she said.

Right at that very moment, a horde of horrible things poured out of the tunnels in front of them. Miri grimaced as she was unable to keep count, for there must have been hundreds of the creatures. Nyx and Rion both cried out in horror, while Jinn silently let out a worried breath. At first glance, their pale forms resembled that of small, hairless children, but that was where the comparisons ended. Their bodies consisted of thin, gangly arms and legs with squat torsos and flaccid, deathly pale skin. What was most terrifying of all were their eyeless faces, with just two small slits where their noses ought to be, with huge, drooping ears dangling by the sides of their abnormally large heads. Each creature had a large mouth with serrated teeth and their hands ended in stubby claws. The entire horde began to shamble forward, their monstrous heads swaying back and forth while their mouths emitted ear-piercing shrieks that seemed to bore into one's skull.

"Orlas," Devos muttered under his breath. It was a name for a tribe that had ventured deep into the bowels of the earth and never returned to the surface. He remembered an obscure, ancient tale that told of a sightless people who were banished by the gods into a dark underworld as punishment for feeding on their own young.

Miri held the war shield close to her body while keeping her black spear in a thrusting position, just above her right hip. The moment when a few of the creatures shuffled closer, she thrust out her weapon and speared the torso of the closest one. The pale being let out an ear-piercing wail as it staggered backwards while clutching its stomach wound, prompting the rest of the horde to stop in their tracks, before turning on their wounded comrade as they ate it alive. Jinn and Nyx quickly did the same, thrusting their spears forward before pulling them back to keep the monsters at bay. Although the swarm of creatures stopped advancing as a few of their wounded brethren cried out to warn the others, it was clear that Miri's group had been surrounded.

Devos continued to rummage through the pile of bones. As he crouched down near the edge of the mound, he noticed that the torchlight he was carrying in his other hand began to flicker as he brought it closer to the cavern floor. That was when he noticed a hairline crack on one of the rock slabs on the floor beside him. There must be another tunnel hidden underneath. He turned to look at the youth, who was standing beside his sister. "Jinn, I found a tunnel underneath this slab, help me!"

Jinn backed away from the front as he crouched down beside the old man. He quickly placed his shield down beside him. "Where?"

Devos planted the torch on the side of the mound of bones to keep it upright, then used both hands to try to pry the stone slab that was next to him. "Over here, help me."

Miri concentrated as she worked with Nyx to try and calm the agitated horde of creatures using their mindsense. The multitude of hostile thoughts were a problem as they each entered a different mind one at a time, only for the other creature to devolve back into a white-hot rage once they moved onto another. Nyx could barely concentrate as she would have to shift back and forth from her mindsense to using her spear in order to keep the swarming monsters from overwhelming them as they edged ever closer. Miri had more experience as she was holding her own, while Rion was almost in tears as he nervously hid behind her.

Nyx jabbed her spear at another blind orla that got too close. She glanced at the quivering boy. "Rion, get Jinn's shield and help me!"

The boy nervously looked down at the floor and found her brother's shield. Rion crouched low and picked it up. The inner straps were much too large for his thin arms so it hung loosely on him as he hefted it up to shield his body. One of the smaller orlas got through the two women as it tried to grab onto the boy. Rion shouted an alarm as he waved the torch in front of him, hitting the side of the creature by the ear. The orla yelped in agony as it retreated back to the others of its kind.

Jinn grimaced in pain as he used all of his strength to pull the slab up. His arm muscles ached as the solid slab began to move up, slowly. Devos silently cursed at himself for being too old to lend his strength. Jinn groaned as the slab was almost lifted, but his arms began to buckle from the strain and the stone started to slide back into place. Reacting quickly, Devos grabbed the spear lying on the floor and began to use its shaft as leverage to tilt the slab back up once more.

This time, the orlas began a more organized advance, as several of them began to edge out towards the sides of the platform that Miri and the others had been standing on. The two Strigas were using their mindsense to instill fear in the horde to prevent it from surging forward, but they were clearly running out of time as they were slowly being driven back. Rion would dart back and forth using his torch to ward off any of the smaller creatures who were not noticed by either Miri or Nyx.

With the spear acting as a lever, Jinn finally got the upper hand as the stone slab came free, revealing a narrow, sloping tunnel that seemed to go even deeper into the ground. The torch that Devos had placed on the mound had begun to flicker violently as a chill draft of wind came rushing out from the hole underneath them. Just as the old man stood up and was about to tell the others about the exit, the frenzied horde of orlas would no longer be denied. The creatures surged forward in a mad rush to get at their prey, their hunger cries at a fever pitch.

Rion screamed as several orlas tired to grab him. He fell onto his back as one of the creatures tore the burning torch from his hands. The boy was able to prevent one of the monsters from biting him as he thrust the shield out in front of him. The orla's fanged mouth had bitten into nothing but hard leather and bone. Miri ran backwards as she grabbed the back of Rion's cloak and pulled the boy upright. Nyx was able to spear a few of the creatures before they grabbed hold of her weapon and tore it loose from her hand. Two of the bigger orlas jumped on top of her, sending the teen girl onto the ground. She used her mindsense to stun one of the creatures, but the bigger one leapt on top of her chest and tried to bite her in the neck. Nyx cried out for help as she used her arms to hold the creature's head back, but it was clear that the orla was winning as its fangs got closer to her jugular.

With a desperate cry, Jinn grabbed his spear and lunged forward, using his weapon as a barrier to thrust at the creatures that were about to devour his sister. The young man's charge pushed about a dozen of the creatures backwards, allowing Nyx to wriggle free and escape. Two of the creatures had gotten to the top of the mound of bones and pounced on Devos, just as the old man was pulling the torch out. The teller struggled with the creatures clawing at him as he thrust the torch into one and pulled out his dagger and stabbed the other, forcing the creatures off of him.

Miri pushed Rion towards the tunnel underneath them. "Go!"

The boy just stood there. He was in shock, and a numbing sense of catatonia overwhelmed his senses as he saw the others struggling against the horde of beasts. Just as a group of orlas ran towards him, Rion was yanked back into reality when Devos grabbed him by his cloak and pulled him along as they both jumped down into the tunnel, leaving the smoldering torch behind on the cavern floor.

Jinn yelled out as he was pulled into the center of the horde. He flailed wildly with his spear, but the strain on the bone shaft was too much and it finally shattered with a loud crunch. He screamed in agony as the swarm of orlas began biting into his flesh and pulled him down onto the ground. One of the creatures bit down onto his exposed throat and tore into his windpipe. Jinn gurgled in his own blood as his senses began fade out into the overwhelming darkness. The last thing he saw was one of the little orlas chewing out his eye.

Nyx only saw the last part of it as her brother was overpowered by the majority of creatures around them. "Jinn!" she sobbed while trying to reach him.

Miri grabbed the younger Striga by her elbow. The rest of the horde had sensed easy pickings as they started to move away from the others to get at the newly slain carcass. "They are distracted. We must go, now!"

But Nyx wouldn't be dissuaded. The young Striga tried to get at her brother until Miri used her own mindsense to calm her down. With tears in her eyes, Nyx said a silent goodbye to Jinn as she went down into the tunnel, just ahead of Miri, who used her spear to cover their escape.

Without torches now, the four of them were in the dark. Nyx and Rion had lost their backpacks, while the only things Devos had in his pack were telling stones and a waterskin. Miri knew they had to increase the distance between their enemies, so they could not tarry. She opened up her mindsense and sent out mental feelers to gauge the tunnel ahead of them. It seemed that the passageway was circular and smooth, with very little obstacles.

"I will lead," Miri said softly. "Rion, grab hold of my cloak and use it guide your way. Devos, take hold of the boy's cloak and walk after. Nyx, are you fit to stay at the rear?"

The teen girl let out a sob, but her mind was focused. Miri sensed that she had accepted her brother's sacrifice. "Yes," Nyx said softly.

"Very well," Miri said as she turned and began to walk along the passageway.

Rion was about to ask where Jinn was, until he realized what had probably occurred. The boy kept his mouth shut as he concentrated on his steps, making sure he would not slip and fall. He sensed the taut tug on the edge of his cloak, and he knew that Devos was following right behind him. Since Nyx could use her own mindsense, she discreetly followed a few steps behind the old man, her stone dagger gripped tightly in her hands. The teen girl was hoping that one or two of the orlas would go down this tunnel so she could kill them, but none of the creatures had come through the hole.

The slight air currents ahead of them became more pronounced as they kept on going. After an indeterminate amount of time, a thin point of light seemed to be up ahead. Now that she had a visual reference, Miri quickened her pace as the dot of luminosity soon became bigger. Before long, they came upon a well-lighted aperture that led out into an open crevasse. Stretched out before them was a flat plain of desert, its vermillion sands spread out as far as the eye could see. They had been underground for so long that each one of them had to squint their eyes from the intensity of the sunlight above. What made the sight even more incredible was the distant outlines of a gigantic black pyramid, just at the edge of the horizon.

Devos was exhausted, but his faith in the telling stones was once again rewarded. "This is the final desert. Beyond lies the Black Redoubt. It is exactly as what the stories have told us."

Nyx sat down along the edge of the cave entrance and wept.

## Chapter 17

When night fell once more, the four of them began to make their way across the twilit sands. Miri figured it would take at least two days of walking before they reached the foot of the Black Redoubt. Nyx had been in a sullen mood, and she refused to eat the remaining scraps of food. When Devos said a prayer to thank the gods as well as Jinn for his heroic sacrifice, Nyx merely walked off to the far end of the cliff wall, not wanting to be part of the ritual. Miri knew that the teen girl was hurting inside, and she did not want to press the issue.

Just before they set out, Miri took stock of their equipment. She still had her black spear, but Nyx had lost hers and all she had was a dagger. Devos had a knife of his own but that was the extent of their existing weaponry. Miri ran her hand along the sides of her torso. It seemed that her leather cuirass had been bitten into, but the orla's attack didn't penetrate the thick armor. They used up one of the waterskins during the day's rest, leaving one full. What little scraps of food they had were now gone as well. Miri had assumed that there would be some sort of nourishment that they could find when they finally set foot in the Black Redoubt, but a gnawing feeling gave her an impression that they might find nothing at all. Jinn's death weighed heavily on her, but she knew that she couldn't second guess her actions, lest it would lead to even more bad decisions. All she could do now was to keep trying her best and move forward.

As the moon was high above them, Miri noticed that Devos was lagging behind. The old man seemed to be limping. Silently gesturing at Rion and Nyx to go ahead, she slowed her walk until she was moving side by side with the teller. "You seem to be slower than usual, Elder Devos," she said. "Is something wrong?"

Devos glanced at her while drawing his cloak closer to his body. She could see his teeth grinning at her. "Oh, I think I twisted my ankle in that last battle we had," he said softly. "Do not concern yourself about me, I can keep up."

"That is one less worry on my mind then," Miri said wistfully. "For I have many more worries still."

Devos nodded. "Nyx is still in mourning, but I am sure she will move on. Even though I am not a Striga, I can already sense that."

"What happened in the caverns was hard on all of us," Miri said. "It was I who made the decision to venture into the lightless tunnels."

"Look around you," Devos said. "The Valley of Stone is several dozen leagues behind us. If we had journeyed on the surface, it would have taken more days, and we would be dead from the heat. You chose the right path. Do not let Jinn's sacrifice be in vain."

"We no longer have any food and very little water," Miri said. "If the Black Redoubt is but a barren ruin, we shall die before we get to the last city."

"Do not fear, the gods have brought us this far. I am sure that fortune will smile upon us again," Devos said.

Despite everything that had happened, the teller's optimism was infectious. Miri couldn't help but smile. "You seem to believe that we will make this journey in spite of all these trials that we have endured so far. What makes you seem so confident?"

Devos reached underneath his tunic and took out a telling stone. He handed it to Miri. "I had Rion with me when we translated all of the telling stones I had in my possession. That one I had kept from you all this time. The reason I never discussed it with you was because it holds a very special tale."

Miri was intrigued. "What tale is that?"

"It tells the story of Kaelr's last words, just before he died," Devos said. "As he met his death upon seeing the gates of Lethe, he was reputed to have said that someone else would come and fulfill the task that he was set out to do."

"Someone else was fated to go to Lethe after him? Who?"

"Kaelr said it would be a boy and her mother," Devos said. "The mother was fated to be a powerful Striga …and the boy was a Magus."

Miri turned her head in surprise. "That cannot be true! Are you saying you believe that the story on the telling stone I am holding right now is about us? Impossible!"

"I used to think that these tales were nothing more than old stories myself," Devos said. "Not any longer. This is why I believe that you and Rion are destined to make it to Lethe."

"But I am not the boy's mother."

Devos nodded. "The word can mean a great many things, it does not have to mean that the boy was born from your loins, it could signify a guardian, or protector as well."

Miri shook her head. "You seem to be stretching the truth in order for the story to make sense. Can you not see that?"

"Perhaps," Devos said. "Or it may also mean that all stories have a certain truth in them that can be adapted to serve as prophecy."

Miri handed the stone back to him. "I thank you for providing a bit of hope with this tale. It would be of great benefit if it came true."

Devos refused to take the stone from her hand. "Keep the stone. There is another story in it that may be of some use for you."

Miri held the carved rock in front of her face. The moonlight reflected off the carvings on its surface, it seemed to glow with its own phosphorescence. "I have not much use for this telling stone. I do not know how to read the glyphs."

"In time you will learn, let the boy teach you," Devos said.

"I have much greater worries right now," Miri pointed to a cluster of rocks out in the distance as she increased her gait, slowly moving past him. "We need to get to those boulders by dawn so we can rest in the shade. Do not lag behind too far, teller."

As Miri moved on ahead, making her way towards Nyx and the boy. Devos gritted his teeth and used all of his willpower to keep up.

They were able to make it to the cluster of boulders, just an hour after dawn finally broke. Miri took the first watch and kept a lookout while the others slept. She could clearly see some details of the gigantic pyramid, for it seemed to be less than a day's journey away from where they were. She wondered as to how many huge slabs of blackened stones were needed to create such a gargantuan structure, for the top of Black Redoubt seemed to stretch upwards towards the misty sky. It must have taken thousands of cycles and an endless supply of manpower to construct such a grand edifice. If that monolith was but an outpost of the last city, she wondered what other wonders to the eye could possibly lay after it. From a distance, she noticed that there were huge openings along its side, indicating that the massive structure itself was hollow. Miri didn't see any signs of movement, but she figured that it was still too far to tell whether it was inhabited or not. What worried her most was the lack of beasts wandering the area and the absence of telltale algae blooms in the sand dunes beyond. If there were inhabitants still living within the Black Redoubt, then there surely must be indications of where they grew and harvested their food. As the sun blazed down onto the sands, Miri wondered if they had stumbled into another dead settlement.

A few hours had passed and the lazy afternoon sun had begun to wane. Miri woke up from her much needed rest and looked around. Nyx was situated near the top of the boulder, keeping watch while still underneath some shade. Devos and the boy slept side by side, using their packs as pillows for their heads. Miri got up, stretched her back and walked over to where the waterskin was. She held the bladder up, testing its weight. There were only a few sips left, and the cluster of rocks that they were resting in had nothing. She looked up at the younger Striga. Nyx noticed her and their eyes met. Miri gave her a faint smile, but Nyx turned her head back to look across the horizon. It was clear that the teen girl still had not gotten over her brother's death. Nyx's enthusiasm had dissolved into a quiet sullenness, her once inquisitive demeanor had been transformed into a heart of stone.

Miri decided not to bother her any further, so she sat down beside the sleeping boy and pulled out the telling stone from her pack. It was but a flat piece of black granite that was the size of her palm. Carved glyphs indicated that it told some kind of story, but until Rion could teach her how to read them, they were nothing more than scratches on a rock's surface to her. Miri ran her fingers along the grooves, marveling at what secrets still lay hidden in its writings. When they had found a bit of safety from the harshness of the land, then she would have the time to learn how to read.

Devos had awoken. The old man pushed himself up into a sitting position. He turned his head and noticed that Miri was looking intently at the telling stone he had given her. "Once you learn how to read, you will want to get your hands on every single telling stone you can find," he said.

Miri glanced at him and smiled. "I hope to the gods that it will be soon, for I am tired of wandering in these wastes."

"The Black Redoubt is but a few walks away," Devos said. "I sense that you will indeed find safety therein."

Miri was tempted to laugh, but she didn't. "So you can sense things now? I never knew you had the power of Vis within you."

Devos just grinned and shook his head. "No, not Vis, but the power of dreams. Just now, I had dreamt that I saw you sitting by a fire pit, being counseled by someone wearing a red robe. The room that you were in had walls of carved black rock. It was evidently within the Black Redoubt, I am sure of it."

Miri arched her thin eyebrows. She remembered Nyx telling her about the very same person, dressed in the same robe. "You dreamt of a man in red as well? That is strange indeed. Nyx had told me the same thing. I am surprised. I have dreamt of him too, but only vague visions."

"The dream that I had was so vivid, it seemed almost like I was scrying into the future," the old man said. "This is why I am telling you that you are indeed fated to make it into that pyramid we see before us."

Nyx climbed down from the top boulder and made her way over to them. "The sun is now beginning to wane. We should be moving out soon."

Miri leaned over her side and shook Rion awake. The boy sat up, rubbed his eyes and looked around. Miri gave him the waterskin and Rion took a sip before placing the tooth stopper back into place. She could sense that the boy was still thirsty, but Rion did not want to finish the nourishing liquid and leave the others without something to drink. The boy stood up and offered the waterskin to the others, but Nyx merely ignored him as she went over to pick up her backpack. Devos just smiled and shook his head.

Another hour passed and the sun had begun its final descent over the horizon. As Nyx and the boy walked to the edge of the rock walls to put on their boots, Miri noticed that Devos continued to just sit where he was. The old man was clearly up to something, but what it was she couldn't be sure.

Miri walked over to the teller and stood in front of him. She adjusted the leather straps of her pack in order to prevent them from digging too deeply into her shoulder. "Come on, teller. It is like you said, merely one more walk until we get to the base of the Black Redoubt."

Devos gave a faint smile as he looked up at her. "I am afraid that my journey ends here, Miri."

Miri was confused. "What? I do not understand."

The old man shifted his torso sideways and pulled back his cloak, revealing two bite marks on his upper leg and thigh. The orlas had evidently taken a fair bit of flesh. Devos had placed a leather bandage on them to prevent bleeding, but it was clear that they had become infected, the skin around the open wounds had turned black. Miri gasped.

Devos gritted his teeth as he eased himself into a more comfortable position, drawing his cloak back around his body to hide his injuries once more. "It took all of my effort to make it this far. I thought I was going to collapse while we made our way here last eventide. The pain has now given way to a feeling of numbness. I believe the orlas must have had some sort of poison in their jaws, much like the norpions do, only their venom is somewhat weaker, but in the end it leads down the same path."

Miri knelt down beside him as she pulled her backpack down. "I may still have some of that poultice that Zedne had given me for the wound in my arm. My arm is fully healed now so I am sure it will be of some use to you."

Devos placed a hand on her trembling forearm. "The poultice is for healing wounds, not for poisons. It is better that you keep your supplies, for you will need them. The journey does not end at the Black Redoubt."

Despite her dehydration, tears began to well in Miri's eyes. "There must be something I could do!"

Devos continued to smile. "You have done well. You have gotten the boy this far. Help him go on to the last city. As for myself, I have lived a long life full of knowledge, and I will take that with me when I at last reunite with my wife in the spirit lands."

The boy and Nyx made their way back and noticed the foreboding scene. Miri wiped away her tears, as she turned and faced the two younglings. "Devos will not be going with us," she said softly. "He will be staying here."

Nyx immediately sensed what had just occurred because of her Vis. She held out a hand of greeting to Devos, and the old man held up his own hand in return along with a smile, indicating that he understood. Nyx gave a snort, then turned around and walked away, her hands over her eyes. She had already lost someone she loved dearly, and could no longer bear it a second time. The young Striga rounded the side of the boulder and was gone. Miri sensed that she stood nearby, but didn't want to be seen.

Rion had noticed the somber mood. When Nyx walked off, he realized the full gravity of the situation. The boy let out a cry as he ran over to Devos and cradled the old man's head. "No, you cannot stay here! You must go with us, we will carry you!"

Devos smiled as his hands lightly gripped the crying boy's forearms. "Worry not, Rion. You are almost at your journey's end. I will stay here, and my spirit will watch over you, always."

Tears ran down the boy's cheeks as he desperately looked up at Miri. "He cannot die here! Not when we are so close. We must seek help at that place and return here with a healer."

Devos knew that it was better to lie to the boy in order to give him some sense of hope. He could no longer feel his legs and he sensed that his time was near. "Alright, Rion. I shall stay here and await the healer from the Black Redoubt."

The boy stood up as he wiped the tears from his eyes. He turned to look at Miri, a sense of desperation in his eyes. "Let us go forth now. We must not tarry. Elder Devos will still be here when we return with a healer."

Miri nodded. "Go and stay with Nyx. I will speak with Devos one last time before we start our journey."

As the boy eagerly ran off, Miri turned to look back at the old man. "Can you truly wait? Perhaps the boy is right, there may be a healer in the Black Redoubt. We can return as soon as possible."

Devos smiled and shook his head. The old man held up a small leather pouch that he had been bringing along. "I can already feel the numbness in my stomach, I can no longer feel anything below my arms. Soon, I shall not be able to breathe. This pouch contains some yellow algae, and I will swallow a bit of it when you leave."

Miri bit her lip. Yellow algae was a fast acting poison. "Why did you bring some of that along this journey? Was it for this very instance?"

Devos shrugged. "I had a sense that I might end up being an unnecessary burden to you and the young ones. I am an old man, and I knew this would be my final trek. There is no need for you to return to this place. Go find the last city. Take care of Nyx and the boy."

Miri placed a hand on his shoulder, then she stood up. "I understand, Devos. Of all the tellers I knew in the tribe, you were the greatest one. I shall not forget you. Farewell."

The old man placed a hand on her boot. "Farewell, Protector Miri. May we meet again in the spirit world some day to tell new tales of our travels as we drink the flowing waters of the gods."

Miri turned around and walked away, out of sight. Devos could hear a distant argument, before silence fell once more. He was now alone. The old man smiled as he breathed in the sights for one final time. Right at that moment, he grew to love the dusty ground around him, the unmoving boulders and the desert air. Life was so precious, existence was but a temporary phase, before passing away in the inevitable sea of time. When the feeling in his fingers began to tingle away, Devos opened the pouch, took out a pinch of the dried yellow algae, and put it in his mouth. That taste was bitter at first, but then his tongue gradually become numb. His body shook and he gave out one last wheeze, then he closed his eyes and was gone.

## Chapter 18

Dawn had begun to break when they finally made it to the outskirts of the Black Redoubt. Miri could see that the base of the gigantic pyramid was honeycombed with numerous open entryways. A number of areas had been covered up by the shifting sands and the whole place seemed deserted. Miri chose the closest opening and walked towards it, followed by Nyx and Rion. Whether the citadel portals were once sealed with doors, she could not be sure, but Miri did notice grooves near the sides that might have held massive hinges for them. She estimated that the doors must have been at least ten yards high and twenty yards across, if such constructs ever existed at one time. Her mindsense failed to detect anything, so she gestured at the others to follow her as she stepped through the entryway and into what looked like a massive hall.

The rays of morning light cast bright columns through the numerous holes along the wall, giving them ample illumination. The floor beneath them was of polished black stone, occasionally topped by mounds of ash that had seeped in from the outside. They could see a few stone tables set along the dimly lit sides of the hall, with numerous corridor entrances at the far side of the area. The interior ceiling must have been at least thirty yards above them, with circular holes that allowed the light and wind to pass through. The place seemed like an old ruin.

Nyx looked around as she stood beside Miri. "I do not sense anything. This whole place is long dead."

Rion ran his hands along the sides of the black walls. He could see ornate glyphs were carved in just about each spot in every part of the surface of the room, there were also writings etched on the granite flooring. It was like looking at a gigantic telling stone. Rion unslung his backpack and let it slide down onto the floor as he tried to read some of the glyphs. "This whole place has got writing everywhere," he said softly.

Miri took off her own backpack and placed it beside Rion's. She then placed her spear against the wall. "Let us rest up for a while. Do not venture through any of the passageways for now. We need to sleep first, then we need to find any source of water in here."

"I am not tired," Rion said as he continued to decipher the writings along the walls. The words that he was able to read from the glyphs were jumbled, but he guessed that they were some sort of dedication to the gods.

Miri sat down, using the side of a stone table as a chair and silently stared at the boy. She had been using her Vis on him all night, slowly making him forget his urgency regarding Devos. By the time they got close to the pyramid, her mindsense was telling her that he had accepted the old man's demise. She felt it better to suppress his emotions and memories of him until they were in a truly safe place. Only then could the proper mourning begin- not just for Devos, but for Jinn as well.

"Neither am I," Nyx said while pointing up at an adjacent stairwell. "I shall see what lies above. I will be in earshot should anything untoward happen."

Miri was too tired to protest. Her head was pounding, and she needed to close her eyes. She saw Nyx make her way up the stone steps and the young Striga soon disappeared out of sight. Rion was at the far side of the room, still looking over the carved writings. Miri leaned back, closed her eyes a second time and was soon fast asleep.

By the time she had reopened her eyes, it was already late afternoon. The sun had drifted over to the other side of the pyramid, and there were long shadows in the great hall. The only thing she could hear was the shrill wind coursing through the holes in the wall. Miri blinked a few times to get her bearings before she got up. She was alone, and neither Rion nor Nyx could be seen. Rummaging through her pack, she quickly took out her leather cuirass and put it on. Even though her mindsense was unable to detect any hostile thoughts, she had a growing sense of foreboding and didn't want to take any chances.

With her armor now covering her torso, Miri grabbed her spear. "Nyx? Rion? Where are you?"

There was no answer.

She knew that Nyx went up to the second level of the structure, but she wasn't quite sure where the boy had gone to. There were numerous darkened corridors at the far side of the hall, leading deeper into the base of the redoubt. She hoped that Rion would have had enough sense not to go into a passageway without any light to guide him, so she ran up the stone steps leading to another level of the building. When she got to the upper landing, she noticed that there were massive open windows around the sides, with tall granite columns buttressing the stone blocks above. Each section of stone had intricate carvings of symbols and hieroglyphs that seemed to glow with a slight green intensity as the fading sunlight reflected off of their surface.

Miri began to use her mindsense to see if she could locate either of the two. Her mental tendrils extended from her thoughts and began to snake along the numerous columns and corridors of the upper level. The whole pyramid was at least several leagues across, so it would be prudent for her to cover more ground using her Vis instead of just finding them through visual means. Within moments, she was able to pick up a faint mental echo of Nyx's thoughts. Focusing her mindsense to locate her young protégé, Miri was soon able to pinpoint her location. Gripping her spear lightly, Miri ran through a shadowed corridor, partially stumbling on a loose rock in the dark, before the passageway opened up towards the other side of pyramid. With the tall windows now facing the glaring sun, Miri squinted as she ran in between more columns, before finally noticing Nyx standing by the ledge of one of the balconies.

As she got closer, she could see that Nyx was looking down below. Miri ran up to her and stopped right behind the girl's shoulder. "Nyx, why did you not acknowledge me when I called out to you?"

Nyx turned and looked at her. "I am sorry. I had been exploring this place. I thought I saw something down below, so I am walking along the sides, hoping to get a better glimpse of it."

Miri kept looking around. "Where is Rion, have you seen him?"

Despite the harsh glare, Nyx's eyes opened wide. "I thought he was with you. You have not seen him?"

Miri let out a deep breath. "No, I was resting. When I woke up, he was not in the hallway anymore."

"That foolish boy! Where could he have gone to?"

As she looked around, Miri noticed something at an adjacent balcony. She dashed over to it and looked down, before letting out a gasp. Nyx ran over and tried to focus on where she had been staring. When the young Striga saw it with her own eyes, she couldn't believe it either. Lying near the side of the pyramid was an abandoned sand sail, its greenish bronze hull glinting in the sun. The leather sails had been furled up neatly. They were not alone.

Miri knew it was the Magi. It had to be. The reason why she could not detect anyone meant that they were using mental defenses to shield their thoughts from her. "I am going back to the lower level to look for Rion. Are there more floors above?"

Nyx nodded. "Yes, there are numerous stone steps leading up into the upper levels, but they are mostly in shadow. We may need torches to explore the places above."

"Do what you can and try to find him up here," Miri said as she turned and began running towards the nearest stairwell leading below. "If you find him then let us meet in the hall where we had left our packs."

"At once," Nyx said.

Rion emerged from the darkened corridor and into another room. He wasn't quite sure where he was anymore, but his innate curiosity won over his caution as he started reading the glyph carvings on the wall beside him. Small, rectangular openings just near the top of the ceiling had cast narrow shafts of light, which gave him enough illumination to study the writings. While the hall that Miri had been resting in seemed to convey nothing more than a dedication of thanks and prayers to the gods, the last few rooms he had explored told a whole different tale. When he had entered the third room a few hours back, the carvings abruptly changed and he began to notice that the symbols of the Gorgons were now craved into every succeeding room that he had walked into. Upon deciphering the carvings in this part of the structure, he was now recounting the history of the Gorgons, from their mysterious origins to the height of their empire. Reading and making sense of the glyphs took some time, but his interest was so keen, he forgot about his thirst and his fatigue.

The boy took a few steps back while he tried to comprehend the whole story. It seemed that the Gorgons were born of incest between brother and sister. The names of their parents were lost in time, but the tale specifically stated that it was from an unholy union of a powerful Magus and his equally powerful sister, who was a Striga. Soon afterwards, the first Gorgons were born at the same time and were called triplets, and would only continue their lineage through more acts of interbreeding with one another. The other tales that he had found etched along the walls were equally astonishing. The true purpose of the Black Redoubt was not to serve as a fortress, but rather as a library to chronicle the history of the entire world. It was here that the accumulated knowledge of mankind would be preserved in stone carvings along the walls of the pyramid.

Rion had been so engrossed with the writings, he did not notice someone else in the room he was in. As he internalized the tale in front of him, the boy heard something utter a low growl behind him. Rion turned and instantly took a step back while he sharply exhaled in surprise.

Standing a few yards away from him was Lord Slane. He had been silently observing the oblivious boy for the past few minutes. His pet canis was sitting on its hind legs and continued to snarl menacingly. Slane bent sideways and patted the beast on its head.

Rion's eyes were almost bulging from their sockets as he continued to backpedal, lightly hitting his back on the carved black wall behind him. "Who are y-you?"

Slane smiled, showing the terrified boy a glimpse of his sharp teeth. "Allow me to introduce myself. I am Lord Slane, chief executor of the Grand Magus. You on the other hand, well, I know you were from Doss, and I have been searching for you for a long, long time."

The boy was breathing so rapidly that he had begun to hyperventilate. "W-what d-do you want?"

Slane pointed at him. "Why, you, of course."

Miri had hurriedly gone down the stone steps, but the area she had run into was unfamiliar to her. Despite being on the ground level of the structure, she was hopelessly lost. While it might have been more prudent for her to run back upstairs and make her way from where she had previously come from, her panic caused her to run through several more darkened corridors that twisted and turned until she could no longer backtrack her way out. Her concern for the boy nevertheless spurned her onwards from one room to the next, hoping that the gods would grant her enough good fortune so as to stumble upon Rion and get him to safety.

The fading light still gave her enough illumination to dash through the numerous rooms and adjoining tunnels. She must have sprinted through at least two dozen hallways, barely stopping just to see if she could find any signs of the boy's passage. The room that she was in had two adjoining corridors to her side, one of the passageways was substantially larger than the other and she could see a massive room at the far end of it. Figuring that Rion would prefer the larger places since they had more carved glyphs on them, she quickly dashed through the bigger passageway and ended up in a great hall, not much similar to the one where they had entered in earlier that day, only this room had an open ceiling, with the second floor gallery just five yards above the ground. But this time she realized that there were others already waiting, her mindsense detected a few stray thoughts coming from the shadowy recesses near two other adjacent passageways at the opposite end of the hall. Miri stopped at the edge of the sloping corridor as two men stepped out from the gloom, into her view.

They both wore black cloaks. The first man was quite tall, with an impressive red beard on his chin. The other man wore a metal mask over the top part of his face. Both were armed, the bearded one had a large metal axe in his hands, while the masked man gripped a steel sword. Miri could tell they wore armor underneath their cloaks as well.

The bearded man stood near the center of the hall. He glared at her with eyes as cold as the night. "Put down your spear."

Miri held her spear horizontally, ready for anything as she began to concentrate on her Vis. "Only after you put your weapon down first."

The man with the mask took a few steps forward as he got closer to the other Magus. "There are two of us. One Striga cannot possibly defeat two Magi."

Miri bent her knees as she got into a fighting stance. "It remains to be seen, does it not?"

The bearded man hissed as he threw off his cloak with one hand. Miri was right, he was wearing some sort of protection underneath. She could see riveted metal plates that had been sewn into his thick leather jacket. If she was going to attack him properly, she would need to strike at his vital areas that were not covered by the armor, a tricky proposition. The other man also threw off his own cloak, revealing a similar type of armor. Both men began to move in different directions, hoping to catch her in between their widening circle.

Just as the battle was about to begin, there was a loud shout coming from the darkened corridor behind the man wearing the mask. Both Magi immediately took a step back as they relaxed their stances. Miri stayed where she was, ready for anything. She could have easily turned around and ran back into the corridor she had come from, but it was clear that the people who were about to enter the room had other plans.

Slane and his pet canis emerged from the corridor at the far side of the hall, laughing whimsically as he pushed at Rion out in front of him, forcing the boy into the room. "Well, well, well! Looks like we are all finally here!"

Miri's heart began to pound. They had the boy. "Rion, are you alright?"

Rion looked around nervously as Slane prodded him further into center the cavernous room. "Y-yes."

"Of course, he is alright. If I had wanted to kill him, he would be already dead," Slane said. "Allow me to introduce our little group here. I am Lord Slane, high executor of-"

Miri cut him off. "I know who you are. I sensed the surface thoughts of your Magus over there," she said, pointing at Turru. "You are Slane, the masked one is called Turru, and that big brute is Baradine."

Slane was taken aback. He gave a menacing glance to Turru before returning his stare at Miri once more. He had not been used to surprises like that, and his anger nearly made him lose concentration over his Vis.

Turru himself looked surprised, even though his mask covered half his face. "Lord Slane, s-she is lying. My thought defenses are still up-"

Slane held up a gauntleted hand to silence him. "No more excuses, Turru, your failure has been noted."

Miri just kept quiet. Her mindsense had detected a momentary lapse in Turru's concentration when Slane made his appearance, and she was able to slip through his lackey's mental armor to delve a quick look into Turru's memory pool. It was clear that they had slaughtered the entire tribe after she had left the settlement. Her own Vis had momentarily ebbed when she felt the pain of loss, but she quickly shunted it away. To reminisce about her murdered friends would be fatal at this point in time. Miri kept channeling her Vis to build up her mental reserves, her desire for revenge tempered with the concern for the boy's well being.

Slane kept one hand on the boy's shoulder. "Well, now that you know who we are, why do you not tell us who you are?"

"Why do you need to know my name?" Miri asked.

"I believe in courtesy," Slane said. "It is simply good manners to know who one is speaking to, is it not? Since you are from the wastes, I had thought that formal greetings are the norm in situations such as this."

"Very well," Miri said tersely. "I am Miri, former protector of the Arum Navar. That boy is named Rion, and he is under my protection. I ask that you let him go."

Slane chuckled. "Former protector? Oh, that is good. Do you know what became of your tribe, Miri of the Arum Navar? They were all killed because of your defiance of the Magi. From what that cowardly elder told me, you murdered our seeker in cold blood. Is that not true?"

Rion let out a shriek as soon as he heard Slane mention the fate of the settlement. The entire tribe was killed because of him. Even though he was exhausted, tears began to drip down his cheeks.

Miri shook her head. She knew that Slane was taunting them, evoking the loss of their tribe to make them mentally vulnerable. Miri used her Vis to calm herself down and she put away the agonizing memory of the loss of her mother for another time. Right now she needed to stay focused if she was to survive. "No, it is not. Your seeker violated the oath of peace and was killed for it. Your patrol has violated the laws of Karma for murdering my tribe. Even if I fall, I am sure that the gods will exact retribution for what you have done."

All three Magi started laughing. Miri sent a calming thought over to Rion's mind, mentally telling him that it was not his fault. She sensed the boy's regret, and used her Vis to alleviate him. Her mental tendrils also drifted over to their opponents as she probed for any potential weaknesses.

Slane's laughter was loudest. He didn't believe in the gods at all, and he found it ridiculous that anyone would think that he would bow down to an ancient curse. The best way to deal with superstitious people was to mock their gods, he believed. "If the gods were truly against my actions, they would have killed me a long time ago. As it happens, I believe I am blessed by them in fact." His tone was flippant, for he believed in mentally toying with his opponents before battle, in order to throw off their concentration. "Look at what the gods have done for me now, they have delivered to me my quarry- this boy, and they have afforded me the opportunity to battle with a mighty Striga. I must say, it has been a long time since I fought against one."

"Let me take her," Baradine said.

"Then let us do this the old way," Miri said to Slane. "You against me. The winner gets Rion, the rest leave in peace."

The canis started growling as it shifted its forepaws back and forth, raking its claws on the stone floor. Slane gestured at the beast to remain calm, and it did. He had an overwhelming advantage against this woman, but he somehow sensed that he would lose respect from his men if he decided not to fight.

Nevertheless, he was a practical man, and he hated having to use too much effort, especially when he didn't have to. "Very astute. You realize that the odds are against you, so you demand a fair duel," he said. "On the other hand, I have quite a significant edge against you and I shall not squander it."

"Then you are a coward," Miri said.

Slane chuckled again. She was very good indeed. This Striga was goading him into anger. He felt a begrudging admiration for her boldness and tenacity. "Desperate words, from a desperate woman. Since you seem to be quite intelligent, I shall offer you the promise of safe passage. If you walk away and let us have the boy, I shall spare your life. This is the best proposal you could ever get from me, so do not take this decision lightly."

"You slaughtered my entire tribe," Miri hissed. "And you expect me to trust you on your word?"

"True, you will be bound to my whims," Slane said. "But it is better to risk staying alive as opposed to being killed in battle that one cannot possibly win, is it not?"

Miri's face was a mask of stone. "I think it is more prudent for you and your men to walk away, and I will spare your lives instead."

Slane smirked as he shook his head. "Well, it seems that all this talk has gotten us nowhere. So it means we fight. I do think it is better this way."

Rion tried to sprint towards Miri, but Slane held out his hand and the boy was violently thrown into the base of the floor. Rion's forehead was slammed violently against the smooth stones and the boy was quickly unconscious, blood oozing from his nose as he lay still. Slane then gestured at his pet canis to attack Miri as he drew his sword. The four-legged beast snarled as it dashed forward, but Miri used her mindsense on it. The canis suddenly stopped, turned around and began growling at the other Magi. Baradine and Turru suddenly stopped their advance and looked at their leader.

Slane's eyes were bulging out of their sockets. He had not expected this. He bent low and smiled at his pet while the canis began to approach him instead. "Calm down, my beloved beast. I am your master!"

Miri extended her mental tendrils right into the beast's set of instincts. Deep in the canis's garden of memories was a time when Slane had slapped it around to teach it how to sit properly. Miri focused on that one memory and increased the beast's aggression by a hundredfold. She amplified the animal's senses from being fearful of its master to one of hate and vengeance. The canis snarled malevolently as it launched itself at Slane, who used his mindforce to throw the animal up into the air just before its jaws got hold of his throat.

Baradine had had enough. He knew that the best way to defeat an enemy was to cut off its head. He used his Vis to leap up three yards into the air. He swung his axe in a downward strike, hoping to cleave Miri in two. But the Striga refocused her mindsense to bore through his lowered mental defenses as she moved sideways. Baradine screamed as the pain receptors in his head overloaded his senses. The large Magus fell to the floor on his knees, his axe clattering beside him. Miri thrust at him with her spear, but he used his reserves of Vis to push himself sideways at the last second, and Miri's attack narrowly missed his exposed neck.

Turru had been confused for a brief moment as he saw Slane trying to use his mindforce to ward off an attack by his own pet at him. Baradine was struggling with the Striga and he was unsure as to who he should help. A part of him believed that he could easily dispatch Slane's crazed canis, but he would have to answer for killing his leader's beloved pet. After deciding to finally help Baradine instead, he gathered his Vis to launch himself into the air to land directly behind that accursed Striga and finish her once and for all. But just as he was about to activate his mindforce, he failed to notice a teen girl dropping down behind him from the upper ceiling.

From her hidden perch, Nyx felt her whole body shake upon hearing that the entire tribe had been slaughtered, and she had nearly lashed out with her Vis right at that very moment. But Miri had been able to sense her presence above them and had instructed her not to reveal herself until the right moment. When Miri had turned the thoughts of that strange beast to attack its master instead, she knew her time had come and she quickly jumped down, right behind the Magus who wore the mask.

Turru suddenly sensed another presence behind him and turned around. Nyx's rage at the thought of the fate of the tribe had now overcome her reluctance, and she grabbed the back of his head and drove the point of her bone dagger underneath the Magus's exposed chin, then she used all her strength to drive the knife up to its hilt. Turru's eyes opened wide as the point of the blade passed through his tongue and into the base of his brain. The Magus fell on his knees and began to choke on his own blood. Nyx noticed Turru had dropped his sword, so she picked it up. Now the battle was even.

Miri and Baradine were at a standoff. The Magus had thought about using his mindforce to crush her skull with just his mere thought, but he was wary of shifting his Vis away from his mental defenses, lest the Striga use her mental powers to overcome his mind once more. Feeling that he had the physical edge over her, Baradine shouted out a war cry as he stepped forward, swinging his axe sideways and hoping to get a piece of her torso. Miri stepped back in order to give her spear an advantage, the axe blade whizzing by ever closer. Baradine kept moving forward, hoping to trap her against the sides of the room so he could shatter her spear and finish her off.

Slane was feeling a mixture of irritation and concern as the canis kept lunging at him, as he used his Vis to throw the beast to the other side of the hallway, but it seemed to make the animal even more determined to attack him. He could not bring himself to kill his beloved pet, so he used his mindforce to keep it at bay. Suddenly, he sensed the slashing of a sword blade as it connected with his back, ripping through his cloak before being stopped by the steel cuirass he wore on his chest and torso. He quickly whirled around and was able to parry another attack with his own blade. Standing in front of him was another female, but this one seemed somewhat younger, and she had Turru's sword.

Nyx cursed at herself for trying to slash the man at his back when she should have swung for his head instead. Now that he was on guard, she had lost the element of surprise. Nevertheless, she was more determined than ever to kill him. "This is for my tribe!" she shouted as she hacked towards his neck.

Slane's rage had finally reached its tipping point. "You are another Striga," he said as he parried another blow with his sword. "There are two of you!"

"Die, you piss drinking dungbug!" Nyx said as she gritted her teeth and used her Vis to smash through his mental defenses while at the same time swinging her sword, hoping the dual attack would be enough to overwhelm him.

Slane had anticipated it as he kept his thought blocks near their limits. He still had some Vis in reserve, so he used it all to redirect Nyx's sword swing towards the canis coming in from the opposite direction. Nyx cried out as she seemingly swung her sword too far, and its blade sliced into the canis, severing its spine. The animal cried out as it fell onto the stone floor, its four legs convulsing in its death throes. Nyx had overextended herself and her body was wide open to attack. Just as she drew back the blade for a parry, Slane crouched down and used his sword in an upward thrust. The point of his blade penetrated just beneath her ribcage and Slane used an extra bit of Vis to drive the edge in deeper, slicing through her lungs and heart. Nyx fell to her knees and dropped her weapon as Slane withdrew his blade from her body.

"No!" Miri screamed as she saw Nyx being mortally wounded from the corner of her eye. Baradine sensed her desperation as he stooped low and lunged forward, this time swinging his axe towards her legs. Miri deflected the swing with the shaft of her spear, then she kicked him in the face since he was close enough. Blood spurted from Baradine's broken nose as he staggered backwards. Miri sent a spear thrust into his right leg, just where his exposed knee was. The spear point tore through the knee cartilage and severely injured the joint before Miri quickly withdrew it, ready to attack again. Baradine screamed in pain as he fell to one knee, his blood soaking the floor around him. The bearded Magus held out his hand for one last attack as he shifted his entire command of Vis into a giant, unseen vise to crush Miri's head in.

Miri suddenly felt something invisible gripping the sides of her head as the pain in her temples increased. Baradine was grimacing at her and gesturing, it was clear he would either strangle her neck or cave her skull in, using his sheer force of will. Her vision became blurry and it felt like a giant boulder was crushing her head. Miri fought the urge to fall down on her knees as her body began trembling from the pain. Sensing that Baradine's mental defenses were down, she refocused her own Vis despite the pain she was feeling, creating a small bundle of reverse agony which she then sent directly into his nervous system. Baradine suddenly lost his concentration as the pain in his torn knee was unbearable. Miri quickly gathered her own thoughts as the pain in her head had subsided, and she dashed forward, plunging the point of her spear through the bridge of Baradine's nose. The spearhead tore through Baradine's eyes and all the way into the back of his skull. Miri fell on her knees beside the dying Magus while using her mental disciplines to recover her senses.

Slane knelt down beside the dying canis. As he looked into its whimpering eyes, he could once again feel the love and devotion of his pet. In its final moments, Slane realized that the Striga's hold over it had abated, and it was back to being his beloved possession for one final time. The canis gurgled one last cough of blood and then its eyes glazed over. Slane fought back tears as he stood up and walked over to the dying young Striga nearby. He could see her breathing had slowed and her life was leaving her.

Nyx tired to say something to him as she lay on her back, but she just ended up coughing out more blood instead. Slane wiped away the moisture in his eyes as he looked down on her, then he swung his blade down onto her neck, severing her windpipe and spine, but leaving a little bit of skin at the back when his blade bounced off the wet floor. As he brought his sword back up to a guard position, he saw the older Striga on her hands and knees across the other side of the room, beside the now dead Baradine. Recovering his Vis, he just stood there, waiting.

Exhaling deeply as the pain still throbbed in the sides of her head, Miri pulled her spear out from the dead Magus and turned around. Nyx was dead, she had already accepted that, but it didn't make the pain she felt any easier to swallow. There would be time to mourn her passing in the coming days, but she had to finish this battle first. She would avenge her, along with Jinn, Devos and the rest of the tribe. Miri focused her mindsense with her desire for revenge, rechanneling her Vis into a powerful reserve.

Slane threw off the remains of his tattered cloak while he faced her. "It looks like you got your wish after all, Striga. It has now come to this duel."

Miri could see that Rion was still knocked out cold. The boy let out a soft groan while lying stunned at the floor. "No more talk," she said while hefting her spear.

Slane extended his Vis, using his mindforce to sense for any loose stone in the redoubt. In less than a second, he soon realized that there were plenty of movable blocks in the upper gallery of the ceiling above him. Miri took a few steps forward, hoping to get in range with her spear while trying to anticipate his moves. Her mental tendrils were trying to get around his thought blocks, but Slane's defenses were formidable, and he countered her probing by singing nonsensical chants in his head.

Just as she got to within range of her spear, Miri suddenly heard a loud, grating noise coming from above her. The moment she glanced upwards, Miri saw a huge block of stone crashing towards her. The Striga instantly rolled sideways on the floor, narrowly evading a chunk of rock that fell onto the spot where she had been standing on. The crashing slab reverberated across the entire floor, and the whole building shook for a brief second.

Using his Vis to propel him in the air, Slane quickly leapt up and landed close to Miri. The executor thrust his sword, hoping to stab her in the neck, but Miri was able to react in time despite being off balance from the crashing of the slab nearby. Her spear shaft partially deflected his attack, driving it to her side as the upper part of the blade tore into her leather cuirass, but the blow was too weak to penetrate the hard leather. Nevertheless, she staggered backwards from his determined attack. Since he was close, Slane elbowed her chin, which sent Miri reeling in reverse, and she crashed down onto the floor. Swinging his sword in a return arc, he drove it down towards her chest while giving it an extra surge of Vis, hoping that there was enough force in his attack to penetrate her chest armor. Miri was able to react in time as she moved her body sideways, but the thrust of the blade caught the side of her arm and it tore a bloody gash as the sword nearly impaled her.

Miri screamed in pain as she rolled away from him. Slane moved in step with her as he wanted to keep her close. He had the advantage since she was on the ground. As Miri held the shaft of her weapon sideways to parry his thrust, Slane used his mindforce to hold the spear down and swung the sharp side of his blade against the shaft of the weapon. This time, Miri's spear was not in a deflecting angle and the steel edge of the sword tore through the ancient, lacquered wood and splintered it. As Miri rolled away for the second time, she realized her spear had been broken in two.

Getting up, Miri now held the lower part of the broken shaft on one hand and had half a spear in the other. Slane used his mindforce to slide forward right in front of her and made a downward swing, aiming for her head, but Miri used both the broken shaft and the half spear in a cross parry and trapped it. Before Slade could withdraw his blade, Miri kicked him in the groin before backing away. She started moving sideways, hoping to get at one of the other weapons lying on the floor.

Slane shrugged as he brought his blade in a guard position once more. His attacks against her had begun to weaken her Vis, and he could now channel his reserves to destroy her. "That kick of yours did not hurt, you know. We Magi have nothing down there."

Miri was only a few steps away from where Nyx's body lay. She saw the sword on the ground and made a dash for it. Slane gestured with his free hand and Nyx's dagger suddenly rose up from the blood soaked floor and whirled through the air, piercing the back of Miri's right leg. The Striga screamed in pain as she fell onto the floor, her broken spear still in her hands. Her concentration broke down, and her mental attacks against him quickly dissipated.

"Oh, so you wanted that sword then?" Slane said as he gestured with his hand once more. The other sword suddenly flew up into the air, as if wielded by an invisible spirit. The moment Miri stood up on one leg, the sword turned horizontal, its blade in line with her body and it suddenly flew right at her. Miri sensed it coming and turned away, but she reacted too slowly and the point of the blade ripped through the leather armor with terrific force, impaling itself on her stomach.

Miri fell on her knees as she tried to pull the sword out using both hands, but some sort of spectral force kept the blade firmly lodged in her abdomen. Blood began to pour from her mouth. The pain was making everything hazy and she could barely move her arms.

"I have yet to lose a battle," Slane said as he sheathed his own sword, this time gesturing with both hands. Miri was suddenly floating in the air, the sword still lodged in her belly. "This is where it ends," he said. "I did so enjoy our duel, Striga, but as you can see, my Vis is superior to yours. Farewell."

Miri was losing consciousness. The last thing she sensed was being thrust out of the window and falling towards the sun baked ground below.

## Chapter 19

Rion woke up as the hot currents whipped around his face. While gathering his senses, he felt being rocked back and forth, caught in a sensation of movement. He opened his eyes and realized his hands were tied behind his back. He was on his side, lying beside a tall metal spar with a large leather sail harnessing the gusts of heated air above him. The terrain slid past him as the vessel he was traveling in continued its slow movement across the flatlands. Judging from the position of the sun up above, it must have been around midmorning. The boy tilted his head up and looked around. He was lying on the top platform of the sand sail, with a flooring of leather and furs serving as a barrier between his bare skin and the hot metal hull of the ship. Standing right behind him was Slane. The Magus held two lines of leather ropes in his hands, while shifting the angle of the sail in order to steer the vessel.

Slane quickly saw that the boy was awake. "You are now a guest in my vessel, boy."

Rion looked up at him. There was some dried blood on his upper lip, but his nose had apparently been healed because he could breathe through it again. "Where is Nyx and Miri?"

Slane smiled and shook his head while concentrating on the sail. He could see the upper spires of Lethe in the distant horizon. "Both Strigas are dead, boy. You belong to me now. I must admit that it was a rather … memorable battle, perhaps the best I have ever experienced. In the end, my power was stronger than theirs."

Rion looked down on the flooring. His lips trembled. The ones who protected him all this time were gone. He was alone once more. Soon, his shoulders began to shake and he let out a dry moan, for he was too exhausted to shed any more tears.

Slane could see that they would make it to the last city within two more days of sailing. Since there were no obstacles directly in front of the vessel, he didn't need to steer any further for now. There were small rock outcroppings nearby, but he could easily steer the land ship in between them. The Magus tied a knot around both lines and hooked their ends near the edge of the mast. Now that both his hands were free, Slane moved forward until he stood over the boy. "Behave, and I will let you live. If you attempt to try and escape from me, then the wastes will swallow you up."

Rion grimaced as he stared into the man's crimson colored pupils. "I do not ever want to lie on that stone slab again! I would rather die!"

Slane knelt down grabbed the boy by the throat, choking him lightly. "You are to cease your complaints. Do not worry, there is no need to place you on a slab to draw out your blood any longer. All the Magi in the citadel where you came from are dead too."

Rion could hardly breathe as the gauntleted hand constricted his windpipe. "What… do you want… from me?"

"This," Slane said as he took his hand away from the boy's throat and used it to draw a dagger from his side. The Magus then sliced a deep cut along Rion's chest. The boy cried out as Slane scraped the blood off his body with the flat part of the blade. Slane brought up the still dripping dagger to his mouth and licked the crimson drops from it with his forked tongue.

The Magus tilted his head back and closed his eyes for a few seconds as the boy's potent blood seeped through his body. He had just started ingesting Rion's blood since early morning, and already he could feel a tingling where his loins once were. Soon enough, he knew he would be a whole man once again, it was just a matter of time. All his life he hated being emasculated, it was a rage that boiled inside of him for as long as he could remember. Slane used his shame as motivation to fuel his extraordinary rise through the ranks of the Magi order. Now that there was no one left to stop him, he would forge his own way across the barren lands, perhaps he would even found a mighty empire of his own.

Rion whimpered as the pain in his chest began to subside. Within minutes the wound had sealed and all that remained was a few drops of dried blood on his chest. Slane looked at the boy's torso closely while running his hand along where the wound used to be. He could not even see any scarring. It was like the work of the gods. This boy was truly special.

Slane rubbed the dried blood on his gauntlet. "See? Your gifts are a blessing from the gods themselves. Your very blood is potent enough to restore my loins and keep me young forever. With your capabilities and my Vis, we can rule this world together!"

Rion frowned and shook his head. "You are an evil Magus! I do not want to go with you."

A flash of anger surged in Slane's mind as he grabbed the boy by his throat once more. "You have no choice! You must either learn to respect my wishes, or you will face a life of endless suffering."

Rion clenched his teeth. If all he could hope for was a life of a being slave at this man's side, then he preferred not to live at all. The boy's thoughts turned from fear into anger. Suddenly he felt time slowing down as something began to stir inside of him. A new sense of awareness began to manifest in his own mind. A power that had previously been dormant had now arisen. Rion could now perceive the directional shifts of the invisible winds around him. His consciousness traveled all along the entire hull of the sand sail. Rion could feel the hundreds of metal nails and screws holding the vessel together. The rolling wheels along the soft sand began to sing out to him, the leather sail high above felt like a living being. All he had to do now was to talk to them, and they would do his bidding.

Slane noticed that the boy's eyes had a blank look to them. His eyebrows furrowed in a brief flurry of confusion. From his own experience, he knew that only the ones with the gift of Vis could have such a faraway look. "What are you thinking about?"

The boy didn't listen to him as he began to gather up his own Vis. It was like scooping handfuls of ether and tightly rolling it up until the whole bundle became more powerful. His first impulse was to try it out. Rion focused his energies on the knots that Slane had tied around the mast to keep the leather ropes fastened. Using his awareness of each time the lines had been twisted together, he used his mindforce to untangle the closest ropes.

After a few seconds, the vessel suddenly began to veer off to the side as several lines that held the sail had unexpectedly uncoiled. Slane stood up in surprise and he nearly fell off the platform before grabbing at one of the metal support struts along the sides. He glared at the boy. "You! You are doing this! Cease your actions or I shall slay you!"

Rion closed his eyes and concentrated once more. He sensed a slightly loose pin along one of the axles that held a portion of the wheels along the side. It had been pounded in by hammers long ago and even though it was slightly unhinged, it would take a powerful amount of force to remotely dislodge it. Rion gathered up his reserves of Vis and consolidated it all before unleashing it against the metal pin. The sand sail abruptly started to shake as the pin was loosened.

Slane grabbed at the loose lines and gathered them before attempting to knot them back to the mast. Just as he was about to tie them together, the entire ship suddenly tilted sideways and he was thrown onto the dusty flats below. The Magus instantly reacted, grabbing at the rope still in his hand as he was dragged along the ground. He had been in a relaxed mood since that morning and he had not prepared a reserve of Vis. Slane roared with rage as he held onto the ropes to give himself a bit more time.

Rion had seen what had happened as he used his mindforce to tilt the sail into the wind. He could see a number of rock outcroppings ahead and it was clear that the sand sail was on a collision course. All he had to do now was to keep the Magus distracted, and he could make his escape.

Slane cried out in pain as his body was dragged through the dusty flats. He had taken off his armor and stored it in the vessel's cabin. As he tried to climb up the hull using the ropes, his right boot was torn away by the increasing speed of the sand sail. Slane slipped and was nearly dragged underneath the stone wheels while he held onto the ropes for dear life.

Rion stood up and used his mindforce to untangle his restraints. In a few seconds, the leather straps that had bound his arms behind his back fell to the floor in a tangled heap. The boy concentrated on keeping the speed of the vessel up when he noticed that Slane was only a few feet away from being caught by one of the wheels. The boy held out his hand and used his Vis to push the Magus down. If he could shove him just a few feet further along the sides of the hull, then it would be a sure death for his enemy.

Just as Slane used his Vis to leap up into safety, a counter force suddenly drove his chest back down onto the side of the vessel. He had to bend his knee in order not to get caught by the massive stone wheel just less than a foot away from him. He looked up and saw the boy's eyes and he knew. "Curse you! I shall make you suffer before you die!"

Rion was using all his power, but he could feel that the Magus was overcoming his Vis. He tried to keep Slane pinned down along the side of the ship, but his enemy had more experience using his own mindforce, and the boy could no longer hold him. Slane roared with rage as he overcame the power holding him down by sheer force of will, his body now slowly rising up into the air, away from the spinning wheels and slowly levitating towards the boy. Slane snarled as he unsheathed his sword. Rion realized he could not do battle with the Magus directly so he used his remaining Vis to dislodge the ropes that tied the sail to the mast. As Slane got to within striking distance, the sail suddenly unfurled and the land ship plunged headlong into the side of a boulder jutting out from the ground in front of it. The front part of the hull collapsed inwards and both man and boy were thrown violently from the platform and onto the surrounding rocks nearby.

For what seemed like an eternity, all she could feel was the cold stone ground beneath her back. Was death nothing more than a long sleep, or was it merely a prelude to a heavenly afterlife that the gods had promised? The answers were not forthcoming as her senses slowly began to instill awareness back into her tired, injured body. In time, the coldness of the stones was replaced by waves of heat that cascaded along her sides. She sensed a painful tightness in her abdomen when her sense of touch returned. Her ears soon began to tell her that there was someone nearby, shuffling back and forth. Her sense of smell indicated a blending of sickly sweet algae and fungi, the kind of things that Elder Zedne used to prescribe when someone in the tribe was sick or injured.

Miri opened her eyes and saw the glowing embers of a small fire being tended to beside her. She tried to sit up, but a sharp pain in her stomach kept her lying on the ground. Crouching nearby was a figure wearing a crimson robe, the shadows keeping its true form hidden from her view. She was in a stone room, and the glyphs on the walls seemed to indicate she was still somewhere within the Black Redoubt. The area had large windows that revealed the night sky. The robed figure sensed that she had finally awakened, and started shuffling towards her.

Miri's memories quickly came back. Her eyes opened wide. Nyx had told her that she dreamed of a red robed man out in the desert. What Miri had never told her was that she had the exact same dream as well. She tilted her head and found that the stranger had knelt down beside her. When Miri spoke, her mouth was dry and her voice raspy. "Who a-are you?"

Two leathery hands pulled back the crimson hood, revealing an old woman's wrinkled face. Wisps of silvery hair hung limply on her head. She gave Miri a toothless smile. "I have come by many names. If you must call me something, then I go by Neth."

"I thought I was dead," Miri said before grimacing from the sudden jolt of pain in her stomach.

"You must lie still for the time being," Neth said as she held her right hand a few inches above Miri's torso. "Your spine was nearly severed, and I needed to rest before resuming the final part of the healing ritual. We might as well finish this now."

Miri was confused. "What?"

Neth gestured at her to be quiet. Miri tilted her to her chest and gasped as she saw a raw, gaping wound in the middle of her stomach. The old woman closed her eyes and murmured a chant in a long dead language. Miri's eyes nearly bulged out of their sockets as she saw droplets of blood seeping out of Neth's outstretched fingers. The drips of crimson floated in the air and soon became a trail of fluid as it slowly flowed down into Miri's wound. The Striga suddenly felt light headed as the old woman's blood mingled with her own, repairing torn muscle, organs and tissue. Neth looked to be in a trance as her blood continued to sew up Miri's stomach until all that was needed was to close the torn skin on the wound. As the fire began to die down, Neth opened her eyes once more and turned away, her heavy breathing indicating exhaustion. Miri looked at her stomach and was astonished to see that the wound had somehow completely healed. She wanted to thank the old woman, but her eyelids suddenly felt heavy and sleep quickly overtook her.

When Miri woke up once more, it was nearly morning. The fire was still smoldering as she sat up and noticed Neth sitting cross-legged nearby, doing a meditative ritual. Miri tried to stand up and nearly fell back down on her first try. Her legs were still weak and her mind was unfocused. She gathered up her Vis, and used it to instill discipline in her body's coordination. When she tried standing up a second time, she succeeded. Looking around, she noticed her backpack was lying on the ground nearby.

Neth opened her eyes but remained seated. "The boy is not far from here. He has finally used his Vis, and he is hiding from the little Magus."

Miri looked at her arm. The gash from Slane's sword had also been healed, leaving a faint scar. The third wound in her leg was also fully healed. "Why are you helping me?"

"You are no longer the protector of the Arum Navar. You are now the protector of that boy. You must get him to Lethe, for it is fated that the great change cannot come about without him. The child is not a mere Magus, he is something more."

Miri began to sob as she sat back down. "I am no one's protector. I have failed my tribe, and I have failed my friends. Nyx, Jinn, and Devos are all dead because of me. My mother is dead because of me."

"This place has not had any visitors for almost two thousand cycles," Neth said. "Your party was the first, then the Magi came after you. You led a long journey across dangerous lands in which many have tried before and failed, for that you are to be commended."

Miri shook her head slowly. The tears continued. "I led them all to die. How can you extol someone who did that?"

"Do not let their deaths be in vain," Neth said. "You have come this far, it is not too late to fulfill your task."

"My task? All I did was to follow in the footsteps of an old legend, a tale that might not even be true! And now my friends are dead, and the boy I was tasked to safeguard is in the hands of my enemy. How could I possibly do anything else?"

"The tale of Kaelr was not a mere legend, it was based on events that really happened," Neth said. "Before he ventured onwards to the last city, he left me here, for he knew I could no longer be by his side."

Miri was shocked. "What?"

"I am sure you have listened to many tales about him, but there were many stories that were never written down," Neth said. "So many memories, all lost through time."

Miri crawled forward, closer to her. She looked at the old woman closely. "Y-you knew Kaelr the Magus?"

"I fought against him once," the old woman said wistfully. "I had nearly killed him. Just as I was about to deliver the deathblow, I happened to look into his mind just to understand why he would even dare to initiate the great rebellion. What I found astonished me, and I spared him."

Miri's jaw dropped. She couldn't believe what she was hearing. "You are a Gorgon, are you not?"

Neth turned and looked at the smoldering fire. "I was one of the first three. We ruled the world for countless generations. They say that you get wiser through time, but that is not true. Memories fade, days simply come and go. In the end, it is but a grey, dreary existence. I can no longer count the passing of cycles. The world is nothing but blinding dust and lifeless stone. My one longing was to be reunited with him, but he told me I must wait. I had to stay here until the child and his mother crossed the silent lands and ventured forth into this forsaken place."

Miri remembered Devos's final tale. "The teller of my tribe said that when Kaelr had died at the gates of Lethe, he had foretold of a boy and his mother would come and succeed at the task he had set out to do. But he never mentioned what that task was."

"You must take the boy to the Maker of Entropy," Neth said. "For he lies beyond the last city."

"If you were one of the first Gorgons and Kaelr started the rebellion, why did you help him? What thoughts did you discern from his mind that made you change your ways?"

The old woman smiled. "Love. When I delved into his mind, I realized that he rebelled out of love. It was in that instance I joined his cause and fought my other sisters. I helped to make him a better Magus, and he aided me to become a more powerful Gorgon. In the end, we vanquished the others, but we both knew there was one final task to be done."

Miri was still trying to piece it all together. "What task was that? What could this Maker do?"

"The Maker of Entropy is the key to restoring this world to its former splendor," Neth said. "The lands around us were once covered in oceans of water, teeming with life. The dry areas were fertile, with beasts and plants. There was food for all and people would thrive. A great catastrophe had happened, and its true cause was lost in the eons of time. The world must be reborn again or else the remaining ones will die."

"So that was why Kaelr decided to travel to Lethe after winning the great rebellion? To restore the world as it was?"

Neth nodded. "But we knew he was not to be the chosen one, it would be someone else. Kaelr tasked me to await the mother, while he went ahead to prepare the way. I have been here ever since."

"Were you the one in our dreams?"

"In a sense, it was I who had guided you to the Black Redoubt," the old woman said. "I used my Vis to send messages into your dreams. I stayed hidden away when you battled the Magi, and waited until the remaining one took the boy. Now that I have restored your broken body, my task is done." Neth began to shudder, and she fell over by her side.

Miri cried out as she quickly moved over to where the old woman lay. She used her mindsense to try and probe for any injuries, but her mental tendrils were telling her that Neth was already dead, it seemed that her body functions had ceased a long time ago, and it was only the Gorgon's Vis that had somehow kept her alive. "Wait," Miri said as she cradled Neth's head in her arms. "You cannot die! There are still so many questions I must ask you!"

Neth's eyes opened slightly. Her lifeforce was slowly draining away. "At last I shall join my beloved Kaelr. It has been far too long. Our lives have been separated by uncountable cycles. It is good to finally let go. I do not know what lies beyond the black entryway, but I go with no further regrets."

"Please," Miri pleaded. "This Magus I fought. He defeated me with ease. I-I am not sure I could prevail against him and save the boy."

The old woman smiled faintly. "Your own strength lies within you. The full power of Vis is largely untapped among its practitioners. Let it flow through you like the wind, and you will find a way. Do not let the limits of your body distract you from your discipline, for the mind is always superior to flesh." With a trembling finger, she pointed to the far side of the room. Miri turned and saw a spear lying against the wall. The shaft of the spear had a smoky grey color, while the blade and tip were inky black. "That was Kaelr's weapon. It is made of a substance called korban firb, a material whose manufacture was lost through time. It will neither rust, nor break. A final gift to you. Use it wisely."

Miri held her breath. The spear seemed like it was made from another time. From her vantage point, it looked like the weapon's shaft had some sort of coating on it. "That was Kaelr's spear? He left it here for me? But how could he have known?"

But when she looked down, Miri realized that the old woman was already dead. With trembling lips, Miri gently placed Neth's head back onto the ground and pulled back the hood to cover her face. She knelt down and said a silent prayer to the gods as the sun began its ascent over the horizon. The fire had also burned out, leaving only faint traces of ash.

Miri stood up, walked over to the side of the room and picked up the spear. It was slightly longer than what she was used to, but it also seemed lighter and more maneuverable. Strange glyphs were carved along the shaft and the flat part of the spearhead. Taking the spear with her, Miri bent down and picked up her backpack before leaving the room.

The place seemed familiar to her now as she walked down several flights of stone steps, back to the ground level of the redoubt. It was there that she walked into the hallway where the previous battle had taken place. Miri walked over to Nyx's body and knelt down once more, carefully arranging the girl's arms and placing them together. She then took one of the tattered cloaks on the floor and placed it over the body. Miri made a second prayer to the gods before she finally left the pyramid for good.

# Chapter 20

Rion crept forward as he stayed low along the sides of the crevasse. He had been hiding throughout the day, and the sun was beginning its descent to mark the onset of eventide. The boy remembered Devos, and what they read about the area from the telling stones. It was apparent to him that the tale of Kaelr finally ended in one of these rock formations. A few leagues out in the distance lay the city of Lethe, and the old teller had surmised that there would be a few islands of stone jutting out from the seas of sand that would mark the final resting place of that legendary hero. If Kaelr had a tomb, then it would have to be somewhere nearby.

Ever since the sand sail crashed against the edge of the nearby boulders, Rion had been able to heal his wounds quickly and made a dash towards the numerous gorges and rock formations in an effort to escape from Slane. The boy wasn't sure if the Magus had been hurt at first, but within moments, he heard shouts and curses carried across the winds. It surely meant that Slane was still alive and somewhere close by.

What kept Rion moving was the voice in his head. It started out as a faint whisper, and it sounded similar to Elder Zedne's. The tone was calm, it instructed him to be quiet and stay out of sight, for aid would be coming soon. Rion had been scared at first when the voice began speaking to him, but he soon surmised that it may have been coming from the red robed woman that he had been dreaming about, ever since they made this journey out into the wastes. The sense that he was not alone, that someone was helping him, gave the boy an added confidence. If it were not for that voice, he might have given up already.

Rion had made it up on a rock ledge, and carefully lay on his chest while he tried to peer down at the wadi below him. He had heard some footsteps nearby and was hoping it was an ally coming to help. But as he took a peep, he quickly saw it was not a potential savior, but his enemy a few yards below. The boy bit his lip and slid his head back, out of sight.

Slane turned when he noticed a slight sense of fiction on one of the nearby rock ledges above him. The Magus grimaced as the pain in his twisted ankle kept him distracted. When the vessel collided with the boulder earlier that day, he had been thrown clear and onto the sand, but was able to use his mindforce to cushion the impact. His quick actions saved him from grievous injury, but he still hurt his ankle badly. Slane hadn't noticed where the boy had ran off to, though he knew that the child had to be nearby, for the flatlands all around offered no cover from the sun and his own eyes. He had been walking around for hours with one boot on, hoping for a sign of Rion's tracks. Slane had a feeling that the boy's latent mindforce was at work, and Rion may have been using his Vis to cover any of his footsteps with loose sand to hide his trail. The lad was clever, but he was even more so, and Slane was confident he would find him soon.

His mouth was parched and he swallowed painfully. Slane could have gone back and retrieved some water from the wrecked land ship, but he felt that he needed to find the boy first. He had been searching along the same area for the entire day now, and still no sign of Rion. When he realized that the sun had begun to set, his frustration increased by the minute. Each time he rounded the side of a boulder, he had expected to find the boy, but every time he looked at a potential hiding place, there was nothing there but sand and stone. He just didn't believe that the boy could have disappeared into thin air, so he kept on searching.

The trail in front of him ended on an incline, leading up to another set of rock cliffs above. When he took the first step, his ankle gave way and he fell onto his knees. Slane gritted his sharp teeth as the pain in his ankle flared up.

"Curse you, boy! Show yourself!" he bellowed. "Look around you, there is nothing but empty dust all around, you cannot hide from me forever!"

Slane stood up as his echo reverberated along the rock walls. "Rion! I promise I will not hurt you, boy! Just come on out and we can agree to an accommodation!"

No response. The boy was being stubborn, even though his actions were hopeless. Slane's frustration was now at a tipping point. Rion was making it hard for him, and he promised a brutal punishment for the boy the moment he would catch him.

Despite his sore throat, Slane's voice was roaring. "Rion! This is your last chance! If you do not come out now I will be merciless with your punishment!"

Still nothing. Eventide had finally set in and the area was now bathed in twilight. This would make finding the boy even harder. The moon above was in its full phase, but he would have preferred daylight. The shadows loomed larger now, the stones and boulders even more concealing. As he rubbed his sore ankle, a new thought came onto his mind. Why not use his Vis to help find the boy?

Slane figured there must be a way. All his life, he had trained to use his mindforce on objects and people that he could see with his own eyes. But what if he could use his other senses to guide his Vis instead? Slane narrowed his eyes as he stood at the edge of the gulley. He had been walking up and down along the entire rock formation for hours, and he more or less knew where the numerous trails led to. If the boy kept changing his position in order to avoid him, then Rion must have left some sort of tracks that he could focus on.

Instead of relying on visual clues, Slane began to use his hearing more as he walked silently along the sides of the boulders. If his ears could pick up the slightest sounds of movement, he would use his mind to visualize the area and use his Vis correspondingly. If the boy was carefully moving away from him, then he was sure that Rion would have to keep him in visual sight in order to anticipate where he would be moving to.

Slane momentarily relaxed his visual senses while using his mindforce to feel the grains of sand among the nearby boulders around him. If he had enough power to throw a person fifty yards into the air, then he surely could seep through a few grains of sand and check if they were disturbed due to someone's weight and vibrations.

Sure enough, his ears soon picked up a slight scratching noise somewhere to his right. Closing his eyes, the sound became even more acute now that he knew where to focus his other senses. Within moments, he realized that someone was observing him from a nearby crag. Slane turned and gestured with his hands.

Without warning, Rion was suddenly thrown up into the air. The boy screamed as he dangled upside down. It was as if a giant, unseen hand had plucked him out from his hiding place and presented him before his enemy. The boy thrashed helplessly in midair as he tried to use his own Vis to lower himself down, but he had no reserves left. Rion had steadily been worn out from a lack of rest and water. He was helpless, and Slane knew it.

"I told you that this would be a foregone conclusion, boy," Slane said, his voice now full of confidence once more. "I gave you a chance earlier to come out voluntarily, but you refused. Your stubbornness will cost you."

"Let him go," a voice coming from behind him said.

Slane turned, his Vis momentarily dropping Rion down into the gulley below. Standing on a nearby flat bedrock was Miri. She had taken off her armor and was wearing only her loincloth and bodice. The spear she held in her hands glowed slightly in the moonlight, the carved glyphs in its shaft seemingly energized by the night.

Miri took a step forward as she bent her knees in a fighting position. Her mindsense told her that Rion was stunned from the fall, but he would be alright in a few hour's time. She remembered what the old Gorgon had said. Miri needed to focus on her mind, for it was superior to her body.

Slane was still in a state of shock, but he instinctively drew his sword. "This-this i-is impossible! Y-you are supposed to be dead!"

"The gods brought me back," Miri said tersely. "Once again we shall have to fight for the boy."

Slane frowned. He knew that he had driven the sword into her guts by the use of his Vis, but he couldn't even see the wound he had inflicted the day before. What sort of trickery was this? He felt it was better to make some small talk while he recovered his reserves of Vis. "I am afraid you have me at a disadvantage, Striga. How is it that you were able to recover from that killing wound I had given you?"

"I had an ally who revealed herself after the battle," Miri said.

Slane furrowed his eyebrows. "Who? Another Striga?"

Miri shook her head. "She was much more. A Gorgon."

Slane snorted. She had to be lying. "A …Gorgon? Surely you jest me."

"She happened to be Kaelr's mate," Miri said. "She had been living in that pyramid for eons, for she was fated to wait until we had arrived."

Slane blinked a few times. Had this Striga gone mad? "You are speaking about the ancient tale of Kaelr, the legendary Magus who had begun the great rebellion against the Gorgons? But that happened so long ago!"

"It did. Kaelr was no mere legend. He was a real man."

Slane chuckled. "Did you not listen to your own words? You are describing a tale that occurred eons ago, yet you are telling me that a Gorgon happened to be Kaelr's mate, and she had waited all this time for you to come visit her? Do you truly expect me to believe that?"

"It does not matter. I am here," Miri said.

"Perhaps you are telling the truth. Why would this Gorgon ally with you?"

"She said I was needed to fulfill a prophecy," Miri said.

"And what prophecy is that?"

"In order for this world to be reborn, I must accompany Rion to Lethe," Miri said.

There was a blank look in Slane's eyes. "This world? Reborn? How could that boy possibly do that?"

"I do not know," Miri said. "All I have are my dreams, and the Gorgon who had passed the message to me and my companions. She is gone now, she used the last of her Vis to heal my wounds. All that remains is to fulfill the task before me."

"Let us make a bargain then," Slane said. "We can share the boy. I need his blood to make myself whole again. We can both live for a long time using his vitae. What do you say?"

Miri shook her head slowly. "He is not a slave, nor is he some sort of potion for you to use. The laws of Karma have also been broken. By you. And my tribe must be avenged."

"Well, since you have admitted that your Gorgon ally is now dead, then I can defeat you once again and take the boy for myself," Slane said. "I think it is better this way. You would be far too dangerous to have at my side."

Miri held the spear horizontally with both hands as she began to circle him. "No more talk, let us end this."

Slane used both hands to hold the sword above his head, keeping the point of the blade at her direction. "Very well."

They both began a slow circle while facing each other. Miri was exhausted from moving across the flat plains all throughout the day. Slane also needed to rest since he had been searching for the boy ever since his land ship crashed. Their respective Vires were at low levels, so each would have to rely more on their fighting skills for this battle. Miri knew that she had the advantage of reach over her opponent's sword, so she took a few steps towards him as she led with the point of her spear. The moment she got within range, Miri began to make sudden thrusts, her right arm acted as leverage while she tilted the direction of the spearhead up and down with a flick of her wrist. Slane knew he was at a disadvantage since she could easily pivot the direction of her weapon and he had left his cuirass in his stricken vessel's cabin. As Miri pushed forward and attacked, the Magus gave ground while parrying her repeated thrusts using his blade and forearm bracers, hoping for a proper opening with which to close and counterattack.

Miri launched another series of attacks, but she had inadvertently lunged too far as her front leg slipped forward on the dusty rock. Slane immediately pulled his left hand back and gestured, sending a cloud of sand up around the Striga, partially blinding her. Miri stepped back and used her right hand to wipe the grains of dirt from her eyes. Slane gesticulated again, using his mindforce to pull her towards him. Miri's boots slid along the ground as her body was suddenly seized by an invisible force and she was pushed towards the Magus.

Slane grinned as he held out the point of his blade, ready to impale the Striga as she was relentlessly dragged towards him. Miri's eyes were still caked with dust, but she could see enough to realize what was happening. The Striga reacted by falling backwards as she slid past him, his blade narrowly missing her head. Miri used the shaft of her weapon to trip up the Magus as she skidded past him, hitting the metal greaves on his shins. Unaffected by the attack on his legs, Slane turned and swung his sword on a downward stroke, hoping to slice through Miri's shoulder while she lay on the ground beside him.

Miri used both hands as she used her spear shaft to block the attack. The point of the blade connected with the middle of the pole, but the strange grey material held. Slane slid the edge of his blade along the shaft, hoping to slice through Miri's fingers, but the Striga angled her spear downwards and let go with her left hand just before the sword connected with it. Slane's blade slid down onto the ground with a loud clang as Miri rolled sideways to get away from him. Slane pulled his sword up and swung again, narrowly missing her back as she got up and moved away.

Both of them stood facing each other once more. Slane concentrated as he gathered up his Vis for another attack. Miri kept her spear at chest level while trying to mentally probe him for weaknesses. She could tell that the Magus was using his reserves of Vis carefully, keeping up his thought defenses at maximum, while occasional shifting his power to attack at the right moment. What she needed was to deliver a mental strike at him right during the time when he made the deviation. The timing had to be crucial.

Miri sensed that Slane was preparing to close in for another attack as he wielded his sword one handed. The Striga hunched her shoulders and started to move forward while readying her Vis, wishing to goad him into using his mindforce once again. Suddenly, Slane used his Vis to thrust himself forward, sliding along the ground in order to close with his sword. Miri concentrated as she lashed out with her mental tendrils, expecting to break through his thought blocks more easily this time. But instead of completing his skid towards her, Slane quickly recalibrated his Vis to increase his mental defenses while he drew a dagger from his waist and threw it at her. Her concentration broken, Miri tried to dodge the incoming blade, but its tip embedded itself just above her right knee.

The Striga cried out in pain as she went into a crouching position. Slane immediately sensed her weakness as the mental attacks against him ebbed. This was just like the last time, when his feints and attacks were enough to weaken her Vis. All he needed to do now was to finish her off. Slane quickly adjusted his reserves back to his mindforce. With a flick of his wrist, he gestured, and Miri was suddenly thrust up into the air.

Slane grinned as he held her upside down. The Striga was now floating helplessly several feet off the ground. He was using his mindforce to slowly crush the life out of her. "As before, you were defeated. It was foolish of you to ever attempt to fight me after you were mortally wounded the first time. You should have stayed in the Black Redoubt instead of trying to catch up with us. You were given a second life, and you threw it away. This is your final mistake. It will take but a few moments to crush your bones, then I will tear your heart out with my Vis alone."

Through clenched teeth, Miri remembered the words of the Gorgon. *Mind is superior to body.* She used her Vis to lock away the pain that was distracting her. Her mindsense was telling her that the Magus below had reinforced his thought blocks and attempting to overcome them would be futile. Miri now realized that she didn't need to attack his mind directly. Using her mindsense, she began to see through his eyes.

As Slane continued to hold and crush her in the air, his vision began to blur. Within a few seconds, his chest started to feel heavy and his legs felt like stones. Thoughts of doubt began to creep into his mind. He narrowed his eyes in confusion. "What?"

Miri could sense that the mental bridge between her mind and his had now been established. She closed her eyes and began to transfer her feelings to the Magus. The sensations of pain and suffering, the pressure on her bones and organs, had now begun to seep their way towards her opponent. Now it was his turn to feel her pain.

Slane gasped. His heart felt like it was about to explode. He felt wracking pains all over his body, it was as if his bones were being ground to powder.

The agony was so intense, he dropped his sword and his knees buckled. Slane fell forward, his face hitting the bare, dusty stone. Blood seeped out from his nose. The crippling pain was too much and he lost his mental concentration.

Miri suddenly fell onto the ground. Her chest heaved great gulps of air as the relentless pressure on her entire body had subsided at last. Her limbs were still aching and she could hardly move them. As she twisted her head sideways, she noticed Slane was lying on the stone slab nearby. Her opponent twitched a little, then Slane pushed himself up slowly with his hands. She needed to kill him now before he recovered from that reverse transference. Miri used her final reserves of Vis to push the pain away from her mind. Suddenly, the aches stopped and she had feelings on her arms and legs again.

Getting up, she noticed the spear lying on the sand nearby. Miri bent down on her good knee and grabbed it before she limped over to Slane. She held the spear with both hands over her head and drove it down towards him. Just before the point of the weapon fell on his throat, Slane twisted sideways and looked up at her, gesticulating with his right hand. The spearhead suddenly stopped in midair. An unseen force held the weapon back.

Slane's eyes met hers and he grinned. "That …was a wonderful trick you just did." He used his other hand to grab at the sword lying beside him and swung the blade towards Miri's legs, expecting to slice through her shins.

But the edge of the sword suddenly pivoted towards the Magus instead. Slane saw the blade of the sword coming towards him and he tried to pull his head away, but it was too late. The razor sharp edge slashed through his windpipe and he began to gargle blood. With Slane's Vis suddenly dissipating, the force holding Miri's weapon was now gone. The Striga drove the spear down onto Slane's face, the edged point piercing through his nose cartilage and into his brain. Slane let out a death rattle of syllables before his head fell back into the ground, blood spewing all around him.

Miri fell on her knees and turned her head. Standing near the edge of the plateau was Rion. The boy had used his own mindforce to redirect Slane's sword to the Magus's own neck. "Miri!" Rion said as he ran over and hugged her.

The Striga let out a deep breath as she held the crying boy in her arms.

Miri looked out into the distance and she could see twinkling lights across the horizon, coming from the last city. Lethe was clearly inhabited, not an abandoned ruin like the Black Redoubt.

Rion looked up at her with longing eyes. "I thought you were dead. I thought I was going to be alone once again."

Despite the pain, Miri smiled and gave him a kiss on his forehead. "You will never be alone ever again, Rion. I will protect you."

Taking the boy's hand, she led him down the plateau. Dawn would be coming soon and their journey would go on.

The story continues in:
# City of Delusions
# The Dying World Book 2
Coming soon!

Join John Triptych's mailing list for the latest news, exclusive discounts, and FREE books!

It's FREE to join in and you can unsubscribe at any time!
http://eepurl.com/bK-xGn

# J Triptych Publishing

## Spellbinding literary entertainment at an affordable price!

**The Expatriate Underworld Series:** John Triptych's gritty, no-holds barred exploration of South East Asia's expatriate underworld, a sordid society in which one man is determined to succeed at any cost. Recommended for mature readers.

    The Opener (Book 1)

    The Loader (Book 2)

**The Amoralist Series:** John Triptych returns to the thriller genre with a new series that focuses on a highly unique assassin who travels the world for all manner of whims and murder.

    A Man of Leisure (Book 1)

    Savage Wanderings (Book 2)

## Science Fiction:

**The Dying World Series:** A mind-blowing, out of this world adventure set millions of years in the future. Mankind has evolved with strange new powers, and only one woman stands in the way of total annihilation.

    Lands of Dust (Book 1)

    City of Delusions (Book 2)

    The Maker of Entropy (Book 3)

# Science Fiction Mythology:

**Wrath of the Old Gods Series:** The entire world is thrown into turmoil as the ancient gods of myth and legend return. An epic, post-apocalyptic series with multiple characters, mythical beings, and world spanning adventures.

**The Glooming (Book 1)**

**Canticum Tenebris (Book 2)**

**A World Darkly (Book 3)**

And more to come!

**Wrath of the Old Gods Young Adult Series:** A complete and standalone series for young adults that ties in with the main Wrath of the Old Gods series. This trilogy centers on a young British boy and of his quest to save his country from supernatural forces.

**Pagan Apocalypse (Book 1.5)**

**The Fomorians (Book 2.5)**

**Eye of Balor (Book 3.5)**

Look for these books in e-book and paperback formats via the internet or by request at your local bookstore.

Please join John's exclusive mailing list! You will get the latest news on his upcoming works and special discounts. Subscription is FREE and you get lots of FREE books! Just type this link to your browser: http://eepurl.com/bK-xGn

Printed in Great Britain
by Amazon